BOOK ONE

LEAFENSONG
FIRST TELLING

BOOK ONE

LEAFENSONG
FIRST TELLING

WRITTEN & ILLUSTRATED BY

J.R. HOOGE

J.R. HOOGE

Saturelle Publishing, LLC
4100 West 12th Street
Lawrence, KS 66049

Cover Artwork and Illustrations: J.R. Hooge
Book Design: mycustombookcover.com

Orders by US trade bookstores and wholesalers: Please contact the publisher at the address above.

Printed in the United States of America

Library of Congress Control Number: 2019908179

ISBN: 978-1-947927-02-5 (paperback), 978-1-947927-01-8 (hardcover)
978-1-947-927-00-1 (ebook)

First Edition

For Orpha, Carol, Claudia and Jenea

LIST OF ILLUSTRATIONS

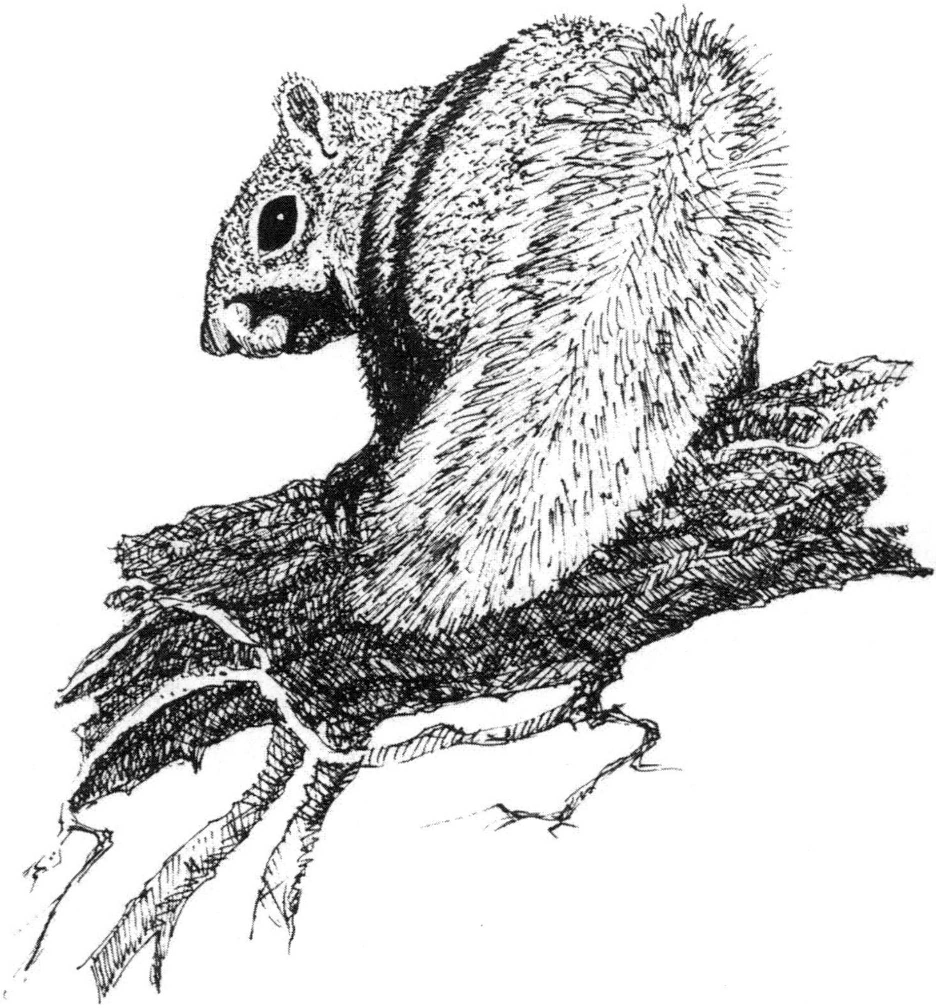

CHAPTER ONE

Year 3072 AA

Day 70

A WHITE-HOT LIGHT FILLED THE EASTERN SKY ABOVE THE TREES. Kooper couldn't resist looking through the bare branches straight into the blinding glare. As a jolt of pain took his sight, he dropped to his knees. His eyes slammed shut, but even so, through his eyelids a bright pulsing orange glowed. *This isn't possible*, he thought. *The clouds are too thick to see the sun.* Confused, his eyes on fire, the grey squirrel was paralyzed with fear. To be blind was the worst possible thing he could imagine, and here he was, helpless to see.

"What is it, Kooper?" Sharani called out. They had been chasing one another through the forest when he stopped. She could see his eyes were now clamped shut, seeping tears.

Sharani crept close and reached out to take his paw in her own. As soon as they touched, she too saw the blistering light. With a gasp, she jerked away to cover her face, hiding behind a tree. But the moment she let go of Kooper, the harsh light disappeared. "What's happening?" she implored.

Unable to speak, Kooper shook his head. The pain behind his eyes had disappeared the instant Sharani let go of him. He was just as bewildered as she. Kooper finally managed to pry open his eyes, looking down and away from the sky, to find the blinding light gone. The sky, the forest, had returned to normal. *Did that really happen?* he asked himself. Kooper's fear lingered, but he wanted to get back to the righted world. Sharani had never before shown him this much attention and he was hungry for more. He knew evening was approaching and his remaining time with Sharani would soon end.

As Sharani watched expectantly, half-hidden from behind a tree, Kooper winked and grinned at her, a wordless invitation, and bolted back into their chase. Sharani laughed over her shoulder and took off just before Kooper could reach her, up an oak tree and across its branches. She slowed to allow Kooper to come close enough to touch her before she quickly twisted away out of his grasp. They threw themselves from branch to bough, scurrying up and down the tree trunks. Wishing to prolong the tantalizing game, Kooper left the image of uncommon light behind as the two reveled in their romp.

Sharani slowed enough for Kooper to come near her again and, with a quick turn and a sudden burst of speed, she darted just beyond his grasp, coyly letting him brush against her. Chests heaving as they panted, Kooper and Sharani sped after each other in a heated dance. Twice they stopped mid-stride—tails twitching and chests heaving—before rushing off after one another again. Kooper didn't want this to end.

Neither of them noticed the eastern sky becoming lighter again until the sun suddenly blazed low above the horizon through the trees, sharp and bright. Kooper's eyes shot skyward and stopped again. Right on his heels, Sharani tumbled into him, flushing with embarrassment at the sudden awkward contact. Kooper stood transfixed as a brilliant gold illuminated the shimmering trees. *This is crazy*, he thought. The day was nearly spent. The sun setting in the *eastern* sky was impossible! Before he could sort it all out in his head, he was startled by a distant voice.

"Kooper, wake up!" barked Boggs, his brother.

Confused, still inside his dream, Kooper didn't respond.

"Wake up! It's the First Light! Koop, wake up!" Boggs shouted, finally resorting to shaking his brother.

Opening his eyes, Kooper saw only pitch black and he bolted upright. His head hit hard on the unyielding oak ceiling of the nest, and he grimaced at the sharp pain.

"The morning of FIRST LIGHT is coming!" Boggs repeated.

Realizing he had been dreaming, Kooper groaned, sorely disappointed that the imaginary romp with Sharani was over. All memory of the intense light was lost for the moment.

"Oh, let me sleep!" moaned Kooper. "If you only knew. . ." his voice trailed off as he closed his eyes and wrapped his tail around his nose, wanting to sink back into his delicious dream.

"It's the First Light!" Boggs persisted, impatience making his voice anxious and shrill.

The import of these words finally penetrated his fog and Kooper jerked himself awake. Scrambling to rise, he narrowly avoided smacking into the hard wood again. Rubbing his still stinging head, he tried to orient himself. He was unable to see anything in the darkness, but he knew from the scents surrounding him that he was in the nest he shared with Boggs.

"First Light," Kooper repeated those words aloud. Remembering the strange light of his dream, he wondered, *could that be what I saw?*

Every winter thick gray clouds completely filled the sky above the forest, blocking all sunlight until the precious sun returned in the spring. It had been so for as long as their Tribe could remember. Ancient tradition held that if one of them greeted the dawning rays of spring's first sunrise from atop the highest tree in the forest with song, it would be the greatest of good omens for both the Tribe and the Singer. However, climbing in utter darkness before dawn was the most fearful thing any of them could imagine. Grey squirrels had poor vision at night making them especially vulnerable to owls. For generations, no squirrel had been courageous enough to dare to make the terrifying climb.

The last remnants of Kooper's dream—of Sharani's fur brushing against his, of her smiling face—vanished as the import of Boggs' announcement fully sank in. "Are you sure it is time, Boggs? How do you know? What do you Sense?" he asked in a rush. Boggs didn't answer.

Kooper reached out and gently touched his brother's back. Boggs was sitting straight up and utterly still in the darkness, facing East. Kooper closed his eyes and concentrated on opening his mind to Boggs and Sensing his thoughts. *Maybe he knows what this all means.* Kooper felt the telepathic oneness with his brother, and for the briefest moment, the bright light of his dream returned before it dimmed and disappeared. Kooper immediately realized that Boggs had also Sensed the strange light in the sky he had witnessed, but only Boggs had realized what it foretold.

A light rain began to patter against the tree outside the nest, quickly increasing. In no time, the wind intensified, the rain became a heavy downpour and the air was charged with electricity. The rain blew through the opening of their nest, drenching their fur, causing them both to shiver. A jagged flash of lightning lit up Boggs' wet face just inside the nest's entrance, water drops sparkling, before everything turned pitch black again. Watching from the back of the nest in the dark, Kooper realized that Boggs' eyes were open wide and bore not a hint of fear.

An immense clap of thunder shook the great tree and, for a second, fire reflected inside their nest from outside the entrance. Terrified, Kooper squeezed his eyes closed after which all was eerily quiet once again. Trembling, Kooper slowly opened his eyes to see only the darkness of their nest. There was no fire, no bright light. The storm was miraculously gone and his fur was dry. Kooper reached for Boggs. He was dry. *Is this, too, a dream?* Kooper wondered.

"Boggs, I heard the storm! I saw the lightning and fire! I felt the rain blow into the nest. We were both wet. But now we're dry?" Boggs remained silent. Kooper tried once again to focus and Sense out his brother's thoughts. Kooper caught a glimpse of a soft, golden sunrise glowing behind a curtain of trees before quickly fading to darkness. In its wake, Kooper became aware of the sadness Boggs was feeling. Instinctively, he reached for Boggs' shoulder. Kooper shared the profound sense of loss his brother felt, as though it was his own burden. Without a word, he gently stroked Boggs' back. Finally, Boggs turned around and spoke softly but urgently.

"You know I cannot be the Singer. It must be you. You have the voice. You have the heart, the courage, the vision. You must be the Singer."

Kooper began to protest, "I can't..."

Boggs cut him off, grabbing his paw. "No, don't argue," he urged. "Go now before it's too late. It will be light soon and you must climb the Singer's Tree to greet the dawn. You must sing!"

Boggs reached out with both paws and gripped Kooper's shoulders. "Sing for both of us, and for Mother." Boggs released his grip and instantly Kooper Sensed that Boggs had blocked him from any further connection. Saddened and subdued, he gently placed his paw one last time on Boggs' shoulder and sighed in resignation. "You're right," Kooper said out loud. "It must be me."

Boggs moved away from the nest entrance to allow Kooper to peer out. A cold north wind struck him in the face, instantly bringing tears to his eyes. Kooper knew the thick, twisting limbs of their grandmother's ancient oak tree stretched out above, but they were invisible in the black night. He knew he would be unable to see anything as he crossed through the trees and climbed the Singer's Tree. Shivering from cold, Kooper listened intently but heard only the moaning of the wind. He wanted to stay with Boggs and share the warmth of the nest and dream again of Sharani, but using all his willpower, he forced himself to crawl out of the nest into the cold night. Though blind and completely vulnerable in the total darkness, Kooper realized his brother experienced the same dangers every day and night. Boggs had been blind since birth.

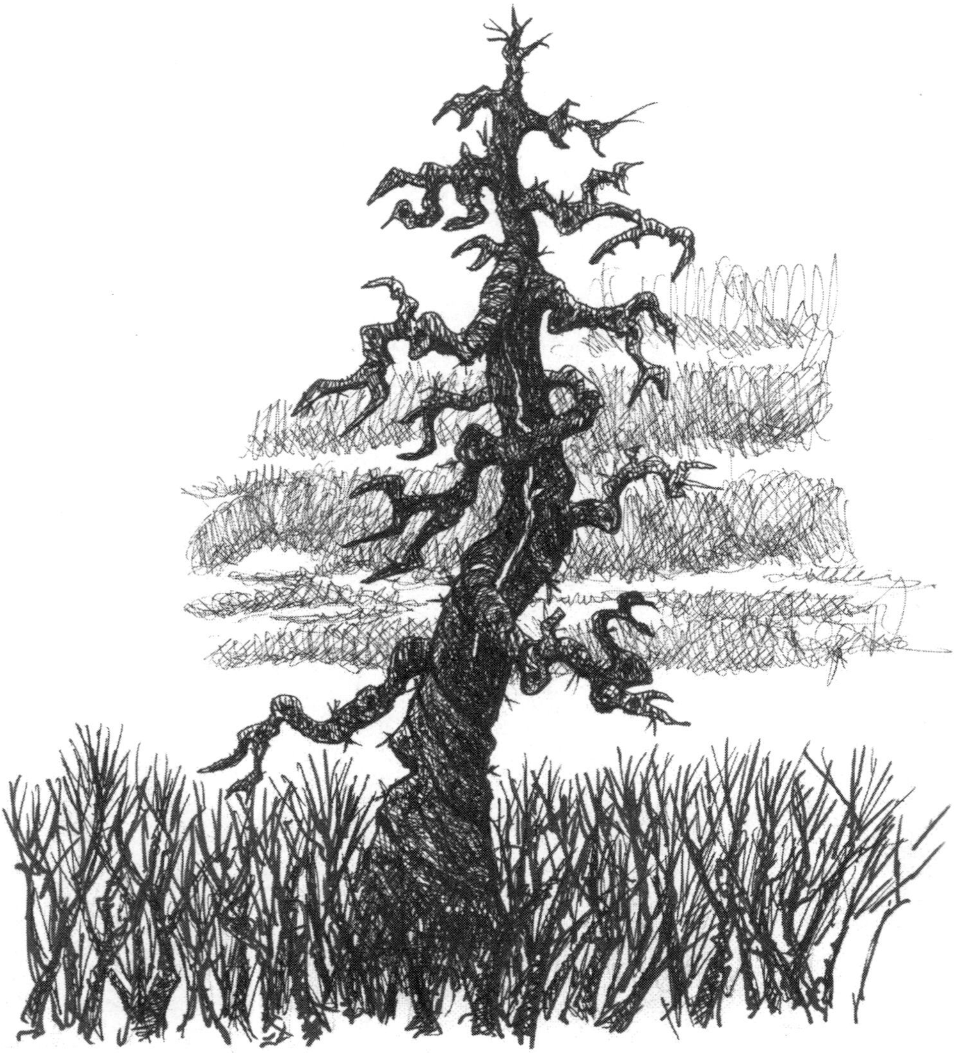

CHAPTER TWO

Year 3072 AA
Day 70

KOOPER SAT SHIVERING IN THE COLD JUST OUTSIDE HIS NEST. Heavy, opaque clouds had hidden the moon and stars all winter long. As his eyes adjusted to the darkness, Kooper began to see the shimmering lacework of light dancing through the tree branches in a cloudless sky. The long-awaited first sunrise of spring was approaching.

Shuddering in the frigid wind which parted his fur, Kooper moved forward along the thick, gnarly branch extending behind their warm nest to the trunk of his grandmother's tree. Beka had inherited this tree as a home for her family long ago. The ancient bur oak was the oldest tree in Leafensong and had lost many branches to battering storms over the years. The remaining limbs on the trunk were thick and bent, spreading and twisting outward like crooked arms. Kooper's sharp claws gripped the shallow crevices of the hard bark as he crawled up and around the trunk. Finally, he reached the branch which he knew was the path to his destination. He took two steps, thinking about what lay before him at the end of the limb and tripped over a forgotten vine, almost falling off. He instinctively grasped the side of the limb with the claws of all four paws and pulled himself up, stopping to catch his breath.

With a heavy sigh Kooper shook himself and fluffed up his fur to wick away the cold sweat from his skin. He reminded himself he had to be careful. He tried Sensing out again to Boggs, but his twin sat still, facing East, wordless, his mind closed to Kooper's attempt to reach him. Boggs could easily Sense not only what was in Kooper's mind and heart, but the thoughts and emotions of any other squirrel as well. Kooper's ability to do the same was limited, rarely attempted. He felt inadequate in Sensing compared to his brother. He knew they were the only two who were capable of the skill, but Boggs was not responding. This quest was his alone.

Shaking off his trepidation, he set out again to feel his way through the darkness, across the familiar bough, reminding himself to step over the vine this time. The limb creaked and swayed in the night wind, making his footing more difficult, but he pushed on to the end of the branch. Once there, he pulled up short in a panic. He realized he'd have to leap blindly to the next tree. Panting, he grasped the bark tightly with his claws as the limb swayed in the wind. It was an easy task in the daylight when he could see his landing place in the neighboring ash tree. There were several small limbs he could choose from if he could see them. But now, peering out into the darkness before him, Kooper was paralyzed. His claws clamped onto the bucking limb as a gust of wind ripped into his fur and bit his skin. His thoughts ran back to the safety of his nest, to the comfort of his brother's warmth. He took a deep breath.

Kooper's heart was pounding so hard he could hear it, but he knew he couldn't abandon this journey. He straightened his shoulders and pulled a steadying breath into his lungs. He thrust himself forward with a cry and leapt into the black void toward the ash tree's trunk.

Just as it seemed he would be suspended in the freezing air forever, he slammed into the side of the ash tree. With a hard jolt, he banged his jaw into the coarse, ridged bark and slid downward, his claws scratching desperately for a firm grasp. Abruptly, his claws dug in and he stopped sliding. He pulled one claw at a time out of the bark, stretching each leg, squeezing his paws, and loosening the cramped sinews and muscles. He raised his left front paw to his mouth and tasted the blood where his skin had torn. He clung to the swaying tree until his head cleared and his heart slowed its crazy beat. He could scarcely believe he was still intact. "Lucient, thank you," he whispered aloud. He wanted to stop and rest, but there was no time to waste. He knew his journey had just begun.

Kooper followed familiar trails along worn branches and vines. At first each step in the dark was tentative. But slowly he became used to navigating in the darkness and began to trust his instincts—the muscle memory of where to step, where to climb—until his uncertainty lessened. He moved faster but slowed before jumping from tree to tree. Once, faced with a particularly long jump, he retraced his steps and took a more circuitous trail to avoid another headlong leap into the darkness.

As he made his way through the forest, Kooper heard the muffled flight of an owl overhead. He stopped and sat, breathless. Unmoving. He imagined long, sharp talons reaching for him in the dark. Owls were silent in flight unless extremely near so he knew when he heard one flying, it was dangerously close. His heart beat like a drum in his ears and there was no relaxing a whisker until he was sure the owl had passed on. Menacing in size, with shredding talons and an awful screech, owls were as evil as Ebyn, as the black night they inhabited. Kooper was aware that in the dark, owls had vastly superior eyesight. Each time he heard their fluttering wings, he stopped moving and had to struggle to continue his terrifying quest.

As quietly as possible, Kooper approached and passed a sleeping nest of squirrels in another bur oak. He could hear the soft breathing of a mother and her family of yearlings nestled in their late winter sleep. He slowed, his mind suddenly awash in the stories about his mother he'd heard so often from his grandmother and aunt. Try as he might, he had no memories of his own. Surely she would have been proud of him. Singer to the Light! He ached thinking of the pain she endured, what the storm stole from them all. He resolved to honor her by completing his journey.

Kooper pressed on through the dark forest, moving tree to tree, across sturdy limbs and shaking vines, moving steadily but on high alert for any signs of danger. Finally he reached the narrow grove of cottonwoods that spread lengthwise west to east in the northern half of Leafensong. He sped up until he reached his objective, the Singer's Tree, that stood west of the center of the grove. From another cottonwood Kooper hopped onto the long, low limb jutting straight out from the massive trunk. The limb was just below the spot where the trunk split into six separate vertical stems. Though younger than his grandmother's bur oak, each of the stems was taller, and four reached higher than any of the other trees. It had grown from a tiny seed, carried aloft by a fluff of silky cotton, to an immense size. At the juncture, each of the six stems was almost as thick as Beka's ancient oak.

Kooper found what he knew was the tallest of the six stems and dug his claws into the soft, spongy bark. Relief flooded his mind and his muscles. He ached all over from the strain he was under. For just a few moments he closed his eyes, breathed deeply and rested. When he was ready to climb to the top, he pulled the claws of a forepaw out of the bark to reach upward. Again, he again heard the unmistakable sound of an owl's beating wings. He knew the owl was almost on him. Certain the owl was about to pierce him with its talons and not knowing where to hide, he sucked in his breath, waiting for the inevitable.

With an awful crunch of branch and bone, he heard the sudden cry of a vole above him. Kooper Sensed the vole's horror and pain as the owl's talon sliced into its body. He heard the second talon scrape at the bark as the owl slid down the shaggy stem, trying to gain a firm grip on the tree while still holding on to the vole. *He's going to land on me!* Kooper realized. The panicked thoughts of the vole filled Kooper's mind as it struggled to free itself from the owl's talon. Kooper felt the air pushed by the owl's wings as it labored to obtain a much-needed meal.

Kooper had never Sensed the thoughts of any animal but a squirrel until now. He felt fully the vole's last breath when the owl's talon closed tight and the air squeezed out of the vole's lungs, causing a final, audible squeak.

The owl's other talon tore pieces of bark as it tried to stop its fall, wings beating furiously. Gusts of wind from the wings flattened Kooper's fur and his skin twitched as flakes of bark fell on him. Kooper was certain the owl would fall upon him any second. Then the owl grasped the vole in its beak and thrust itself away from the tree with both legs to fly off into the night sky. In an instant the muffled sound of its beating wings was replaced with silence.

Even though Boggs had tried to block out Kooper's Sensing, Boggs heard the vole's fearful shriek as Kooper's emotions overpowered the barrier Boggs had put up in his mind. For a sickening moment Boggs thought Kooper had been attacked by the owl, and he cried out Kooper's name. But Boggs quickly realized another animal had been the owl's prey. Relieved, Boggs let down his barrier as Kooper's frantic fear and giddy relief melded together in each of their minds.

The woods now were silent except for Kooper's ragged breathing. It had been almost too much for him to handle. His heart thumping, his thoughts racing, tumbling through his head, Kooper clutched the tree bark with a death grip. He couldn't stop trembling. Needing the release, he called out into the night air, his voice ragged and hoarse.

"Boggs, I don't think I can do this."

Kooper lifted his face upward, eyes still closed, hoping that Boggs would respond, needing his reassurance. Instead of Sensing Boggs' thoughts, a vision of Beka's tree slowly took shape in his mind. A faint light glowed behind the old oak's sprawling limbs, and he heard the sounds of his family singing softly: Boggs, Beka, Claryn and Spinner. The scent of spring and new life in the forest filled him. The light intensified, not to a painful burning but a warm spreading radiance. His breathing slowed and his trembling and panic ceased. His vision of Beka's tree and the sky glowing behind it diminished until they disappeared.

Kooper was calm enough now to refocus. He understood that he had to resume climbing despite the dangers. Although it was invisible in the darkness, Kooper somehow Sensed the tall cottonwood reaching toward the sky and he opened his eyes. The shadowed stem to which he clung filled his eyesight. He lifted up his head and looked straight up. It was still total darkness but, as his eyes adjusted, he began to see stars, uncovered by clouds. First Light was indeed coming. More and more stars glimmered through the branches swaying above him, hiding and then exposing the tiny points of light.

Kooper knew it was up to him to climb to the top of the tree and greet the dawn for the Tribe, for his family, his brother, for their mother. With new determination, he once again reached up with a front paw to sink a claw into the thick, pithy bark and pull himself up, one step at a time.

The old cottonwood was one of the few trees with its topmost branches unbroken, soaring above the surrounding forest. Kooper made his way steadily through the irregularly spaced limbs when a sudden gust of wind rose. The tall, flexible stem creaked and bent precariously as Kooper tightened his grasp of the soft bark, waiting for the wind to subside.

Once the wind stilled, Kooper climbed higher. The bare branches above him had thinned, exposing more stars, and he stopped to stare. Never in his life had he seen the clear night sky from such a vantage point. Dumbstruck, he watched as shooting stars, one after another, sped to earth. *Could this be First Light?*

Kooper approached the highest branches of the cottonwood when the wind suddenly rose again, twisting and bending the spindly limbs to the limits of their endurance. Branches creaked and cracked. Kooper had to hold onto the stem with all his strength as the wind tugged at his fur, nearly yanking him loose. When the wind died down, he crept upwards again, carefully considering each step. The bark itself had thinned, and he could no longer sink his claws into its meager remains. He had to find fissures and small ridges he could grasp until even those disappeared as he neared the very top of the tree. But he realized the stem he climbed had turned more horizontal than vertical. He took two more steps to confirm this and then retraced them back to the last branch that seemed to be heading upwards and climbed this one instead, heading higher.

The limb he climbed was thin and Kooper could only pull himself up by grabbing the small branches sprouting from it with his sweating paws. He slipped and scuttled backward. His heartbeat pummeled his ribs as he desperately fought for footing, finally stopping, his front paws gripping small branches. Stars began to spin dizzyingly around him. Barely able to hang on, he inched down the trunk until he felt his hind paws on a branch and wrapped his front paws around the slender stem. His stomach heaved and he leaned over to retch. Convulsing, panic once again washed over him. He closed his eyes to shut out the overwhelming expanse of glittering sky. Thoughts tumbled over themselves in his head. *If I fall, I'm dead. And what will become of Boggs?*

"No! No!" he shouted to himself. "I cannot let go!" It was a defiance, a plea, a declaration that he couldn't suppress. Once it was expelled, Kooper was better able to calm himself. He breathed deeply, remaining rooted to the same place, even though he was still uncertain. *How high must I climb? Am I high enough?* he wondered.

Before he could answer himself, Kooper heard the soft whoosh and rustle of an owl's wing feathers, this time passing below him. Instinctively Kooper froze, slowly curling his body inward to become as small as possible, scarcely breathing until he heard the owl fly on, leaving silence in its wake.

He wanted to stay put, but Kooper saw the faintest glow of the approaching dawn and knew that he had to move quickly. He felt he had to climb as high as possible. That was the objective, the highest treetop. Reaching up, he found a fork between two small branches and slipped his right front paw through, pulling himself up enough to reach another, smaller limb with his left. He tried to keep calm and focus solely on a way to take one more step and then another. Just one more step. One. Slowly, he pulled himself up with his front paws, his rear paws stretching up, straining his back legs, claws scraping at the bark until finally he was able to get a hind paw on the slender limb. Circling the thin stem with both front paws, he carefully pulled and pushed himself up until both rear paws were on the narrow branch, which bent precariously under his weight. He could go no further.

It was his good fortune that the wind gusts had diminished into a constant, steady breeze. Facing East, he now was above all of Leafensong and its entire surrounding forest. It was nearly sunrise. The view stunned him, stole his breath away. Kooper watched in wonder as the sky just above the horizon began to lighten. A smile crept across his face while vivid pinks and shimmering oranges spread across ribbons of clouds low in the morning sky. *The sun must show itself soon,* he thought. *What will that be like?*

But his smile was replaced with wide-eyed fear when he recalled the burning light in his dream of racing through the forest with Sharani. *Will it be like that? Will the First Light be painful, or worse? Will it blind me?* He shook his head fiercely, trying to steady his mind. The twig he clung to swayed and bent, but righted itself again. *Was that the First Light? Was it only a dream? Was it something else entirely?* He felt a shudder run through his body. He had overcome his greatest fear of being exposed in the treacherous night, completely unprotected. But now he feared even more that the sun's first blazing rays might actually blind him. *Is that the price of greeting the first dawn?*

He willed himself to slow his pounding heart and push away his rising alarm. He purposefully turned his eyes away from the rising dawn in the eastern sky and looked westward. His eyes fell on the Dark One—the lone giant tree towering far to the west of Leafensong. He could just make out the top of the mammoth, faintly illuminated against the black sky. The forbidding ancient tree loomed above every tree in the forest, dwarfing even the Singer's Tree.

Kooper had never seen the Dark One before, other than a quick glimpse through the branches of the forest. His grandmother and aunt had warned him and his brother and cousin not to climb too high in Leafensong's trees. "Don't look upon that tree, Kooper! It is Ebyn, evil, dark and vile. Its dark shadow can swallow you like the hawks that fly through its branches." No one in the Tribe dared to look upon the Dark One, nor did they speak openly of the tree, knowing that doing so would cause the squirrel to fall prey to the wickedness it embodied.

But Kooper could not take his eyes off the great tree. He sat transfixed as it slowly became more visible moment by moment, a dark gray behemoth looming in the half-light of a new day. Despite a creeping cold twisting in his gut, Kooper stared fixedly at the enormous tree, unable to look away. It's few short, broken limbs, twisted and misshapen, reached for him like menacing claws.

Kooper felt the rise of panic within him once more. Uncertainty multiplied. *What have I done?* He tried to look away from the Dark One, but couldn't. Gasping out loud, unable to catch a breath, his whole body turned weak. A hind paw slipped off the thin branch on which he was standing, and he was barely able to hang on with his front paws. He reached around the thin stem as far as he could, grasping his own fur with his front claws, piercing his own skin. His stomach heaving, chest pounding, he finally summoned enough willpower to close his eyes to the Dark One and turn his attention back to the East. Once again, an image of Beka's tree appeared in his mind, surrounded by a halo of soft pink and orange light. He heard Boggs desperately calling his name far in the distance within his mind. He fought to balance himself on the spindly branch beneath his hind paws. Forcing himself to draw in long, slow breaths, the pounding in Kooper's breast began to subside until he could open his eyes again.

Dawn was finally blooming on the eastern horizon, becoming noticeably brighter. Far below, a bird began to sing to greet the new day. He steadied his breathing, following Beka's instructions for calming himself, then worked to banish uncertainty and dread. He needed to focus on the birds singing far beneath him and on the luminous light of a new day of spring. His task was to welcome it.

The sun began to emerge over the shadowy world of dormant trees and patches of dirty snow. The top edge of the shining globe rose above the horizon with sudden brilliance, mirrored by a thin line of clouds above the sun. Kooper gasped, momentarily taken aback by the bright light. But it wasn't painful and didn't blind him; his concern vanished, replaced with the realization that he had reached his impossible goal. As he watched the sun slowly climb above the horizon, he began to sing the song that had been taught to every young squirrel of the Tribe; they were to sing it if they were so fortunate as to greet spring's new dawn. From barely a whisper, his high, winsome voice projected through the forest, growing louder, welcoming the sun's return. He knew the sun would now return each morning until the next winter. He lost himself in the joy of singing, growing bolder. He kept his eyes steady on the rising sun as it became a full, bright red sphere just above the horizon of trees. Streaks of clouds above glowed red and pink, brilliant against the still dark sky. He felt the barest caress of warmth on his fur and skin, realized how much he had missed the warmth and light of the sun, and immersed himself in the delight of this long-awaited morning.

Kooper looked up and saw the first rays of the now fully-risen sun light up the silvery bark of the limb above him. It was the highest branch on the tree. *I must reach that*, he thought. With his right paw circling the slender vertical stem, he stretched his left foreleg and paw above his head and just managed to grip the limb. As he did, a sudden blaze of light exploded across Kooper's chest and belly and exposed the dark markings on his alabaster fur.

Every banded squirrel bore some manner of the Tribe's distinguishing dark markings, but Kooper's and Boggs' markings were unique to them, and identical to one another. Starting low on Kooper's belly, a black flame spread out and upward, glossy and iridescent in the morning sunlight. The tallest tendril curving under his chin and across his left cheek, ending just below his left eye, pointing toward his nose and mouth. The blaze throbbed on his chest as he filled his lungs and sang his heart out.

Dawn has brought new life to our land.

To hearts grown faint in the long dark night.

With joy we lift up our song of spring,

And give thanks to the promise of warmth and light.

High above the only world he had ever known, lost in song, Kooper didn't hear the waking Tribe join in. His song penetrated their sleep, and they sprang from their nests. Spring had finally returned! Their beautiful voices rose in joyous harmony as they watched glittering sunlight filter through the trees of Leafensong. It was the first time the revered song had greeted First Dawn during any of their lifetimes. They rejoiced in their good fortune as they, too, heralded the sun that would welcome every morning through spring, summer and fall.

Most had no idea who the singer was. But his family did.

"Mother, that's Kooper singing!" said Claryn, shaking Beka. "He's climbed the Singer's tree! He's singing the Song to First Light!"

"No, it couldn't be," replied Beka as she strained her ears to hear, pulling her creaky body out of her inner nest, across the porch to where Claryn and Spinner sat at the outer opening.

"It's Kooper," Spinner said simply in a hushed whisper. Beka knew it was true but couldn't say anything. Incredulous, all three started singing, blending their voices with Kooper's and all the voices of the Tribe.

Kooper's singing awoke Sharani, also. At first, she thought it was only a dream. But a slight smile crept across her face when she realized her Kooper was the Singer.

As the Tribe sang along exuberantly, no one else knew that the new Singer was one of the twins marked by a black flame. They didn't know that he was singing not only to the new dawn, but also in remembrance of the mother he had never known and in honor of his blind brother.

***

One witness did see the Singer. Far to the east, between Leafensong's eastern border and the rising sun, a female red-tailed hawk was already awake when she heard faint singing. Shakti was sitting between two male red-tails in the top of another cottonwood. It was almost out of her range of hearing and the other two hawks slept on. Shakti turned her head towards the sound. Her binocular vision instantly focused upon Kooper's chest, glowing like a hot ember, lit up by the first golden rays of the sun. She could see that Kooper was a squirrel, but it made no sense to her. She had never seen a squirrel in the highest treetop at dawn, let alone a squirrel with a black flame on his belly and chest. She shook her head and blinked, trying to sort out the meaning of this vision as she watched and listened warily.

Shakti's companions were wakened by the rising chorus of voices joining Kooper in song.

"Do you hear that?" one of the other hawks whispered as they, too, focused their eyes on Kooper, who appeared to be on fire.

"Is that a squirrel?" asked the other.

Shakti replied simply, "Yes."

All three of the hawks sat still, watching and listening, un-certain, but aware that they were witnessing something special.

***

Yet another witness to the north of Leafensong listened as Kooper sang, although he couldn't see the Singer. Ragnar was just settling in his bed of soft grasses within his midden of sticks piled up at the base of an old hedge tree. He had been up all night. The wood rat did not share the squirrels' appreciation of Kooper's singing. He hated Leafensong's squirrels and their constant racket more than anything. He too realized something was unusual, because he had never heard a squirrel sing so early in the day. As the other squirrels joined in, a second wood rat approached him.

"Do you hear that?" asked Ivar.

Ragnar spat on the ground. "Yes," he snorted.

"There are so many. Do you think Skag will bring enough soldiers?"

"Yes. And it won't be long now," said Ragnar.

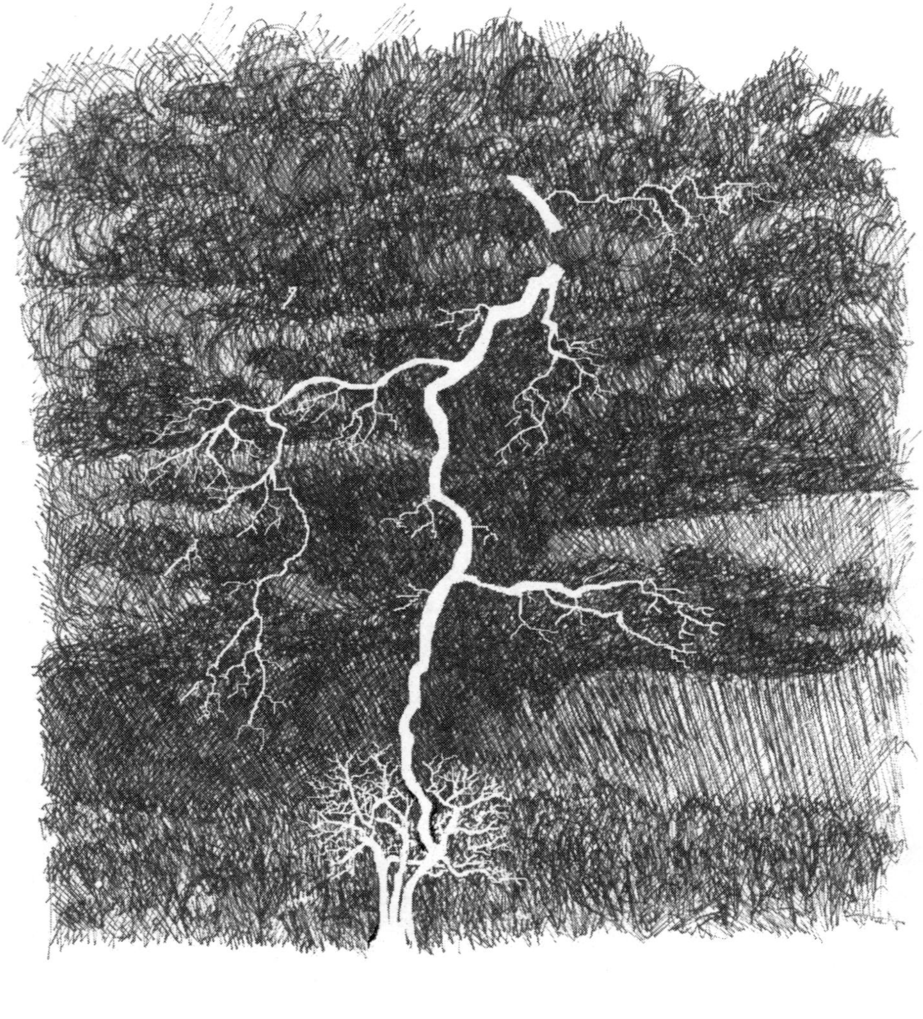

CHAPTER THREE

Year 3072 AA
Day 70

AS THE FIERY SUN LIFTED INTO THE MORNING SKY, RIBBONS OF
CLOUDS DRIFTED IN FRONT, SOFTENING FROM A DEEP RED TO
IRIDESCENT ORANGE AND SHIMMERING PINK. The kaleidoscopic
colors were reflected in the patches of snow and ice below. From
his perch atop the forest, Kooper sat unmoving, transfixed by the
changing colors and brilliance, trying to comprehend it all.

Suddenly, his heart lurched and his chin shot up as he quickly
scanned the sky in all directions. He realized that, unlike among
the thick branches below, there were none here to conceal him.
Hawks and eagles will be flying anytime now! What are you think-
ing? Go! As quickly as he dared, he wound his way down the stem,
careful to find strong footholds, but also watching the sky.

By now, many in the Tribe had gathered in the lower limbs
of the great cottonwood or beneath it on the ground, waiting to

see who the new Singer was. The massive tree's thick canopy of leaves in the summer blocked the sunlight from the forest floor and few trees had been able to grow beneath it to any size. Only stunted saplings grew here and there, opening up the view from the ground to the now bare limbs of the huge cottonwood. The squirrels had all been taken by surprise, then were captivated by the long-awaited song to First Light. Every one of them had been taught that this song brought with it a season of great fortune for their Tribe. The air was alive with chatter as the squirrels gathered, the anticipation growing, everyone anxious to learn the identity of their new Singer to the Sun.

But as Kooper came within eyesight, their excitement vanished. Kooper saw the shock on their faces. Their chatter changed to a rumble of whispers.

"Is that the blind one? Surely not!" an old buck said.

"No, it's his brother, Kooper," chimed in a doe.

"It's one of Beka's grandsons. Surely he can't be the Singer!"

Many left, unable to accept that this was their new Singer.

Kooper ignored their whispers and focused on descending safely, offering a simple nod to the squirrels he passed. As he approached the junction of the stems, he tried to Sense for Boggs, but once again received no response.

Only Kooper knew that by rights Boggs should have been the Singer this morning, that Boggs was the one who Sensed it was First Light. But Kooper also knew that it would have been impossible for Boggs to climb to the top of the Singer's Tree. And the Tribe would never accept Boggs as their new Singer to the Light.

Kooper had heard their birth story many times and had memorized each word and image. Clinging to the cottonwood's thick bark, he stopped for a moment to let the story wash over him, and heard Aunt Claryn's voice in his head, beginning the familiar narrative.

He and Boggs had been young pups, naturally curious about their absent mother. Claryn had left Spinner with Beka and then gathered Boggs and Kooper to her in Beka's sleeping nest. Kooper could feel the warmth of his brother's body held tightly against his on that late spring day the year before.

"The time has come to share with you the whole story of how you came to be born. You need to know and remember this. Your mother, Chaska, had a soul as beautiful as her face, and a loving nature that could not be suppressed. Everyone felt blessed just by being in her presence. She was overjoyed to be having pups for the first time. She so wanted to be a mother. She loved you the moment her womb quickened.

"One afternoon, Chaska had gone too far from your grand-mother's tree when she felt a sudden drop in her belly, signaling your impending birth. She knew she couldn't make it back to your grandmother's tree in time. A storm was brewing, darkening the sky; the thunder turned from a low growl into deafening explo-sions in a matter of minutes.

"She had to settle into a small nest she found in the sycamore next to your grandmother's tree. We knew none of this and re-mained in your grandmother's nest. We were tending to my own new pup, Spinner, who had just been born.

"The oak trembled with thunder all around, while we waited for Chaska to return, but she didn't come.

"Outside, the storm grew more fierce. Rain was driven nearly horizontally by the winds and lightning tore across the sky, drawing ever closer. With each burst, the trees would light up more. We were looking out the entrance of our nest, watching for Chaska. We knew she would have come to us if it was at all possible. Her absence was more frightening to us than the storm itself."

Claryn paused a moment, overcome by the sorrow of remembering. But she was determined that her nephews know their mother's heart through her telling of the story. Kooper and Boggs sat transfixed before her, urging her to continue.

"What did she do?"

"Yes, what happened next, Aunt Claryn?" they both clamored.

Claryn drew in a sustaining breath, smiled warmly at each of her young charges and whispered, "Now listen carefully. I'm about to tell you the most amazing part.

"Her babies were coming too soon. She couldn't stop what was happening. Her body bore down until she felt her first born slip into the nest below her. Kooper, it was you who appeared first. But, then C – R – A – C – K!!!

"A huge bolt of lightning from high above split the dark clouds, sliced down through the rain and lit up everything. The three white trunks of the sycamore right next to us blazed like a beacon before everything turned black again. It frightened us terribly. We'd never been so close to lightning. The rain soon lessened and we could see that the lightning had struck one of the trunks of the sycamore. It had caught fire and was burning fiercely. The crackling of the flames and the smell was horrifying.

"We were waiting for the rain to stop, to go look for your mother, when your grandma and I heard it at the same time."

"Heard what?" asked Kooper and Boggs in unison.

"You two," replied Claryn with a smile. "We could hear you

crying, the unmistakable cry of newborn babies. We rushed out and went straight toward the sound, realizing it was coming from the sycamore trunk that was on fire! There was a nest just beneath where the fire was burning. That's where your mother gave birth and where we found the three of you.

"Your mother was terribly weak and bleeding badly, barely alive, but she was smiling, trying to suckle her babies. You two."

Overcome with grief, Claryn paused. Each of them was enveloped in a deafening silence. Kooper and Boggs were at a loss as to what to say or how to feel. Claryn herself was adrift for a moment in the memory.

In that dead space, Boggs spoke up, "She stayed with us even though the tree was burning?" he asked.

Claryn nodded. "The rain was keeping the fire from spreading for the moment, but it was still burning, the flames flickering, the smoke thick. But there was no way your mother was leaving you."

"She must have been brave." said Kooper, his eyes full of tears. "We wish we could have known her."

"I wish you could have too," Claryn replied. "She was strong and fierce in her love for you." Claryn cleared her throat, determined to tell her nephews the whole story, no matter how painful the memory.

"Your grandmother and I knew your mother was dying, that we couldn't heal her. We knew that she would not live to watch you grow or be able to protect you from that which might bring you harm. Your mother knew it, too. After she told us what had happened, her voice faded into silence. There was nothing Beka and I could do but cradle her to ease her passing as she held on to both of you. But she managed to say one more thing. She made your grandmother and me promise that we would raise and protect her babies. That we would love you as if you were our own."

Boggs was stunned. In a strangled voice he asked, "So I killed our mother?! If I hadn't been born..."

"No!" groaned Claryn. "No one is to blame in any way. No one caused this. Bad things happen to everyone, some worse than others. No one is immune from pain, sadness, suffering. But some injuries simply cannot be healed. It was very hard to accept losing our beautiful Chaska, but her death was no one's fault!"

Kooper and Boggs lowered their heads and nodded.

"Of course, your grandmother and I did not hesitate to make the vow Chaska asked of us. We gently stroked her fur and rocked the three of you until her last breath. The pain of losing her was raw, but we knew she'd gone in peace. When the storm had dwindled into a soft rain, your grandmother and I took you away and brought you back here."

"What about Mother?" asked Boggs.

"By the time we got you two safely here, she was already gone. The rain stopped and the fire grew larger, engulfing the tree trunk. We couldn't get her out. Remember I had just given birth to Spinner. I wasn't much help. It was all we could do to save you. The fire burned up the tree trunk above the nest. It burned all the next day and night.

"And we set about raising you both as your mother wished, devoting ourselves to protecting and loving you, just as she would have."

Neither Boggs nor Kooper responded, trying to absorb what they'd been told. Finally, Kooper said, "I have a question. Boggs' and my markings are so different from everyone else's. We've heard the whispers that we were marked by the fire that killed Mother. What do our markings mean?"

Claryn sighed. "I don't really know, dear. Yes, your markings resemble flames. The lightning killed your mother. I don't know if your markings mean anything except to remind you of your connection to the extraordinary mother with whom you were blessed, as well as each other. But your grandmother and I knew that you would both be special as soon as we saw you! After we got you into your grandmother's nest, right here, I gathered you to me. I fed you along with Spinner. Your grandma and the other does made sure I had enough good food to make the milk I needed for three. They welcomed both of you until the day your eyes finally opened. It was then we discovered that Boggs was blind, and everything changed."

Kooper and Boggs were speechless. And humbled. And grateful. And sad. And afraid. All at the same time. Claryn reached out to embrace both of them.

"You had to hear this important story, the beginning of your story. Yes, it was terrible. But, you must never forget that your mother gave life and love to you. There is no love more powerful or pure than a mother's love! And your grandmother and I share that same love for both of you and your cousin, Spinner."

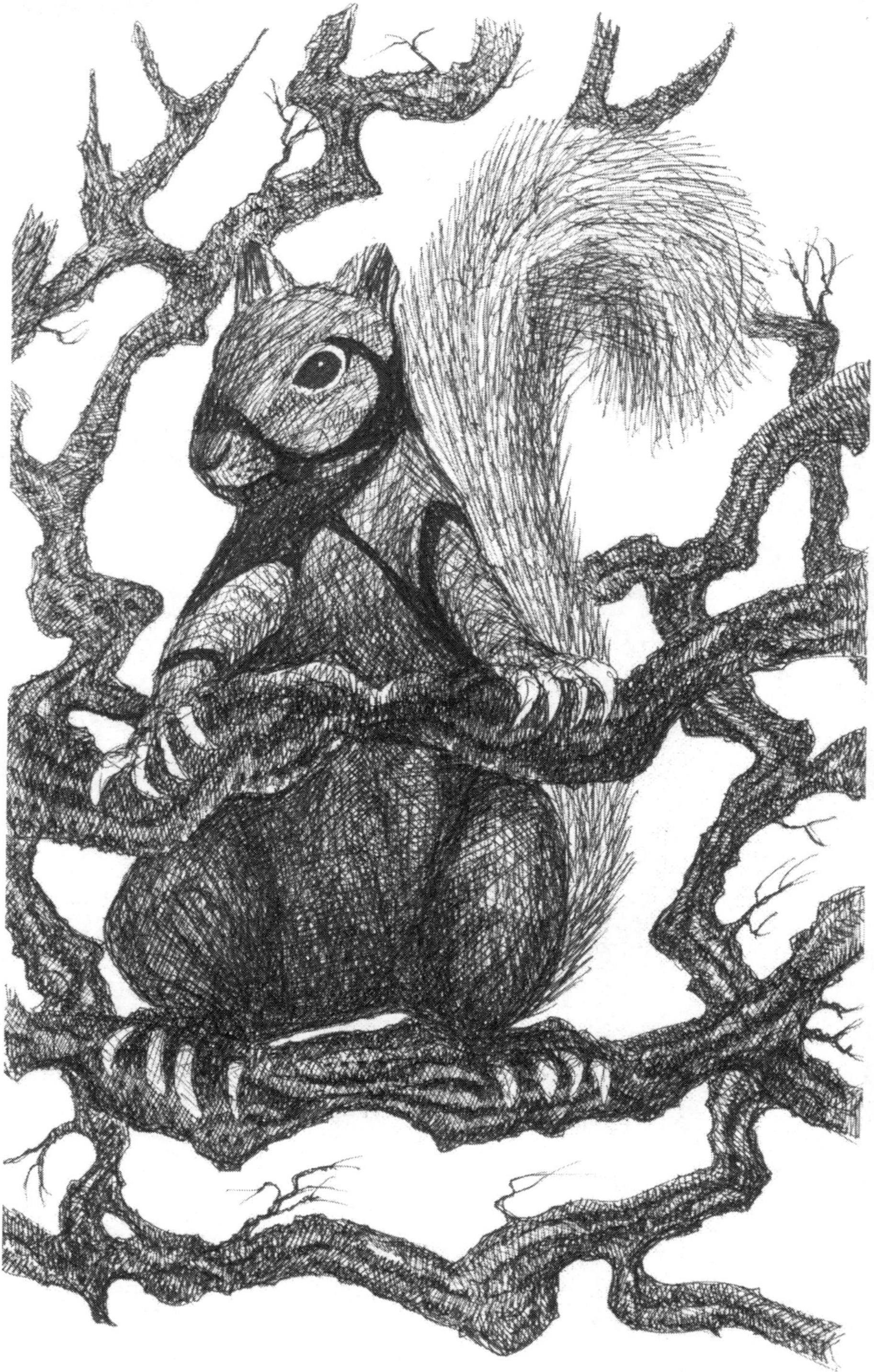

CHAPTER FOUR

Year 3071 AA
Day 101

AN UPROAR ROSE AMONG THE TRIBE ONCE IT BECAME KNOWN THAT ONE OF CHASKA'S PUPS WAS BLIND. This blindness, coupled with the fact that each was marked with a black flame, made them outcasts.

"What do the marks mean?" squirrels asked one another.

No one in Leafensong had ever had such a mark, and many contended this was a mark of Darkness, of Ebyn, especially those on the Council.

The grey squirrels knew no greater fear than that of being outside at night. To them, Light, Lucient, was goodness and life while the darkness of night was absolute evil, Ebyn. A storm at night full of lightning was as terrifying as an owl. To deal with this troubling situation, word went out for all the Council members to gather at the Council Oak, their meeting place.

The great bur oak tree had fallen decades earlier, its roots pulled partially from the ground. It angled up, stretching to where its upper trunk had wedged tightly between two other oak trees. It lay near the center of Leafensong, east of Beka's tree and south of the Singer's Tree. It had been the site of Council meetings for many generations of banded squirrels.

Within minutes, each Counselor climbed through the oak's upturned roots and found his seat upon bark which had been worn smooth by generations of squirrels. The eldest sat higher up while the youngest sat close to the crown of roots at the bottom. The rest of the Tribe quickly filled the surrounding trees. Guards positioned in the highest treetops kept watch for hawks in the sky above.

Strap, the Leader of the Council, rose on his haunches at the upper end of the Council Oak, pausing to let the murmuring below die down. He was a large, muscular buck with two broad stripes running from his shoulders down his back to the end of his tail. His commanding presence and long-held position had led him to expect the deference shown him. He looked about, pleased to see the large number of squirrels surrounding the Council. He enjoyed a sizable audience. Once he had their full attention, he opened the meeting, speaking in a powerful voice that resonated through the forest.

"Welcome, my fellow Counselors and all tribal members, to this special meeting. Singer, please invite the Light."

Strap dipped his head forward toward Torn Ear, who had been Singer of the Council for years. Torn Ear rose from his position close to Strap to face the large assembly and lifted his eyes toward the bright sunlight filtering through the bare trees.

His voice rose, beautiful and soaring.

> "Oh, Giver of Light,
>
> Shine down on our land,
>
> Bring wisdom and sight to
>
> The new day at hand,
>
> Release now your Power
>
> To inspire and revive
>
> Each spirit made faint
>
> In the shadows of night.
>
> We offer great thanks
>
> O Giver of Light."

The Counselors all murmured their approval as Strap intoned, "Well sung, Torn Ear."

Torn Ear had barely retaken his seat when an argument erupted among several Counselors about the blind orphan pup.

"We can't have a blind squirrel within the Tribe!" said one. "It's too dangerous. That twin is obviously Ebyn. We can't allow that in Leafensong."

"The blind pup must be banished!" said Caleb, a senior Counselor, rising on his hind feet just below Strap. His tail twitched angrily, and he jabbed with his front paw as he spoke. "And his brother with him! They both bear marks that look like black flames, like the fire that killed their mother. They have to be Ebyn!"

"Banish them! Banish them!" shouted most of the Counselors.

Banishment meant taking the pups outside the homeland,

where they would be abandoned to face certain death.

However, other Counselors were not so sure this was something they should even decide.

"You're asking for trouble if you try to take any pup away from a doe," said one hesitant Counselor.

"That's right. Bucks don't have anything to do with raising pups. This is none of our concern," sniffed another. "Better to just let the does handle it."

"They won't like our interference. They'll say this is none of our business."

"It is the Council's business!" argued Caleb. "It's a matter of Lucient and Ebyn!"

The arguing grew louder, more heated.

Strap had returned to his seat and was listening without comment. It was the Council's tradition to find consensus for important decisions, but Strap was not above cajoling or even intimidating the Counselors to force a decision he favored.

Keeping Ebyn out of Leafensong was one of the main responsibilities the Council took upon itself and a frequent topic of debates. But Strap usually left such discussions to the others. He wasn't really that interested in the age-old preoccupation with the meanings inherent in Lucient and Ebyn. He was concerned with the Tribe's well-being and enjoyed wielding the power of the Council. And his own.

Strap finally rose and when the Counselors quieted, he spoke.

"I hesitate to interfere with our does who are raising orphaned pups. Ordinarily this would be solely a family concern. But I hope the does understand that we can't allow this blind pup and the dark shadow he carries to remain in Leafensong. It's our responsibility as the Council to protect our Tribe from Ebyn. We must be ever diligent and that duty takes precedence over rights of family.

"After giving this much consideration, and as Leader of the Council, I hereby decree, with the Council's consent, of course, that the blind pup must be banished. We know he is touched with Darkness. But do their black marks which look like fire mean he and his brother are both Ebyn? We don't really know. This is something we haven't faced before. I believe the pup with sight should be allowed to remain. This seems reasonable and fair, and should satisfy the does. Do we all agree?"

Immediately most of the Counselors affirmed Strap's pronouncement, "Yes, we agree. Banish the blind one!"

Caleb and a few others were not happy, wanting to banish both, but did not object. Others were also hesitant, uncertain how the does would react, but remained silent. No one wanted to openly disagree with Strap.

Strap glanced at the most senior Counselors—Caleb, Beecher and Abel—who sat just below him. They looked back and forth at one another frowning. Finally, Caleb spoke.

"We'd be allowing Ebyn to remain among us if even one of the two pups remained. Are you sure you want to be responsible for this, Strap?"

Strap could see the slightest twitch in the corner of Caleb's mouth, not quite a smirk.

"This is a decision of the whole Council, Caleb, not mine. I am merely offering this as a solution to a vexing problem. Do you want to try and take the pup that sees from Beka's daughter? Do you want to explain why you think that's what needs to happen?"

Caleb's mouth straightened into a thin line. Those who didn't know him well would think he had no feelings about this.

"Well?" asked Strap, fixing his eyes on Abel and Beecher also. "Do you want to tell Beka or her daughter that both these pups must die?"

Abel and Beecher looked at one another as the other Counselors behind them murmured warnings.

"I wouldn't do that," said one.

"No way," added another.

"No," blurted out Abel. "Banish the blind one. That will get rid of Ebyn."

"Yes, that should be enough," added Beecher.

Strap now stared at Caleb waiting, allowing Caleb to see the small smile on Strap's face.

"Well, Caleb?" Strap asked, "What do you think?"

"I agree," replied Caleb, sullenly.

"It is decided then," said Strap.

A few of the does in the surrounding trees muttered their objections under their breath, but most kept quiet and simply left.

Locating Rak, a Counselor and Captain of the Guards, who sat on the Council Oak not far below him, Strap ordered, "Captain, gather some of your guards and take the blind pup outside the tribal area at once. He is to be banished!"

Rak, who hadn't said anything, now jumped into action.

"Yes sir," he replied.

Rak motioned to two of his guards, Matson and Daker, who sat in a tree next to the Council Oak, to follow him as he walked down the length of the leaning oak and exited between its upturned roots. Without another word, the three of them set off through the trees, west toward Claryn's nest to carry out Strap's decree.

Strap was quite satisfied with this compromise. *A blind orphaned pup won't be missed*, he thought. All the squirrels deemed blindness a terrifying curse. He knew does would fight to the death to ensure the safety of their children, but this pup's mother was no longer living. The blindness clearly made the pup Ebyn. And the Council was, after all, generously allowing the blind pup's twin to live. Surely their authority and decision wouldn't be seriously questioned. *After all, what is most important is protecting the Tribe from Ebyn, isn't it?* he sniffed. *Even Beka has to understand that this is a matter for the Council to decide, not the does. They all have to understand that.*

Happy to have led the Council once again to his decision and confident his decree would be carried out, Strap watched the Council and audience slowly disperse. A smirk finally appeared on Strap's face as he watched Caleb leaving quietly, and Strap put the issue of the blind pup out of his mind.

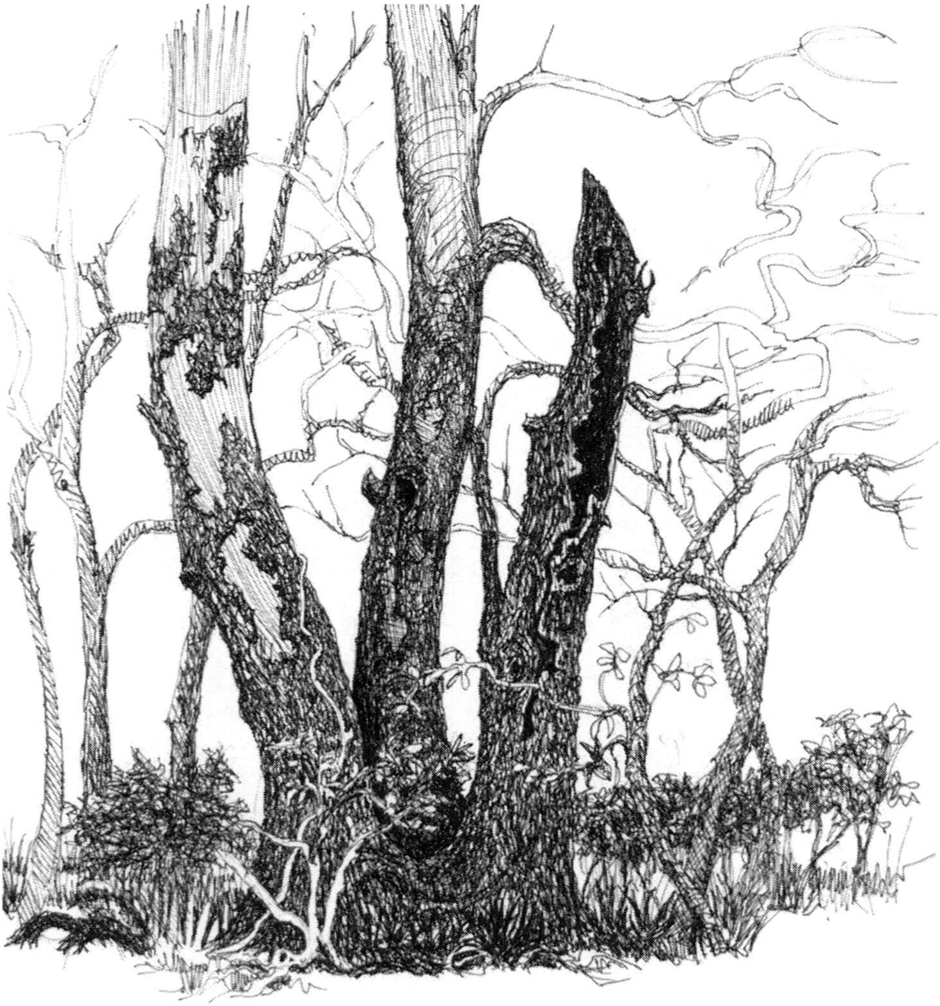

CHAPTER FIVE

Year 3071 AA
Day 101

RAK AND HIS GUARDS, MATSON AND DAKER, MOVED AT A STEADY PACE, HEADING WEST. Focused upon safely crossing limbs and vines, climbing and descending tree trunks and jumping from tree to tree, they ignored the forest around them that was bursting with new life. The leaves were turning more vibrant green; the songbirds were singing of hope and rebirth. And they tried to ignore the does trailing behind them who were muttering angrily. But the complaints were growing louder and the does were becoming more agitated as they distanced themselves from the Council Oak.

I can't believe this, Rak thought to himself, annoyed. He finally stopped, determined to put a stop to the does' meddling. He turned around, but was surprised to see well over a dozen does following close behind. He raised a front paw and shouted a warning, "Turn back! The Council has the final word on this, and it has been decided. There will be no further discussion. Go back to your nests at once!"

But instead of dispersing, the does became even angrier. One old doe approached Rak, yelling vehemently, "You leave Chaska's pups alone! This is none of your business!"

"That's right," said another doe. "The fate of these pups is a family matter and Claryn and Beka will decide what will happen with the pups!"

I've never seen does so angry, Rak thought as does sprinted ahead through the trees on either side of him. As other does continued to harangue him, Rak glanced at Matson and Daker and could see the worry in their darting eyes. He didn't say anything, simply motioned with a paw for them to follow.

Rak, Matson and Daker continued on as more does chased alongside and behind, some now yelling almost non-stop.

"You leave Claryn alone!"

"You've got no business taking a pup!"

"How dare you interfere with a family!"

Rak didn't respond. When he considered where Claryn and the pups were staying, the fur on the back of his neck tingled.

As the Tribe's venerated Healer, Beka held the greatest stature among the does of Leafensong. She had inherited her tree from the Tribe's last Healer, her great-great-great grandmother. The bur oak had stood in Leafensong for centuries, its thick trunk angling up from a broad base at the ground, covered with deep furrows and pronounced ridges. Much of the dark bark had been worn smooth by multiple generations of clambering squirrels. Its branches were thickset and strong, few shortened where they had broken off in storms, but most sprawled out like well-muscled forearms, covered with small, light green leaves growing larger and darker every day.

Beka's bur oak was just past the burned sycamore, which came into sight first. The tops of its two remaining trunks, taller than Beka's oak, gleamed white with the sun, in sharp contrast to the burned out stump of the sycamore's third trunk. The sycamore stood just beyond an ash tree which Rak, Matson and Daker entered, jumping and crossing a long limb, circling the trunk and following a branch to the far side of the tree, looking directly at the sycamore. There they stopped and stared.

The repulsive stench of charred wood filled the nostrils of Rak and his guards. The blackened stump was the closest of the three trunks and reminded them of the violent storm and firebolt of lightning which had taken Chaska's life. Rak and Daker had each been curious enough to have already gone out of their way to see it, but observing it so close up was a jolt to their senses. Rak heard Matson gasp and whisper, "How did these pups survive? No wonder one was born blind."

Even though outwardly he seemed completely composed, inwardly Rak shuddered. Like everyone in the Tribe, he harbored an instinctive fear of lightning and fire. But no fear had ever prevented him from performing his duties. He had become Captain of the Guards years ago because of his size and strength, athletic prowess and courage, but also because of his intelligence and tenacity. Like Strap, he was not easily intimidated. But now, facing the burned sycamore with Beka's oak looming behind, and with the horde of loud, angry does surrounding him, Rak hesitated, uncertain.

Daker spoke up, "You don't think she'd still be here, do you, Cap? I'd think by now Claryn would be nesting in Beka's tree."

"I agree, Cap," said Matson.

Rak could tell by their voices that Daker and Matson did not want to go into the sycamore. He didn't either. Turning around to face his guards, Rak said in a low voice, "I agree. She's surely taken the pups into her mother's tree. But, if we check out the sycamore first, it might intimidate the does. They don't want to go in the sycamore any more than we do. And we need to get them to back off."

Neither Darker nor Matson moved. Matson's eyes pleaded for Rak not to order them into the sycamore.

Very well, he thought. "You two stay here," Rak said. "I'll go in and check out the nest." Rak could see the relief wash over Matson's and Daker's faces. He only hoped they did not see his fear.

Chapter Six

Year 3071 AA
Day 101

RAK TOOK A DEEP BREATH. IN ONE STEP, HE REACHED THE END OF THE LIMB AND JUMPED THE SHORT DISTANCE TO A LONG, ARCHING BRANCH OF THE SYCAMORE, LEADING TO ITS MIDDLE TRUNK. Instantly, the does hushed and the forest became eerily silent. As Rak assumed, the does were also deathly afraid of the Darkness the sycamore represented.

Deliberately, he descended the trunk until the nest opening on the burned trunk was directly across from him. He forced himself to jump the short distance to the stump, landing on the crumbling bark next to the small opening where he knew Chaska had given birth. He poked his head inside, his stomach lurching. As he expected, he detected no other scent than that of burnt wood. No one had been in the nest for some time.

Rak backed away from the opening and looked around at the silent does. His eyes fell on Rayna, an older doe he knew only in passing, perched high up in a neighboring hickory tree. *Maybe she knows where Claryn and the pups are,* he thought. He jumped back to the center trunk of the sycamore and climbed to another limb, ran across it and jumped over to the hickory. With a few hops he came alongside Rayna, who hadn't moved. Leaning in close to her face, Rak bellowed, "Where is Claryn? Where is she nesting?"

Rayna cowered, her eyes darting back and forth.

Several does shouted at her, urging her to keep quiet. "Don't tell him anything, Rayna!"

"I. . .I'm not sure," Rayna stammered as she backed away from Rak. She turned to flee only to find that Daker and Matson had come up from behind. Daker grabbed her shoulders roughly. Thrusting his face close to hers, he narrowed his eyes, shouting mere inches from her face.

"The Captain asked you a question! Now, where is Claryn's nest?" he barked.

Rayna extended a trembling paw and pointed. Daker, Rak and Matson all swung around to see that she was pointing toward a hole in the shape of a crescent moon high up on the trunk of Beka's tree.

Outwardly, Rak showed no expression, but inwardly he cringed. He had assumed that Claryn would have taken the pups into her mother's tree. But seeing Rayna point to the bur oak, he now faced the fact that he had to enter the one tree that was most sacred to the does. The does, seeing Rayna point to Beka's tree, realized the bucks fully intended to enter her tree to take the pup. Once again they screamed their objections.

"You have no business there!"

"Stay out of Beka's tree!"

"That's the Healer's tree; you can't go there!" Feeling guilty for having betrayed Claryn, Rayna was now angry with herself and Daker. Emboldened by the other does, she lunged at Daker. Hissing wildly through her teeth, she raked her claws across his flank, drawing blood. In pain, and furious that she had dared to harm him, Daker lifted a clenched paw to strike her. But Rak reached out past Rayna to grab Daker's paw and stop the blow just before Rayna was struck in the face. Rayna quickly shot out from under them.

"Daker! Get yourself together!" Rak ordered. "We're here to get a job done. That's all. We don't need to make enemies of the does!" He nodded toward the does now gathered in trees all all around them. Daker looked about, realizing that the number of does had greatly multiplied. The three guards were completely surrounded by does filling the limbs of the hickory and adjacent trees. Their furious voices had become a barking chorus,

"You can't enter Beka's tree!"

"Stay out! Out!"

The does grew ever bolder and angrier, inching closer, their voices at a shrill pitch. Matson's and Daker's tails twitched and jerked nervously.

From a branch above them, a doe dropped, landed directly on the limb behind Matson, and spat at him.

"How dare you! You've no right to go there!" she screamed. "You can't take orphaned pups away from Claryn. She promised Chaska she'd protect them! Shame on you!"

Outwardly, Rak forced himself to appear calm, but inwardly his trepidation mounted. *This was a mistake*, he now thought. *I shouldn't have agreed to do this.*

The doe behind Matson was still berating him and had backed him up into Daker, who was now face to face with Rak.

"What are we going to do, Cap?" asked Daker, uncertainty plain in his voice.

Composing himself, Rak barked sharply, "Like it or not, we've got a job to do. Follow me and stay close." Rak kept his eyes focused straight ahead as he led Daker and Matson towards Beka's oak. Rak drew in a deep breath to fortify himself and jumped from the hickory onto a branch of the bur oak, followed by Daker and Matson. Outraged by the audacity of the bucks to enter Beka's tree, the does instantly surged forward and leaped onto the limbs of Beka's tree, surrounding Rak and his guards on every side, below and above them, screaming their defiance. But the three bucks plodded on, pushing does aside as they climbed the tree's trunk towards the nest Rayna had pointed out. Rak glanced at Beka's main nest below and was relieved not to see her. As he approached the moon-shaped entrance to the nest, Rak spoke up, trying to make himself heard above the furious din, "Claryn, we're here for the blind pup. The Council has decided . . ."

He was interrupted by Claryn's muffled but heated response from deep inside the nest. "No! The twins are mine! Both of them! Go away and leave us alone!"

Claryn's declaration didn't surprise Rak. Although he had never known Claryn to be aggressive, he knew nothing was more fierce than a doe protecting her pups and the wrath of the does made her reaction, at this point, expected.

Rak spoke up again, "Claryn, the Council has decided you can keep the healthy pup. But the blind one must go. He is marked by Ebyn. He is not really yours, anyway."

Still not showing herself, Claryn spit out angrily from just inside her nest, loud enough for all the does to hear.

"I said NO! I've adopted them! They are now mine. Both of them. You can't have either of them!"

Claryn's bold defiance was immediately followed by the does increasing the volume of their objections to a deafening roar.

Rak's shoulders fell in frustration. He saw that the does' fury and Claryn's responses were feeding each other and the situation had spun completely out of control.

Before he could change his mind, he pushed ahead, motioning to Matson and Daker to follow.

But just as Rak reached the mouth of the nest, Claryn sprang up from inside to block the entrance. Her incisor teeth bared just inches from Rak's face, she hissed at him in defiance.

"You'll have to kill me to take either of the pups!"

Instinctively, Rak backed into Daker, who couldn't move with Matson right behind him. Two other does clawed Matson's rear haunch, drawing blood as they screamed, "Get out of Beka's tree!"

In pain, Matson jerked around to fend them off as another doe dropped from a higher branch onto Daker's back, clawing wildly, cutting gashes through his fur. Frantic, Daker shook her off, and the doe slid down the trunk. Both Matson and Daker were now thoroughly terrified as the rabid does closed in on them from all sides, screaming that they leave.

"Get out of Beka's tree!"

"You have no right! Get out!"

"You'll have to kill us all to take either pup!"

Rak was now frozen by confusion and fear himself, when he heard the calm, confident voice of an older doe above them.

"Captain, stop. Call off your guards and leave. Claryn and I both have adopted these pups as our own."

Rak looked up to find Beka. She was sitting on her haunches, peering down from a higher branch of the gnarled oak. She rose and began to carefully crawl down the furrowed trunk toward Claryn's nest while Rak quickly scanned the crowd of does circled around him. None spoke further, their eyes focused on their beloved Beka. For the first time, he noticed the members of the Council and other bucks gathered in the surrounding trees. Silent and wide-eyed, they were as shocked as he was by the does' behavior. It seemed to Rak as if the entire Tribe had gathered. He shifted in the uncomfortable quiet, unsure how to proceed.

Beka broke the inertia when she approached the nest opening where Claryn was still standing her ground. Without pausing, Beka moved boldly past Rak into the nest as Claryn backed further inside. Beka turned and laid down, her head and shoulders protruding from the large opening. She could not have physically prevented Rak from forcing his way into the nest, but Rak realized neither he nor any buck could disobey her authority, not here in her own sacred tree and not now, given the fanatical support of so many does.

Her eyes wavering only from age, Beka locked eyes with Rak, and spoke again in a voice that was calm yet strong enough for everyone to hear.

"The Council has made a mistake. It does not have the right to banish any pup. It has always been the right of does to make decisions regarding our young. We have performed that task ably, and the Council has never suggested that we should not do so.

Until now. But the Council has no say in this. These pups are adopted by both Claryn and myself!"

Rak was completely taken aback. *They **both** have adopted the pup? I've never heard of such a thing.* His thoughts were now a jumbled mess. He craned his neck toward the surrounding Council members, searching for thier leader. Strap was standing on a small branch of the ash tree next to the sycamore, higher than Rak and looking down, his paws resting on another branch. Rak waited for him to say something.

On the surface, Strap appeared to be unfazed, as composed as ever, not showing his inner emotions. But he was as shocked as Rak and the other bucks. When his eyes finally met Beka's stare, Strap realized he had to respond. He knew the Council members were waiting to see how he handled this, and that none would come to his aid. After all, it had been his decision to banish the blind pup and he had bullied consensus from the Council. His gaze flickered across to Caleb, who was openly smirking.

Strap began making his way toward Beka's tree, keenly aware of the eyes of the entire Tribe upon him. With a veneer of bravado hiding his uncertainty and anger, he strode across the sycamore's limbs, until he was directly across from Beka's perch in the oak. With all the steadiness he could muster, Strap broke the silence.

"Perhaps the Council should discuss this further. The Council will meet again and . . ."

Beka interrupted him in a firm, stern voice, "It doesn't matter what the Council discusses. I say again, a decision about the care of pups is only for does to make. This takes precedence over the Council's concerns. The twins have been adopted by both Claryn and me and are now under our protection. It is done."

Seething within, Strap scoured the crowd but no Council member said a word. Struggling to control his voice he replied as calmly as possible, "Very well. I believe I speak for the Council. We concede to Beka's wishes. However, I point out that if any misfortune befalls our Tribe as a result of the Darkness brought here by the blind one, the fault will be Beka's alone."

Without waiting for a response, Strap turned from Beka and crossed back through the sycamore. The uncomfortable silence was ended by does breaking out in song, celebrating family and the bond between mother and pup. Strap fumed as all the does joined in. His gut was churning as he thought to himself, *You can have your blind pup for now, but you won't be around that much longer.*

Without a word, Rak motioned to Matson and Daker to join him as he left Beka's tree, crossing through the hickory and avoiding the sycamore. Eager to escape the does' celebration, the Council members followed Strap as he headed back to the Council Oak. No one spoke up until they were out of earshot. A few grumbled about Beka's declaration. Others griped about Strap.

"This should have never happened. It sets a bad precedent."

"They both adopted the pups?"

"Strap didn't let us think this through. This is his fault!"

But Strap didn't hear them. He was too lost in his own angry thoughts. *You just wait, Beka. Your time will soon be over.*

In the midst of the laughter and singing all around her, Beka watched Strap leave. She knew Strap's capitulation was only a momentary respite and Boggs could still be in danger. She retreated into the nest where Claryn was nursing the pups. "We must be careful," she warned Claryn even as she embraced them. "Bucks and does alike will still feel threatened by Boggs' blindness."

"Do you think Strap or the Council will try again to take Boggs?" asked Claryn, fretfully.

"We don't know what the future will bring," Beka replied. "At least for now, though, Boggs is safe."

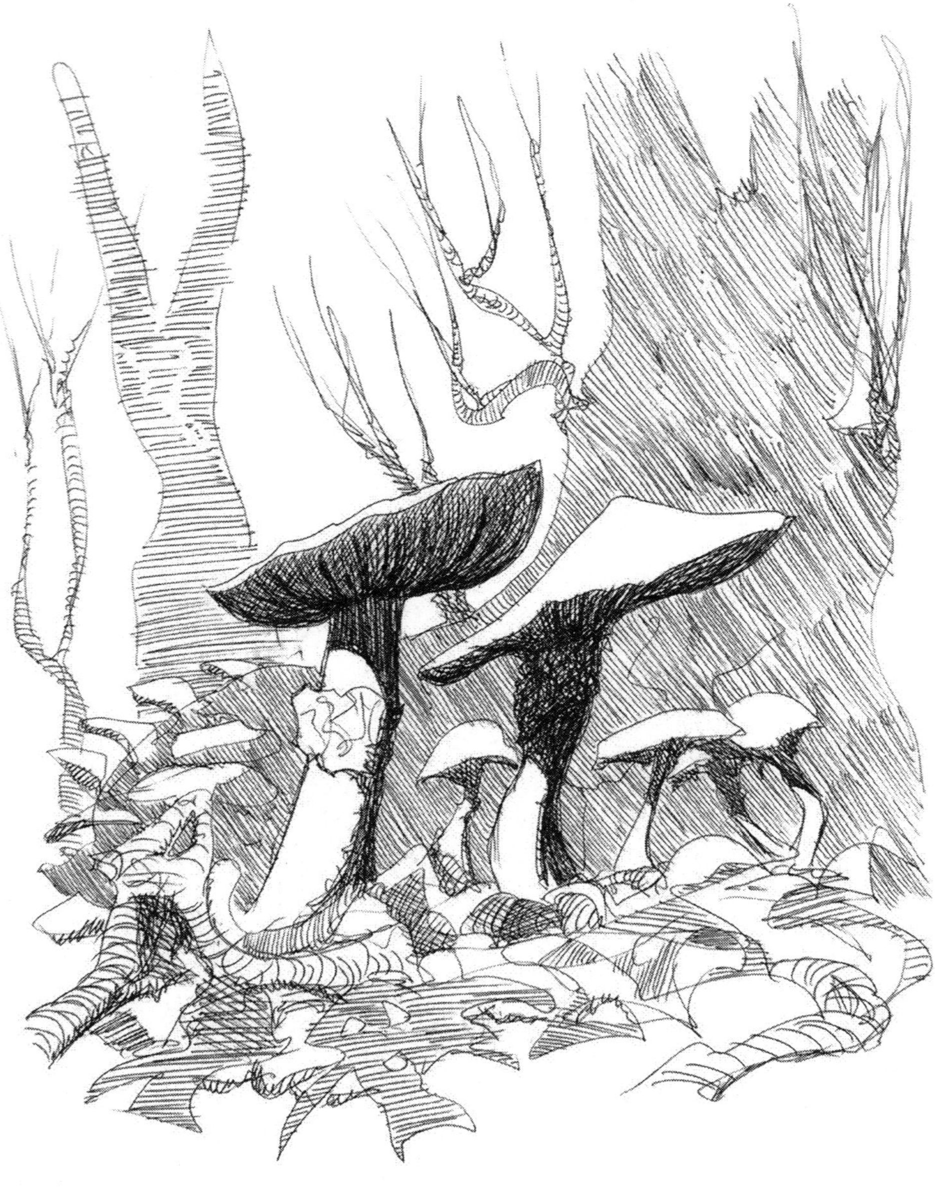

CHAPTER SEVEN

Year 3071 AA
Day 176

BEKA AND CLARYN'S FAMILY WAS LEFT TO ITSELF, AND THE PUPS GREW STEADILY AS SPRING PROGRESSED TO SUMMER. Days grew longer and warmer. The leaves on the trees filled out, changing from light to a darker green, and the sunshine so abundant in early spring was now, for the most part, blocked by the dense canopy. The squirrels had gorged themselves on the abundant food. They especially enjoyed the plentiful silver maple buds and flowers that turned into crunchy seeds, each with two small wings, that twirled as they fell, delighting the playful pups. Many seeds were also gathered by Claryn and stored in dry holes in Beka's bur oak, just as acorns and nuts were in the fall. But they were too plentiful to all be eaten and stored. A host of pale green maple seedlings shot up from the forest floor, but most soon died from lack of sunlight. Only where a tree had fallen or a branch had broken off did enough sunlight find its way through the canopy to allow the young trees to continue to grow.

The maple seeds that were, still on the ground with the arrival of summer had begun to decompose and were no longer good to eat. So the squirrels turned to finding last year's acorns and nuts under the leaves on the ground. Claryn stopped nursing the rapidly growing pups and began teaching them where and how to find good things to eat.

"Can you smell any acorns?" Claryn asked the pups one day.

"Here's one," said Kooper as he dug down, pulled out a bur oak acorn so large it was obviously from his grandmother's tree and brushed away dirt, only to find it had a small hole. He held the acorn up to his nose and sniffed warily. Disappointed, he threw it aside "It's bad. It's got a worm in it."

"I've got a good one," said Boggs as he held up an acorn free of worms, brushed it clean and proceeded to gnaw the thin shell off with his long front teeth. He handed bits of the nut meat to each of the others.

"How come Boggs can find so many good ones?" asked Spinner, as he quickly ate his portion, then buried his snout in the leaves beneath him, looking for his own acorn. His tail twitched as it hung over his back and he dug with his forepaws.

"I think being blind has heightened his other senses," replied Claryn, as she looked up to see Beka watching from the entrance to her nest. Beka glanced down at them, caught Claryn's eye, smiled, and then looked up, checking again for any hawk flying under the canopy, hunting for its own meal.

"You mean his hearing might be better, too?" asked Kooper proudly, his own snout close to the ground as he tried to catch the scent of another acorn.

"Possibly so," said Claryn.

"Here's another good one," said Boggs, happily tearing off the hairy cap and handing it to Kooper.

"Yep, no worm in this one," said Kooper, turning the acorn over in his paws as he sniffed. "I have a hard time smelling the difference between a good and a bad one when they're still under the leaves or dirt. They pretty much all smell alike to me until I can dig them out."

"To me too," said Spinner. "I think Boggs does have a better nose."

"Here's a smaller acorn. A black oak I think," said Kooper. "It's a good one."

"I don't like those as well as the bur acorns. The black oak acorns are really bitter," added Spinner.

"They don't taste as sweet as a bur acorn," agreed Claryn. "But, they last longer before spoiling. A bur acorn will start decaying in one year, but the black or red oak acorns last an extra year even if buried in the ground. I think that's why the bur acorns taste better. But, if you store any acorns or nuts up in a tree and keep them dry, they last much longer."

"How about if we find some mushrooms to eat?" asked Spinner.

"Okay," said Claryn. "Remember, you've got to be careful eating mushrooms. Some kinds will make you sick and others will even kill a squirrel. Pay attention so you learn which mushrooms are safe to eat and where the good ones grow."

"I know there are some mushrooms over here," said Spinner as he led them to a walnut log that was rapidly decaying into dark brown dust. "Right here on the other side of the log. Are these good, Mom?"

"Those are. But these over here are not. See the difference? They smell different also. Here, take a whiff."

"So if I ate those, I'd get sick?" asked Kooper.

"Or worse. You do not want to eat those, believe me. Boggs, can you smell the difference between these?" Claryn held up two mushrooms that looked fairly similar under Boggs' nose and he smelled one at a time, his nose crinkling.

"Yes, this is the safe one to eat," Boggs said pointing to one of the mushrooms. He turned his head towards the sound of a doe squirrel singing in the distance and then a second doe joining in.

"Do you recognize the difference in the voices of the squirrels singing, Boggs?" asked Claryn.

"Yes," replied Boggs, still listening. "I've heard these voices before."

"I wish they'd be willing to let us sing with them," said Spinner. "When I try to join in, they usually stop."

"It's probably your voice," joked Boggs. Kooper guffawed. But all of them knew the reason was Boggs and Kooper.

"Give it time," Claryn said smiling. "Just keep singing yourselves. Hopefully, they'll come to accept you."

"I don't care if they do," said Kooper. "I'm fine with them leaving us alone."

"It will take longer for the others to accept you and Boggs. But, I think eventually they will."

"It's me they're afraid of," said Boggs out loud. "Everyone thinks I'm Ebyn."

"They think that about me, too," said Kooper. "We both have

the same marking on us. I think when anyone sees us, they think of fire, lightning and darkness. I've heard them say so."

"Yes, that's what some think," replied Claryn, "But they're wrong. Just because you have your unique markings doesn't mean you are Ebyn."

"I think your flames are great," said Spinner. "I wish I had one."

Claryn laughed. "You were named after your markings, Son. You're one of the few squirrels with a band that spins around your body and your tail."

"I thought it was because I was such a great spinner."

Spinner twirled himself around and around until he got dizzy and fell over.

Kooper and Claryn laughed. "Maybe that too," giggled Claryn. "Now let's look at these mushrooms again. I don't want you to eat any unless you're sure they're not going to make you sick. Until you are sure, ask Boggs."

Claryn continued to teach the pups when and where to find food which was plentiful in Leafensong. Members of the Tribe rarely ventured beyond its boundaries because their territory was home to plenty of good food trees, especially bur oaks. And no bur oak had better acorns than Beka's tree.

***

"Grandma, I've brought you an acorn," Boggs said as he entered her nest one afternoon. Beka's nest was at the end of a stout limb that had broken off many years ago. It was equidistant between the highest branches and the ground, and no other limbs with leaves were near it, making it easy to see the surrounding trees and ground below from the nest opening. At the front of the nest was a deep, wide porch. The large opening had three deep cuts in the lip but otherwise was smoothly rounded by years of use. The entrance to the inner nest was in the center of the wide back wall of the porch.

"Well, thank you, dear," replied Beka, grateful. "I was getting hungry." It was late in the day and Beka had spent all afternoon treating two does and a buck with ailments, who had just left. Boggs usually stayed away when others came to visit her. "Oh, this is a very good one," said Beka as she chewed the bur acorn, contentedly. "This must be from my tree."

"It is," he said with a grin.

"Claryn told me that you're able to know which acorns beneath leaves and even soil are good by smell, even before you dig them up." Boggs nodded. "Can you always tell?"

"Almost always," Boggs replied happily.

"Even acorns buried deep in the ground?"

"Yes, ma'am."

"You must have a great sense of smell. I don't know anyone else who can do that."

A big smile lighted Boggs' face. "I guess I'm pretty lucky then."

"Yes, you are.…Say, can you help me with this moss? I haven't had time to separate it since Claryn and Spinner gathered it. And can you tell me how many different kinds there are?"

Boggs hopped over and put his nose down into the large pile. *Two…no, three,* he thought.

"Three," said Boggs eagerly. "Two smell a lot alike, but I think there are three different kinds. Is that right?"

"Yes," Beka said happily. "I need these separated and then each divided into smaller amounts rolled up inside sycamore leaves."

"Why do you use sycamore leaves, Grandma?"

"Because they're larger than most kinds of leaves and can hold the right amount of moss without spilling. I've got a stack of leaves right here."

Boggs and Beka divided the moss into three piles. "There. Now we pull each type of moss apart into smaller sections, like this one."

Boggs took the clump in both paws and held it up to his nose to examine it and then handed it back to her. He separated another portion into two halves and held them up for her to see. "Like this?"

"Perfect. And we wrap each up with a leaf and tie it off with a piece of vine." She wrapped a leaf around the moss and tied the slender vine around it before handing it to him. Boggs turned the bundle over with both paws, feeling how the vine secured it.

"I see," said Boggs, raising his head as soon as he said it, realizing it didn't make sense. After a moment, they both giggled.

"You do see but with your paws and nose, Boggs. Probably better than many squirrels see with their eyes." Both smiled as they started to work.

"What are the names of these mosses?" Boggs asked.

"Carpet moss, forked moss and white-tipped moss."

"What do you use each of them for?"

"Carpet moss is used as a dressing for wounds. It reduces swelling and infection. It's a great medicine, and I use it often. Fortunately, it's pretty abundant." Beka handed him a clump.

"I recognize the smell and feel of it," said Boggs as he held it up to his nose. This grows in lots of places, on logs and on the sides of trees, especially oak and maple trees, doesn't it?"

"Yes, that's correct," said Beka, nodding. "How about this forked moss? Do you recognize it?"

"Yes," said Boggs, now smelling the ball of moss Beka handed to him. "This only grows on really rotten walnut logs and branches on the ground. And hackberry logs too."

"You're right, and very observant. This forked moss reduces pain. So I often use carpet moss and forked moss together when an ailing one has a cut."

Holding up a paw full of the third kind, Boggs asked eagerly, "What about this kind? You called this white-tipped moss, right?"

"Yes. This is used mainly for toothaches. The patient packs it in his or her cheek next to the tooth. Now, let's put these bundles on my shelves."

On either side of the opening to the inner nest along the broad, back wall of Beka's porch, shelves had been cut deep into the hard oak wood from floor to ceiling. Most had been there since long before Beka had inherited the tree, carved by the teeth of earlier Healers. The shelves were packed with bundles of leaves, bark, and other medicines with rolls of thin vine used to tie off the bundles.

"Can you figure out which kind of moss goes where?"

"Yes, ma'am." He proceeded to put each package away, deciphering where each went by smell and touch.

"Thank you, Boggs."

"You use other things for medicines than just moss, don't you?" he asked, touching the other packets stacked on the shelves.

"Yes," Beka said as she sat down on all four legs in the middle of her porch. "I use lots of things for different reasons. Leaves and stems of plants. Here, smell this bundle. These are dried paw paw leaves picked in early spring. Claryn gathered these from the patch of paw paw trees west of here. These will repel fleas from a nest. I use different leaves picked at different times, dried flowers and berries, and a number of kinds of bark. Usually I have a patient chew bark. You have to know how much of each kind to give a patient so they don't chew too much. Some medicines help calm down an upset stomach, others will reduce a fever or settle nerves. Like I said, lots of medicines for different remedies."

"Do you mind telling me what they all do? What they're used for? And how you use them?"

"That's a lot of information. You sure you want to know all that?"

"Yes," Boggs said excitedly. "I really do."

"Well, okay," she said. "If you really want to know." She picked up a package of carpet moss. "As I told you, this reduces swelling and infection. It has to be held against the wound, tied on with a piece of vine if possible. It will soak up the infection and has to be replaced several times a day."

I guess I will need more of this, Beka thought to herself. Boggs jumped, surprised. He had heard Beka's thought and realized she wasn't actually speaking. He couldn't see her face, but somehow he knew the difference between hearing her voice talk out loud and hearing her voice in his head. He didn't know why he realized this, but he was sure she had not spoken.

"What is it, Boggs?" Beka asked, seeing him jump.

"Nothing, Grandma. What about the moss that reduces pain?" he picked up another package. "This is forked moss, right?"

"Yes. Can you smell the difference? It's somewhat similar."

"Yes, ma'am. This isn't as bitter. And it smells a bit like a ripe hickory nut."

"Yes, it does," said Beka, surprised, her nose held against the bundle. *That's a good way of putting it,* she thought. *I wouldn't have described it that way myself, but now that he says it, I think so too.*

Boggs realized once again he was hearing Beka's thoughts. But, he didn't mention this to her. He wasn't sure what to think. *I haven't heard of anyone else doing this. Am I the only squirrel who can?* He normally didn't like being different from the others. But this ability to Sense someone's thoughts was intriguing. *Is this like my ability to smell so well? Can I do this because I'm blind?*

Beka noticed that Boggs was deep in thought. "I think that's enough talking about medicines. How about if we sing awhile? Boggs, are you listening to me?"

For a split second Boggs thought about telling Beka he could Sense her thoughts but immediately decided against it, uncertain how she would respond. Instead, he said, "I'm sorry, Grandma, yes, let's sing."

***

Beka and Claryn had already taught many of the Tribe's songs to the pups. Like most does, Beka and Claryn were constantly singing or humming. Hearing a squirrel singing in the distance, others would join in, some singing the melody, others harmonies, and soon the forest was filled with song. Beka and Claryn encouraged their young charges to sing as soon as they were able.

"Can you sing with me, Spinner?" Claryn had asked when the pups were only a few months old. "Listen to the words and the melody. Hum along until you get it."

"Let's sing harmony, Boggs," suggested Beka. "And you too, Kooper. I think we five will make a great choir. I'll start off."

By the middle of summer, Spinner, Kooper, and Boggs sang without the need of encouragement. They had learned how to weave their sweet, young voices into beautiful harmonies. They loved singing so much that even when they weren't you could hear them humming contentedly to themselves, just as Beka and Claryn did.

To everyone in the Tribe, music was an integral part of their daily lives—as necessary as food and air. The Tribe did not know why singing had always been so important, although Beka had an idea. She believed singing was natural for any squirrel because it made one happier. She also knew music helped healing.

As summer wore on, Kooper started watching over Boggs more and more. He was determined to make sure Boggs was safe whenever Boggs was down on the ground searching for food. Boggs didn't need any help from Kooper in finding nuts. So Kooper came to be his brother's watcher, staying above, usually in Beka's tree, looking back and forth from Boggs to the sky through gaps in the canopy and all around through the tree branches, watching for hawks.

Spinner tried to watch out for Boggs also, but Kooper had realized that his cousin was an unreliable watcher. Spinner was hyperactive and more interested in having fun. He had a difficult time paying constant attention to Boggs or anything else.

Claryn helped watch Boggs also, but by the end of summer, she and Beka had come to accept that Kooper would always be on the lookout when Boggs descended the trees to forage for food or just explore the forest floor, or when Boggs moved through the branches of the bur oak and surrounding trees he had now memorized. Kooper's protective feelings towards his twin were obvious.

"Kooper is so attentive!" Beka said to Claryn one warm late afternoon as they sat on her porch eating a snack.

"He certainly is. Twins often have a special bond."

"It's more than that," replied Beka. "And it's not just twins that feel that way. You and Chaska felt the same way about each other."

"Yes we did. I don't think I'll ever get over her loss."

"Me either, but it will get easier. When I lost my sister and your grandmother, it took a long time to feel all right again. But life goes on and at least we have Chaska's pups with us."

Time did help heal their hearts. Time, as well as being so busy caring for patients, gathering medicine or food, and teaching their young family all the ways of their Tribe. And singing, sometimes mixed with tears.

***

When summer ended, leaves on walnut trees turned yellow, falling with the green husk-covered walnuts. The long twigs holding the leaves and nuts also fell, making for a tangled, dirty mess below any walnut tree. The larger leaves on sycamores became mottled and curled up before turning completely brown, fluttering down whenever a strong breeze rustled the branches. Hard maple leaves began their transformation to red and gold. Ash and cottonwood leaves turned two shades of yellow. The days were still warm but nights were beginning to cool. And it was time for gathering and storing as many nuts for the upcoming winter as they could.

"We've filled the topmost storage holes, Aunt Claryn," said Kooper, hanging upside down and looking in Beka's porch, framed by the bur oak's leaves that were beginning to turn a dull, reddish-brown.

"Good," replied Claryn happily. She and Beka were bundling together thin pieces of bark each tied with bits of vine. "Now we can start filling the next lower ones. But first you and Spinner need to clean out the nuts from last year. Throw out any spoiled ones and put all of the good nuts in one spot. Those will be the first we eat. We don't want to waste any of them, especially our acorns from this tree."

"Thank you for helping, Kooper," said Beka. "You all are a big help in this. Especially as I'm having a harder time gathering food."

"And, Kooper, keep the silver maple seeds in one hole by themselves," Claryn added. "Your grandmother really enjoys having some of those in winter."

Beka smiled at that thought and added, "Yes, I do!"

Boggs arrived with a bur acorn clamped tightly in his teeth and a walnut under a foreleg. Since he didn't move as quickly, he couldn't store as many acorns as the others, but he kept at it, moving at a steady pace. He removed the acorn from his teeth and set it on the porch floor with the walnut. It was obvious he had pulled the soggy husk off the walnut just moments before. The fur on his forelegs and chest was still damp and stained from the husk's dark brown juice.

"You're a mess, Boggs," laughed Spinner, who had joined them. He dropped the two large bur acorns he was juggling on the porch floor. "You've got walnut stain all over you."

"I like walnuts," said Boggs defensively. "They're my favorite."

"You keep pulling walnut husks off, you'll be as dark as walnut juice."

"I like them too, Boggs," said Beka. "I hope you're storing some walnuts for us."

"Yes, ma'am," replied Boggs proudly. "I've stored plenty so we can have some all winter long."

"Thank you. That will be tasty on a snowy day."

"Do the other families store as many nuts as we do?" Boggs asked.

"Not always," said Beka. "And many are sorry they didn't. That's why we gather so many. This tree always has more acorns than any other tree, enough that we never eat all we store. In late winter we'll have surplus for the families who didn't save enough."

"That doesn't seem fair," said Spinner with a frown. "We do extra work for others?"

"For ourselves and others," replied Beka. "That's part of being members of this Tribe. With your mother's help, I heal others who are sick and injured, and we share food because our tree has more and better acorns than any other tree. We're fortunate. This family has never gone hungry, even in the coldest part of winter. You'll appreciate having all our food when the snow comes."

Boggs listened in his mind to Kooper and Spinner's thoughts about winter, which they had heard so much about but had never experienced.

I like it when it's cooler, thought Spinner. *I don't see why getting cold would be so bad.*

I want to see snow. I bet it's beautiful, thought Kooper.

Boggs still hadn't told anyone he could Sense. Although he was beginning to appreciate this ability, it was another thing that made him different. *Am I the only squirrel able to do this?* he wondered. *What would they think if I tell them? Should I keep this to myself?*

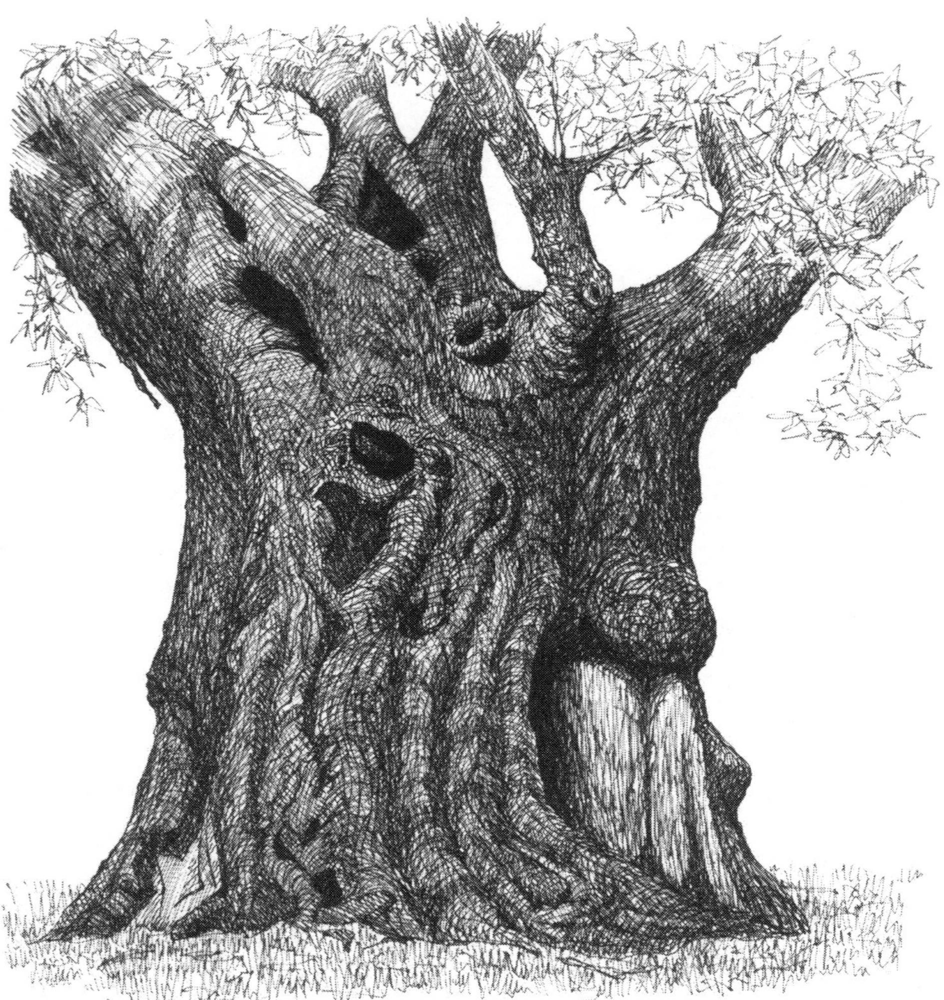

CHAPTER EIGHT

Year 3071 AA
Day 250

IT WAS EARLY AUTUMN. Beka wrapped Eljo's upper foreleg with a poultice of carpet moss in long paw paw leaves and secured it in place with a piece of vine. Eljo was a healthy two-year-old buck, only recently accepted into the Guard with his brother, Kuel.

"I've made that same jump plenty of times, Beka."

"I'm sure you have, but that's a problem with silver maples. The limbs split so easily. You're lucky the broken branch only pierced your skin. Fortunately, no bone was broken or chipped. I've pulled out all the splinters and cleaned it. Now you need to let it heal." She finished tying off the vine and held his paw as she spoke.

"Now you take it easy," she told him sternly, "No more jumps until this heals up. Come back before nightfall and I'll change this dressing. It needs to be changed three times a day for a week. And sing every chance you get. I know your mother has a beautiful voice; she'd love to sing with you."

"Mom does have a nice voice," said Eljo. "So does my brother, Kuel. I'll go find them and see if they would like to sing together."

"Good. Do this often. And lie on a tree branch way up high when there's a breeze and listen to the leaves rustle and the branches moan. Listen to the birds sing. Hum along with the cicadas—there are a few still singing. All of that will do you good."

"Thank you, Beka. I'll be back before nightfall to get this changed."

"Before you go, I wanted to thank you."

Confused, Eljo asked, "Why?"

"Rak just named you and a good number of other guards."

Eljo brightened into a big smile. "Yes, ma'am! Twenty of us! The older guards say it's the biggest number of new guards since after the Great Battle."

"You should be proud of being named a guard."

Eljo beamed.

"But, do you know why Rak has named so many new guards? Is he worried about something?"

Eljo's smile vanished. "The Captain told us he's concerned about what may be happening outside Leafensong. He hasn't told us what exactly. But some of the older guards have been talking. Seems pack rats have been sighted just across the border."

"Pack rats!" Beka shuddered. "I thought no pack rats had been seen for years."

"Not until a few months ago. But now every few days one or two is seen at dawn or dusk."

Beka raised her eyebrows, "Are you sure the Captain would want you telling me this?"

"He knew I was coming here to get my wound treated. He told me if you asked to tell you. He said 'keep no secrets from Beka.'"

Beka caught her breath and almost choked.

"He feels bad for last year, Beka. He doesn't talk about it, but the guards know. He respects you and appreciates your healing us."

Beka was speechless. She had no idea Rak thought like this.

"There's talk the Cap may add even more guards. He's sure got us working hard. We train every day, morning and afternoon, learning how to fight, paw-to-paw combat, how to jump and leap properly, and we're learning the commands our officers would use in a fight. Sergeants Gist and Karmer and even the Captain are doing the training. They don't allow anyone to slack off. They push us and we're determined to be the best guards possible."

"Good for you," said Beka but inwardly she cringed, realizing Rak was preparing for a fight and knowing what could happen. "Now you be careful in your training. You tell the Captain I said no leaping for you until this wound closes up. Not until I say it's okay. I expect you back here later today so I can change this dressing."

"Yes, ma'am. And thank you."

Beka watched Eljo move cautiously as he left her tree. He stopped to sit in the neighboring ash as yellow leaves fluttered down. She heard him join in with other squirrels as they sang along with the thrumming of cicadas. But not a hint of a smile crossed her face.

The next morning, high above Beka's nest, Kooper sat still as he watched Boggs below. Dew left by the lifting fog glistened on leaves and bark. Boggs was sitting on the end of a stout limb seemingly staring at the damaged sycamore next to Beka's oak. Many of the sycamore's leaves had dropped, exposing the thick, rough squares of scaly brown bark at the bottom of the tree. The bark quickly turned into a creamy-white, smooth surface extending to the top of both the center trunk and the one closest to Beka's tree. Each was twice the height of Beka's oak. The far trunk, though, was a stump, the top black and charred. The ragged opening to the nest where the pups had been born was just beneath what was now the top of the stump. The scar left by the lightning bolt extended through the opening to the ground, a white gash across the blackened wood and brown bark.

Boggs had done this several times over the last few days, and it was making Kooper nervous. *What are you doing?* Kooper asked himself. *You can't see the tree, what are you thinking?*

As Kooper watched, Boggs got up and moved across the limb, down the oak's furrowed trunk to the forest floor and then straight to the base of the sycamore. He looked up as though he could see the tree's three trunks above him, making Kooper even more nervous. *You're not thinking of climbing that tree, are you?*

After hesitating only a moment, Boggs began to climb the trunk closest to Beka's tree, crossing the bottom section and quickly reaching the smooth bark above. The going was slow as there wasn't much texture for Boggs' claws to grip. He was especially careful moving across what remained of loose scraps of light green and grey bark that curled up and easily pulled away.

Boggs methodically explored the trunk and its branches. He went out as far as each long, curving limb would support his weight before returning to the trunk and moving to the next higher branch. He ran his paws over every loose flake of bark, knothole, adjoining limb and clump of twigs.

Kooper had seen Boggs do this in all the surrounding trees and realized Boggs was memorizing the sycamore as he had the others. But Boggs' explorations had never caused Kooper's stomach to push up into his throat as it did now. Kooper himself hadn't been in the sycamore since Claryn and Beka had first removed them before their eyes were even open.

Boggs continued to methodically inspect every branch and section of the thinning trunk. Finally he reached the top and after a moment's rest, descended until he was directly across from the burned out birth nest. There he sat for a few moments before climbing back up and across to a limb of the center trunk. He began inspecting all its branches. Kooper stretched and laid down, breaking his watch for only a moment to retrieve a bur acorn from a nearby hole in Beka's oak. He tore off the top and munched the nutmeat absent-mindedly as he returned to his duties.

The sun had marched across the sky by the time Boggs reached the top of the center trunk and once again descended until he was even with the top of the scarred third trunk. After hesitating for the briefest moment, Boggs hopped across to the charred bark and approached the old nest just below it's jagged edge. Kooper didn't look away this time but his heart thumped as Boggs climbed inside, disappearing from Kooper's view. Although he had half expected this, Kooper's heart sank. *No! Why, Boggs, why?*

Boggs Sensed to Kooper. *Because I don't want to be scared, Koop. And I want to see if it will help me remember Mother.*

It was as though Kooper had been struck in the head with a falling branch. He knew he shouldn't be able to hear what Boggs said from inside the sycamore nest, but he had heard Boggs' voice clearly, as though Boggs was right next to him. He stood up, his hind legs wobbly, and he instinctively looked all around, up and down, to see if Boggs was in Beka's tree, though he knew he wasn't, and then back towards the sycamore, when he heard Boggs' voice again.

I'm here in Mother's last nest, Koop. And yes, you're hearing my thoughts. I'm not talking out loud. Can you hear me?

Kooper was at a complete loss. Externally, he appeared fine, still standing on his hind paws, unmoving, but internally his mind was racing. *This can't be!* he thought to himself. *I must be dreaming.* Dizzy, his hind legs unable to hold him up, he sat down and grabbed a thin branch with a front paw to steady himself.

You're not dreaming, replied Boggs. *I'm sending my thoughts to you from my mind. And I can hear your thoughts. Can you hear my thoughts, Koop? Can you?*

In disbelief, Kooper reluctantly thought, *You can hear my thoughts?*

Yes, Sensed Boggs.

Kooper reluctantly but intentionally thought, *Then what am I thinking?*

You're asking me what you're thinking. Yes, it's true, I can hear your thoughts just as you can hear mine. If you're still watching, you're going to see me leave this nest now.

As Kooper watched, still dumbstruck and frozen in place,

Boggs stuck his head back out for a moment, glanced toward Kooper's general location and then came completely out of the nest, and steadily stared at him.

Boggs Sensed to Kooper again, *No, I can't see you, but I can hear your thoughts if I focus upon you. I know this is hard to accept, Koop, but it's true. I really can do this. And it's becoming easier and easier.*

Kooper shook his head but otherwise didn't move.

Kooper. Are you still there?

Reluctantly, Kooper allowed himself to think, *Yes, I'm here.*

I know it is strange, but it's really a good thing, I think.

"No!" said Kooper out loud, defiantly, but then merely thought, *How can something so...so strange be good?*

I'm strange, Koop. Everyone says I am; some say I'm Ebyn.

You're not Ebyn, thought Kooper. *But, this...I've never heard of such a thing, and I don't understand it.*

I don't understand it either, Sensed Boggs. *Maybe the lightning caused it, just like it caused my blindness. Or maybe my blindness somehow did this. I know my sense of smell is better than anyone else's. Maybe this is like that.*

Kooper didn't know what to think, what to say.

I know you're confused, Sensed Boggs.

You seem to know what I think even when I don't, thought Kooper uneasily. *Do Aunt Claryn and Grandma know you can do this? Have you told them?*

No, Sensed Boggs. *I'd like to tell them, but I don't know how they'd take it. You're the only one I've...Sensed this to.*

Is that what you call this? Sensed? Sensing?

Yes. Seems as good a description as anything.

I've got to think about this, thought Kooper. *And I don't want you to...Sense my thoughts for now anyway. Please stop it! Just speak to me out loud.*

I'm sorry, Koop. I'll stop Sensing right now.

Kooper was quiet. He was dazed, still in shock. *Can this be real?* He wondered. *And if so, is it...is it Ebyn?*

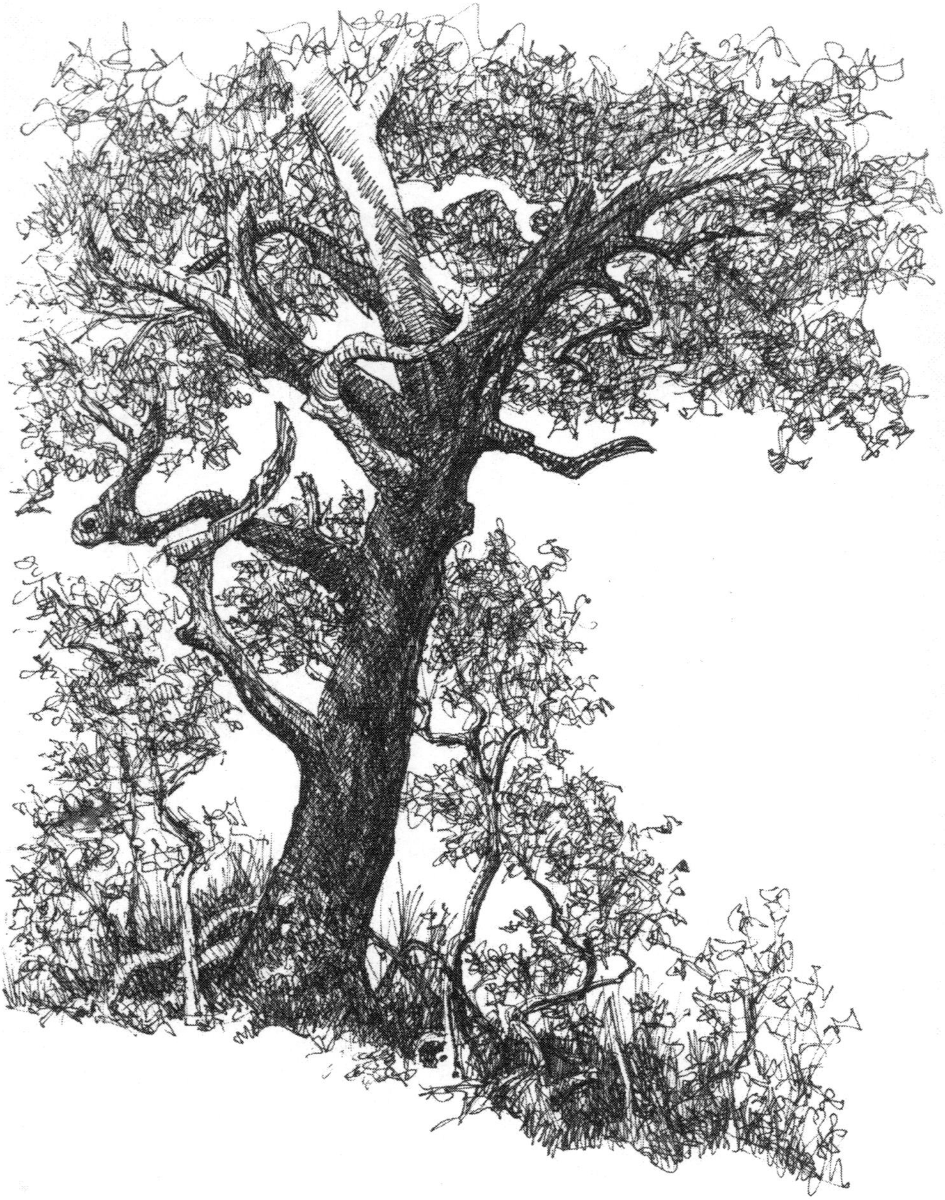

CHAPTER NINE

Year 3071 AA
Day 251

LATE IN THE AFTERNOON THE NEXT DAY, BOGGS JOINED KOOP-
ER AND TOGETHER THEY WENT DOWN TO THE FOREST FLOOR
TO GATHER ACORNS AND NUTS UNDER A NEIGHBORING BUR OAK.
YELLOW, GOLD, GOLD, AND RED LEAVES WHIRLED AROUND WITH
EACH STIFF BREEZE UNTIL THEY SETTLED ON THE GROUND. The
cheery songs of other squirrels and songbirds filled their ears, but
they remained silent. Neither had spoken all day. Boggs purposefully avoided Sensing Kooper's or anyone else's thoughts and kept
his own uncertain thoughts to himself. *Should I tell Grandma and
Mom?* he wondered. *Is this Ebyn? It doesn't seem wrong. Is the sycamore Ebyn? Am I?*

Kooper's thoughts were totally jumbled. He tried to focus on
his work and watching for hawks, but he couldn't avoid wondering,
Is Boggs really Sensing my thoughts? Is this real? Is any of this real?

Looking out the entrance of Beka's porch at his cousins below, Spinner whispered to Beka and Claryn, "Something's up with Boggs and Kooper. They're not speaking to one another and barely willing to talk to me."

Claryn looked up from the bundles of moss she was tying. "We noticed it too. Do you have any idea why?"

"No idea," he replied.

"Why don't you stay and help us, Spinner?" asked Beka. "If we leave them alone, I'm sure they'll resolve whatever is bothering them."

As dusk fell, Boggs and Kooper climbed into the nest they'd been sharing in Beka's tree. They settled in as usual, back to back, but neither spoke, and Boggs continued to keep his thoughts to himself. Kooper was still upset and confused, angry at Boggs, but he also felt guilty for feeling this way.

As darkness closed in fully, the low, steady rumbling of a distant storm reached their ears. Kooper pulled himself up to the nest's entrance to look outside. Through the thinning canopy of leaves, lightning beyond Leafensong lit up the sky every few seconds in a narrow blue arc above the nearly black horizon.

What would happen if lightning hit this tree? Kooper wondered. *Would it blind me?* Even though he had told Boggs he didn't want him to Sense his thoughts, Kooper abruptly thought, *Boggs, if you are Sensing me, I don't care. Are you listening to the thunder?* But instead of Sensing a reply, Kooper felt the rumbling of Boggs snoring, echoing the thunder in the distance. Kooper smiled to himself, *Well, at least you're not afraid,* he thought. *Maybe being in the sycamore has helped you.*

The rhythmic rumble of Boggs' body against Kooper's was

soothing, and Kooper's muscles relaxed even as the distant thunder continued. *Boggs can't be Ebyn,* Kooper thought. *My brother's never done anything that's bad, let alone Ebyn. Everything about Boggs is good, so his Sensing must be a good thing. And maybe being in the sycamore is the right thing for him. I probably just need to get used to it.* Kooper let out a long sigh, his mind finally at peace. Soon he too nodded off and joined Boggs in deep sleep with the thunder rolling on like a slow lullaby.

The next morning Boggs and Kooper still said nothing as they awoke and moved down to the ground to find something to eat. Boggs located a good walnut beneath the top layer of fallen leaves. He easily pulled off the dried husk and handed the hard inner nut to Kooper, who could keep quiet no longer.

"You Sensed to me that you went into mother's old nest because you didn't want to be scared. The tree has always frightened me. It scared you too, didn't it?"

"Sure, when I first entered it," said Boggs.

"Does it now?" Kooper asked.

"No, it doesn't," replied Boggs, somewhat surprised at the realization.

"You also...Sensed that you hoped being in the nest would help you recall memories of Mother," said Kooper. "I've never had any. Do you really think being in that nest might bring back memories of her?"

"I don't know," said Boggs. "But somehow being in the nest does make me feel closer to Mother."

Kooper mulled this over as he chipped away pieces of walnut shell exposing the pungent nutmeat. He broke off a piece of shell and spit it out. Using his tongue, he pulled out some nutmeat and chewed. Neither spoke nor Sensed to one another about the sycamore or their mother as they spent the rest of the day gathering and storing nuts. They had almost filled the storage holes in Beka's tree. Beka and Claryn had remarked how fast the job had gone this year with the pups' help.

As darkness fell, the two brothers once again settled into their nest in their grandmother's oak, back to back. Kooper spoke up, "Were you Sensing my thoughts today?"

"I did a few times. It's hard not to. I'm sorry if you didn't want me to."

"It's okay if you do," said Kooper. "I don't understand it but I guess there's nothing wrong with it."

Boggs eagerly Sensed back, *I'm glad you're okay with it. Maybe you can do it too, Koop, hear the thoughts of others and even Sense your thoughts to them. I've wondered if you could.*

"No, I don't think so," replied Kooper out loud. "And I don't want to try."

Boggs didn't respond or Sense anything else for several minutes until he blurted out loud, "I ask myself over and over what could be the reason I was born blind."

"And why I wasn't," Kooper responded uneasily. "I don't think there was a reason. I heard Grandma tell Jesska that sometimes in life bad things just happen. She said some squirrels have a hard time accepting that because they're afraid of questions that have no answers. I'll never accept that there was a reason you were born blind. It could have been me just as easily." Kooper paused before adding, "And it's okay with me if you want to sleep in the nest in the sycamore from time to time. Just not all the time, okay?"

"Thanks, Koop. No, I won't sleep there all the time."

The next morning was cooler, but the day had warmed by late afternoon. Resting after hauling nuts into Beka's tree, Kooper was high up in the oak eating a bur acorn, listening to the singing of birds and squirrels, humming along. Dull, red leaves were beginning to fall from the oak and more and more leaves were dropping from the sycamore, making the white and stark black tree stand out from the rest of the forest. Kooper realized for the first time that he wasn't avoiding looking at the tree. Gazing down, he watched Boggs climb the oak with a walnut clamped between his teeth and an acorn held against his chest.

As always, Boggs moved slowly but deliberately until he reached Kooper and the storage hole next to him. Boggs pushed the acorn into the last spot available in the storage hole and patted it in tightly. He sat down, holding the walnut in both front paws, and cracked it open with one crunch of his front teeth. He offered some of the nutmeat to Kooper, and both ate delightedly. Holding the remains of the nut in his front paws, Boggs asked Kooper timidly, "What do you think about both of us sleeping in the sycamore nest tonight?"

"No. I don't want to do that," replied Kooper, his voice rising. "That's just too much for me. You can sleep there yourself, though. I'm okay with that."

Boggs finished eating his walnut meat and dropped the remaining shell over the edge of the limb. *Thank you, Koop,* he Sensed and reached out with a front paw to lightly touch his brother on the shoulder. Boggs kept his paw there until he moved again, methodically climbing down the oak's trunk to the closest limb that stretched all the way to the sycamore, crossing several limbs until he reached their birth nest. Boggs glanced back and then climbed in and disappeared.

Kooper thought about finding Spinner or joining Beka and Claryn but decided against it. Sullen and lonely, he retreated to their regular nest in Beka's tree. While he didn't object to Boggs sleeping in the sycamore, he missed terribly the comfort of being together. Tears came to his eyes and he fell asleep, solitary and feeling empty.

Kooper slept fitfully. Each time he awoke, he realized he had been dreaming but couldn't remember the dream. It just left a sour taste like a rotten walnut in his mouth.

Boggs slept in the sycamore for two more nights. Kooper remained in the same nest in their grandmother's oak but slept poorly, waking up irritable and remaining that way each day. Boggs was sympathetic but determined to continue to sleep in the sycamore.

After the third night, early in the morning Kooper was barely awake when Boggs Sensed to him, *Koop, can we talk about both of us sleeping in the sycamore?*

Immediately, Boggs Sensed Kooper's heated reply, *No! I don't like it that we're apart at night but there's no way I'm joining you there! I don't want to discuss it!*

Boggs sighed and thought to himself without Sensing to Kooper, *You're just being stubborn.* Immediately, Boggs heard in his mind Kooper's angry response, *I am not being stubborn! You are!*

Boggs was stunned. For the first time Kooper had heard Boggs' thoughts without Boggs intentionally Sensing to him. And Boggs had heard Kooper's thoughts without trying. *He can Sense also,* Boggs realized. Boggs scrambled out of his nest in the sycamore and Sensed to Kooper, *Where are you?*

In our nest in Grandma's tree. What do you care?

He knew no one was watching out for him, but Boggs was too excited to wait. He exited his nest and hurried to Beka's tree and to the nest Kooper was in. Once he reached the entrance, Boggs spoke out loud, "Koop, do you know what you did? You Sensed my thoughts and then sent your thoughts to me! I wasn't trying to send you my thoughts or hear what you were thinking. You've never done that before. You can Sense just like me. Koop, do you hear what I'm saying?"

Boggs waited expectantly and after a brief moment heard Kooper's claws scraping the oak as he came to the entrance of the nest and looked out at Boggs.

"You didn't make me Sense your thoughts?"

"No!"

"And you heard my thoughts without trying?"

"Yes!" said Boggs excitedly. "You can Sense like I can! And I bet you can Sense what other squirrels are thinking also."

Kooper wasn't sure what to think. Boggs had never lied to him and Kooper believed him. But Kooper wasn't sure he liked this.

"Well, don't tell Mother or Grandma," he finally said out loud.

"What about Spinner?" Boggs asked.

"I don't know. If it's true, I don't want to hide this from him. But don't tell him yet. Let me think about it."

Boggs didn't Sense to Kooper at all that day until the afternoon, uncertain how Kooper would react. But Boggs couldn't wait forever and was anxious to share his Sensing ability with his brother. *This can't be Ebyn,* Boggs thought. *This must be a good thing!*

Boggs had just finished putting acorns in one of the last storage holes in Beka's tree, and Kooper was down on the ground when Boggs Sensed to him, *You want to try and send me your thoughts, Koop?*

Boggs waited anxiously for a reply without trying to read Kooper's thoughts. Finally, Boggs Sensed Kooper's faint thoughts in his mind, *How's this? Can you hear...Sense what I'm thinking?*

Yes! Boggs Sensed back. *You definitely can do this just like me.*

Boggs waited to see if Kooper would Sense his thoughts again but if he did, Boggs didn't hear him. Nevertheless, Boggs had a smile on his face the rest of the day. *It may be just the two of us*, he thought, but the loneliness he had felt since first realizing he could Sense had evaporated.

That night, Boggs returned to their regular nest in Beka's tree curling up next to Kooper, back to back, without a word. Kooper could smell the odor of the burnt sycamore wood on Boggs' fur but didn't care. He was happy to have Boggs back with him. Kooper intentionally Sensed to Boggs, *I've missed this.*

Me too, replied Boggs eagerly in his mind. Their contented sighs spoke volumes.

Kooper had hoped Boggs would stop spending nights in the sycamore nest. But the very next morning before either was up, Boggs Sensed to Kooper otherwise, *I want to sleep in Mama's last nest again tonight, Koop. Do you want to join me?*

Kooper didn't respond at first but finally Sensed back, *Maybe, I don't know. I'd rather not, but if you want to sleep there, I'll try. I just don't know if I can.* He waited a moment and Sensed again, *Are you trying to hear my thoughts or do you think I am Sensing again? Can you tell the difference?*

Yes, you're Sensing on your own, Boggs replied. *The more you do this, the easier it will become. At least that's what happened with me.*

It still makes me feel uncomfortable, replied Kooper.

Give it time. There's no hurry.

Kooper's thoughts that day weren't about Sensing. Instead, all day long, Kooper's thoughts kept returning to the idea of sleeping in the sycamore. Whether he was on the forest floor looking for nuts or in Beka's tree, his eyes would wander to the white tree and the dark nest entrance. In the past, he would have averted his eyes; merely looking at the tree made him uncomfortable. At some point mid-afternoon he thought to himself, *It doesn't frighten me like it used to do. I'm no longer afraid of the tree.* He Sensed to his brother, *Okay, Boggs. I'll sleep in our birth nest with you tonight.* There. He had finally said it. Boggs didn't Sense back any words but instead Sensed a feeling of total happiness to Kooper. It was the first time Boggs had Sensed a feeling instead of words and Kooper couldn't help but smile. *Thanks, Boggs,* he Sensed, knowing Boggs would hear him in his head.

That evening, Kooper did join Boggs in the sycamore, following Boggs into the nest. As he entered, Boggs turned and smiled at his brother, *It's a dry nest, Koop, not bad at all. You get used to the burned smell.*

Entering the sycamore and approaching the nest hadn't been too difficult for Kooper, but as Boggs went into the nest Kooper hesitated. His nerves were on edge and, for a split second, he almost turned and left.

It'll be okay, Boggs Sensed gently. Kooper exhaled deeply, pushed past his fear and climbed through the entrance.

Boggs' own scent had infused the nest, reducing the odor of

the charred wood; it made the smell bearable to Kooper, but just barely. He laid down with his back next to Boggs' and tried to relax. He could feel his pulse racing. Remembering Beka's instructions to patients, Boggs began to hum a slow tune. Kooper realized Boggs was helping him calm down and joined in the humming, taking deep breaths as Beka had also taught patients. Soon both were asleep.

The two continued to nest in the sycamore the next several nights, and Kooper became halfway used to the aroma as his own scent infiltrated the surrounding wood. The fire hadn't reached the very bottom of the nest where the two lay. There was now an unspoken understanding between them that if Boggs desired it, they would together sleep in the sycamore, not only because Kooper needed the closeness of his brother, but he now also wanted to find out if he could somehow glean memories of their lost mother.

It must have been terrible for Mother at the end, Sensed Kooper one evening as they settled in.

Yes, both the physical pain and the realization that she wouldn't be able to raise us, Sensed Boggs. *At least she had to know Aunt Claryn and Grandma would take good care of us.*

In the middle of that night the deep rumble of thunder woke them. Kooper jumped up, fear pumping through his veins. "Do you hear that?!" he whispered out loud.

"Yes, and I think it's coming this way fast." Boggs replied. The thunder had awakened him a few minutes earlier and he had been listening. Thunder rolled again, this time louder.

Lightning brightly illuminated the trees outside the nest and the thunder clap came quickly, this time causing the whole tree around them to vibrate. Small shards of burned wood filtered down on them as electricity filled the air, and the fur on both Boggs and Kooper crackled.

Kooper moved so he could look outside the nest's entrance. The wind had picked up all at once. Enough leaves had fallen that he could see the trees whipping back and forth with each flash of lightning. He could feel the sycamore tremble, and with the next flash, a corresponding tingling in his skin. "Do you feel that?" he asked fearfully as the thunder boomed, more lightning split the sky and his skin prickled again.

"Yes," said Boggs. "I've never felt this before."

Neither understood what was happening but they realized the tingling in their skin happened each time lightning pierced the sky above the canopy of leaves. Kooper backed as far away from the nest entrance as he could, with his back tight against Boggs. Edgy and nervous, both laid still, listening intently as the storm raged on, jerking slightly as static electricity jumped from one to the other.

"There's lightning in that storm," Kooper said, his left ear twitching nervously. "Mama must have been scared before the lightning hit her." Boggs didn't answer but Kooper felt him Sense a mixture of feelings, both comfort and sorrow.

Both stayed wide awake until the storm passed over, the wind dying down as suddenly as it had risen. The booming thunder receded along with the tingling in their skin. Exhausted from lack of sleep and tense muscles, they finally relaxed.

"It wasn't really so bad in here," offered Kooper bravely, unable to sleep. "The storm wasn't any worse than being in Beka's tree, I guess. I'm glad we were together."

"Thank you, Koop. I'm sorry it's been so difficult for you to be here. But I'm glad you are!" he said with a smile.

"But I don't want to sleep here during a storm again if we can help it."

"No, I agree." Boggs answered.

After that, no words were spoken between them, but neither did they sleep. They lay back to back in the nest, listening to the now barely audible thunder. Each recalled the story Claryn had told them about their mothers' struggle to birth them, and for the first time ever, their thoughts merged and became one, in sync, as if they were the thoughts of one being. Both remained wide-eyed and fully awake as they felt the wind and rain of the storm that killed their mother, trying to accept what was happening but saying and Sensing nothing to one another. The thunder finally died away completely, and without another word or thought, the two fell into sleep, exhausted. Long after midnight, the thunder resumed, this time far to the west, the sound carried on a steady wind. Neither Kooper nor Boggs stirred, but their bodies twitched with each muted rumble, a slow, rhythmic beat that continued for hours. Finally, close to dawn, the thunder faded completely away.

Kooper awoke well after dawn broke. He smelled the musty aroma of the wet, charred wood, stretched and opened his eyes. He could barely make out Boggs in the muted interior of the nest. It was a bleak day, the clouds not letting much light through the trees.

"Did you dream of thunder, Boggs?" asked Kooper after Boggs stirred.

"Yes. You did too?"

"Uh-huh, but I don't think it was a dream."

"You were awake?"

"Part of the time." Kooper shook his head, trying to remember what he heard. *Was it a dream?* he wondered.

"I've never heard thunder like that, dream or no dream," Boggs said.

Kooper slouched down, his back against Boggs. "I'm still tired," he said. "I'm going back to sleep unless you want to go get some food."

"No, I'm not hungry," replied Boggs, pausing before asking, "Did you hear anything else?" Kooper didn't respond, and Boggs raised his voice slightly. "Koop, did you hear anything else?"

"Like what?" Kooper responded drowsily.

"Voices...singing."

"No." Kooper was almost asleep. "Just thunder. Just a storm."

Boggs tried to relax and go back to sleep himself, listening to the sounds of morning outside their nest. Birds and squirrels were singing, and limbs creaked in a slight breeze. There was the crack and final thud of a branch weakened by the storm breaking completely loose and falling to the ground. But there was no more thunder, nor voices.

Boggs couldn't decipher the words he had heard, but he was sure he had heard voices singing. *Kooper obviously didn't hear them,* he thought. *Did I really hear them, or was I just dreaming?*

Kooper's breathing was deep and regular. He had turned around and now held a front paw around Boggs. Sound asleep, Kooper's body involuntarily jerked and his paw tightened, his claws pricking Boggs, but Boggs did not react. He was exhausted like Kooper but couldn't sleep, his own thoughts swirling about. *Someone, more than one, was singing. At least I think it was singing.*

Or was it the wind? he wondered. The voices confused and unnerved him, but he was grateful for the closeness with his twin and, finally, he too fell asleep, oblivious to the sounds of the new day.

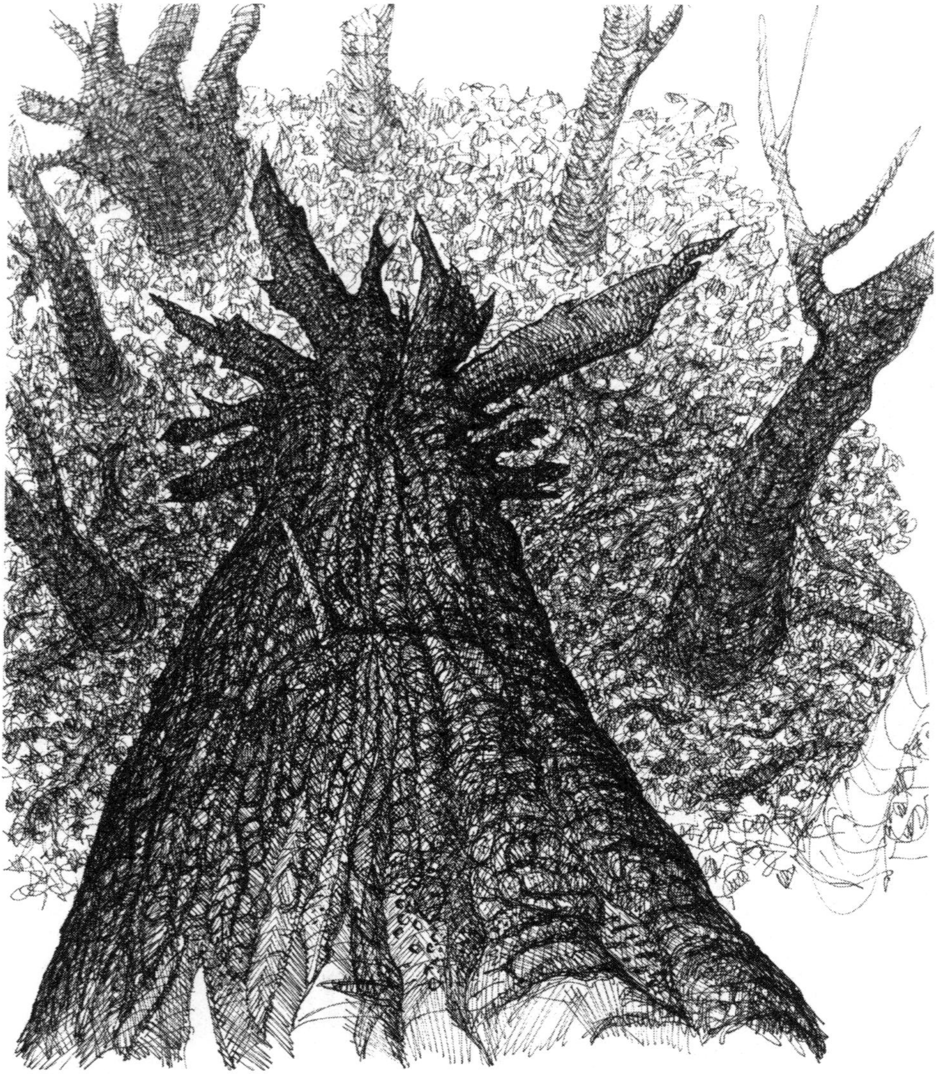

Chapter Ten

Year 3071 AA
Day 258

INEVITABLY, THE FACT THAT THE TWINS WERE SPENDING TIME IN THE SCARRED SYCAMORE WAS DISCOVERED, AND GRUMBLING AROSE. Most of the Tribe were still fearful of the damaged tree and what it represented. They all remembered the fierce storm that caused Chaska's death and Boggs' blindness. The burned out trunk was a constant reminder most avoided even seeing. But heated conversations took place at the Council meetings.

"Those pups should never have been allowed to even enter that tree, let alone sleep there," griped Fitch, an older buck who sat high up on the Council Oak.

"Well, it is right next to Beka's tree," pointed out his friend, Ing, sitting next to him. "They see it every day, and it would be pretty difficult to leave her tree without crossing through part of the sycamore."

"And it does seem natural that they would be curious about where they were born," added another.

"The part of the tree they were born in, what's left of it, is as black as night. It's Ebyn, and they should know better than to be in that tree!" Fitch nearly shouted. "Every time I pass by and see that burned out stump, it makes my skin crawl. I'd sooner die than to cross onto those limbs. You'd think Beka would have made what's important clear to these pups."

Most of the Council members stiffened at the mention of the Healer's name in relation to the sycamore, reminded of the standoff Rak and Strap had with Beka and Claryn. Voices fell into an uneasy murmur.

Without mentioning her name again, several Council members began to speak in worried whispers, "Do you think Ebyn could be drawing her grandsons to that tree?" one of them wondered out loud.

"Their bands look just like flames of a fire. Like the fire that burned up most of that tree trunk. That has to be Ebyn."

"I doubt they mean any harm by spending time in that tree, but it sure does seem dangerous!"

Their voices were muted not only because of this coupling of Ebyn with Beka but also because they didn't know what Strap thought about this. They kept looking for him to respond but he remained silent, looking away into the forest, a blank expression on his face. But the longer he remained silent, the more assertive some became.

Sitting in front of Strap, Caleb asserted loudly, "The Council should forbid any of the Tribe to enter the scarred sycamore. It's a dangerous invitation to Ebyn. If Beka doesn't do something, then we have to. It's our duty."

Strap finally looked out at the members, one by one, except Caleb who he pointedly ignored, and raised himself to speak.

"I have heard and considered your concerns. We all know that our does have usually decided any matter dealing with their pups. However, if something affects the balance of Lucient and Ebyn in Leafensong, then the Council should be involved. Still..."

The bucks below him on the Council Oak waited expectantly. Strap was quiet for a long moment, mulling over how to proceed. He was hesitant to get the Council involved in what could once again cause chaos with the does. He chose his words carefully as he thought out loud, "When the Council realizes that Darkness has begun to affect the Tribe..." He paused, noticing the Council members below parting to make way for someone. He leaned sideways for a better look and glimpsed Beka herself.

Seeing Strap finally aware of her, she stopped, drawing herself up. She waited until all had ceased speaking, their eyes now looking back and forth between her and Strap, anticipating. It was so quiet one could hear a lone acorn fall as she looked at each Counselor, most of whom squirmed under her scrutiny. Satisfied that she had everyone's full attention, she broke the silence. Speaking calmly and deliberately, continuing to make eye contact with the members, she said, "As your Healer, I have considered all sides of this issue. My Chaska's two sons must be permitted to occupy their mother's final nest, because that tree has special meaning to them. Sleeping in the nest is helping heal the emotional scars of their mother's death and that whole dreadful time."

Council members shifted nervously, glancing at Strap, not

sure if the time she was referring to was the confrontation when Rak tried to take Boggs away from Claryn.

"As Healer and the grandmother of Boggs and Kooper, and having adopted them along with my daughter, Claryn, I know it makes sense for Boggs and Kooper to spend time in the sycamore, even sleep there. Just as the sycamore was scarred, so were they. Sometimes unusual healing methods are necessary in unusual situations."

By declaring that this was to be done for the health of the two pups and reminding the Council that she, along with Claryn, had adopted the twins, the Council realized Beka was rejecting the notion that the Council had any say in this. All eyes fell on Strap, wide with anticipation.

He cleared his throat and responded, "Beka, I hear what you are saying. We're all aware that lightning struck the sycamore, killed your daughter and blinded your grandson. But now Boggs, with his blindness, is tainted with Ebyn. We certainly need to limit that. That's the job of the Council."

Strap noticed that those nearby were nodding, which fueled his decision to continue. "It's the Council's obligation, as well as mine as Leader, to ensure the protection of the entire Tribe. It is evident that the Council has jurisdiction here. A mere health concern for a pup or two does not take precedence over preventing Ebyn. Your grandsons' sleeping in that tree is a threat to the Tribe. It is our job to prevent that." With that he stepped back, the stony look on his face meant to discourage any dissension and to hide his uncertainty. He hadn't really given this much thought, but his anger over Beka thwarting his prior ruling regarding Boggs had long festered.

Beka remained undaunted. She now held Strap in a direct stare, long enough to make the other Council members fidget in the awkward silence. Underneath her steely glare, Beka struggled to hide the depth of her fury. *My grandson is NOT a threat! If you fools only knew who he really is!*

But she couldn't tell the Council the truth about Boggs. She knew it would be too much for them to comprehend and accept. After taking a moment to compose herself, Beka began to speak softly, "Strap, knowing I have long been the proven Healer of this Tribe, do you really question my ability to understand, diagnose and treat those who need my help? It is what I've done all my life. That's my job."

Though he worked to keep his composure, the air was charged with tension, evident in Strap's measured response.

"Of course we know what an honored position you have as Healer and all the good work you have done for the Tribe, Beka. But it is the responsibility of this Tribe's Council to discern what possible harm might come to us all if Ebyn is not confined. The well-being of the whole Tribe is more important than that of one or two pups. Your daughter was struck by lightning in the night and your grandchild was born blind, opening our world to Ebyn. You chose to allow it to remain and the Council has to deal with this issue!"

He was flushed and breathless now. Beka let his words evaporate into the air before speaking.

"Are you sure the Council fully understands the significance of Chaska's death?" she asked.

"What do you mean? Of course. Everyone knows that story."

"But do they understand it? What about the lightning, Strap?" Beka asked, eyeing him intently.

"What about it?" barked Strap hoarsely.

"Lightning is as bright as the sun. Even though it was during a storm, and in the middle of the night, it was the lightning, pure light, that killed my daughter. While that was horrible and frightening, it doesn't follow that Ebyn was the cause of it. Chaska and the twins were not touched by Ebyn, they were touched by Lucient."

Until now, Beka had remained calm, keeping her emotions in check. But now she couldn't rein them in, and words tumbled out in a free fall.

"Ebyn did not cause what happened to Chaska or to Boggs! Ebyn had nothing to do with it! The Council doesn't even understand what happened or what it could mean. You're just guessing! And even if you did know, you have no right to declare that my grandchildren are forbidden to enter, or even nest in, the sycamore."

Strap was not prepared for Beka's harsh torrent of words. His fur bristled, but he couldn't speak. A thousand thoughts raced around in his head all at once, rendering him mute. It had never occurred to him or anyone on the Council to consider the concept of lightning not being Ebyn. *Lightning was Lucient? Light killed Chaska?* None had given any thought to that either. *What could that mean?* he wondered. And how was he supposed to proceed at this point? From the looks on their faces, he could see that the entire Council was as confused as he. Before he could form a response, Beka took advantage of his silence and went on.

"Since it would appear that neither you nor the Council seem to understand what you're discussing, perhaps the Council should be more concerned with matters it does understand, and leave the well-being of these young ones to the discretion of your Healer and their adopted mothers. It is Claryn's and my intent to let Boggs and Kooper heal. They're doing well now. They are allowed to visit their mother's sycamore as needed. Any time they wish."

She turned abruptly and slowly started her way back down the Council Oak in total silence. The bucks couldn't move out of her way fast enough. Without another word, she carefully stepped through the oak's crown of exposed roots where Claryn met her to help.

The Council members were as confused and taken aback by Beka's outburst as Strap. They turned toward him, silent, waiting for his direction. Inwardly, Strap seethed. Whether the lightning killing Chaska was Ebyn or Lucient didn't really matter to him, but Beka's insolence, her refusal to acknowledge the Council's and his status outraged him, and his anger overtook him. He rushed forward down the Council Oak, shoving bucks out of his way, through the roots and jumped in front of Beka and Claryn.

"How dare you question this Council and me?! You've always ignored our rightful position as leaders of this Tribe!"

"You call yourself a Leader?!" Beka shot back. "Being a Leader isn't about you; it's about the Tribe! You have the same job I do, to protect this Tribe, and that means protecting every single member, buck or doe, young or old, and that includes those who are ill or blind! It's a poor Leader who won't protect the squirrels who need help the most. Shame on you!"

Turning toward the Council members who now faced her and Strap with jaws agape, she shouted even louder, "And shame on all of you! You argue about Lucient and Ebyn when you have no idea what you're talking about! Do you expect the Tribe to listen to you when you make no sense? When you go along with Strap when he wants to kill a helpless pup? You should have spoken up for Boggs but no one did. None of you deserve to be on this Council. You're a disgrace!"

Her fury spent, Beka twisted back around to face Strap again, her voice now lowered but stern, each word measured, "If you are going to be the Leader of this Council, then lead them properly. Do what's right for everyone and stop thinking about yourself. Now get out of my way!"

Beka pushed forward and Strap backed off, mute, as Claryn helped Beka away from the Council Oak.

Strap was dazed as he watched them go. No one had ever spoken to him like this. His own anger spent, he couldn't reconcile Beka's certainty compared to his own confusion. He realized that he'd lost face due to Beka once again and that the Council was expecting his response. But the last thing he wanted was more discussion. He now sought to have the last word and be done with it. Barely able to raise his voice enough for the whole Council to hear, he croaked, "We will go along with Beka for now. And we will revisit this issue if and when it's deemed necessary."

With that, Strap also left, moving in the opposite direction that Beka and Claryn went, and the meeting came to an abrupt end. The Council members looked around at each other, just as uncertain. They too had a jumble of thoughts to sort out.

We should have protected a blind pup?

Light killed a squirrel?

Lightning isn't Ebyn but Lucient? Could she be right?

Fall leaves silently drifted down around Beka and Claryn

as they continued slowly on their way. Claryn whispered to her mother, "Lucient killed Chaska? Are you sure of that, Mother?"

"No one is certain of anything regarding Lucient and Ebyn. These fools certainly don't know." Soon the two were out of sight.

CHAPTER ELEVEN

Year 3071 AA
Day 302

CLARYN SNIFFED THE WARM BREEZE BLOWING MORE OF THE BUR OAK'S LEAVES DOWN AROUND HER AND HER THREE YOUNGSTERS. She knew there wouldn't be many more warm afternoons like this. Clouds were building in the west. The first blast of winter was on the way. Soon the squirrels would be hunkered down in their leaf-filled nests, staying as warm as possible. Claryn knew the entire Tribe would be well fed this winter as the many storage holes in Beka's tree were now brimming with food. Never had this much been stored before. Spinner, Boggs and Kooper had worked hard all fall to achieve this.

"That's enough work today," she said, smiling and rubbing soil off her front paws. "Why don't you three go for a walk. Do something fun."

Spinner brightened and turned to his cousins.

"Let's do it. You guys hardly ever get away from here. Let me show you what's up north."

Boggs and Kooper agreed and soon the three were well out of sight of Beka's tree. They found an old mama opossum asleep, nestled in a wide fissure on top of a branch of a massive hedge tree. Its long, curving limbs sprawled away from the deeply furrowed trunk. The orange-tinted bark on both the trunk and branches had split open long ago and deep crevices exposed the dense heartwood which had turned black. But the tree was still strong and healthy. The base of the tree angled outward with roots spiraling over and around each other on top of the ground. Even after the limbs died they would hang on for decades.

Spinner hung upside down by his back claws from the limb just above, his head close to the large gray opossum, almost touching her, and started snoring loudly. He feigned waking up and expressed surprise at the sight of the mama opossum next to him.

"Well, hello there. You must have joined me while I was asleep. Wanted to get to know me better, I bet."

The opossum ignored the bothersome squirrel, which only spurred Spinner on to gleefully continue his game.

"You're pretty cute, though a bit larger than the ones that normally interest me. Maybe you should watch what you eat. What about you? You like skinny fellows?" Spinner stretched his body to make himself appear even thinner. "You have any boyfriends? How about guys with bushy tails?" He twitched his tail just above the opossum's nose.

Even Boggs was getting a kick out of this game, laughing out loud as he listened to Spinner's ongoing, one-sided conversation. Still trying to sleep, the opossum turned away with a snort.

But Spinner continued, "Well, Big Mama, if you're going to date squirrels, you need to be choosy. Watch out for the ones with a nervous twitch."

All three squirrels laughed at this old joke. All squirrels twitched. They couldn't help it.

Spinner switched roles, pretending to speak as the opossum, changing his voice to an exaggerated high pitch as he replied to himself, "Yes, young fellow, I have noticed how well you shake your tail. You certainly are handsome."

Finally the old opossum had heard enough. She opened one eye, just to a slit, glanced at the irritating squirrel, and with a surprisingly swift kick, knocked Spinner off the branch to the ground. With a single "Humph!" the opossum slowly got up and lumbered across the branches away from the bothersome brats.

Spinner lay buried under a thick pile of leaves on the ground. He popped his head up with a goofy grin on his face, moss and leaves atop his head. "Maybe it was something I said," he lamented in mock dejection. His cousins burst into laughter.

On their way back to Beka's tree, the three youngsters heard another group of squirrels chattering and singing not too far away. The others were approaching and would soon be close enough to see them.

"Let's go," urged Kooper.

"No, let's wait and say hi," Spinner argued. "I recognize some of their voices. Those does are our age!"

Anxious to leave at once, both Boggs and Kooper started to walk away but Spinner grabbed their forelegs.

"Don't leave," Spinner pleaded. "I know them. It'll be okay."

Boggs remained silent but Kooper answered, "No. They're not interested in us."

"I can introduce you. If you just say hello…"

"We'll frighten them, Spin."

"That's 'cause they don't know you."

"And they're not going to. They think we're Ebyn."

"If you just say something. No harm in trying. They were all leery of me but now most are friendly 'cause I am. Come on, meet some does."

"No."

Boggs spoke up, "Koop's right, Spin. They sure don't want to talk to me."

"Well, maybe not you, Boggs. But, Koop…"

"I'm not saying hello to anyone who won't do the same for Boggs."

"I know how you feel, but you're never going to get them to talk to you if you don't try."

"I don't care if they do," Kooper barked.

"Some of them might not care to talk to you, but I bet there are a few who will."

"They'll take one look at the flames on our chests and they'll be gone."

"That's not a big deal."

"Being blind is," Boggs reminded them.

The does suddenly came into view as they scampered around the thick trunk of an old silver maple, a short distance above the ground. Spinner called to them, "Hello, girls. Whatcha doin'?"

The four does saw the three young bucks and stopped in

their tracks, hanging onto the shaggy bark of the maple tree. None of the does responded, but Spinner moved closer.

"Hey Jone, Marissa. You looking for food?" Boggs and Kooper stood silent and still.

Jone answered, "No, we're on our way to visit my cousin. How are you, Spinner? What's up?"

"I'm great! Boggs and Kooper and I have been messing around with a opossum. Just having fun."

The girls had no response so Spinner added, "We found some good nuts here. Boggs has a great nose for them."

The bucks could see that the very mention of Boggs' name made the other three does nervous. They began to back away when another doe appeared and joined the others. It was Sharani.

"Who's that?" she asked.

Jone responded, "That's Spinner. And his cousins."

"They're the ones with black fire on their chests, aren't they? And one of them is blind?"

Uncomfortable with her directness, Jone replied simply, "Yes."

"Hi, Sharani," Spinner greeted her with a smile.

Sharani didn't answer. Instead, she dropped to the ground and approached the three males.

"I've heard about your flames. Can I see them?"

Kooper and Boggs nodded, stunned. No doe other than Beka and Claryn had ever spoken directly to them before. The other does stood still as Sharani moved past Spinner, right up to Kooper and Boggs to examine their markings, looking back and forth at them. She reached out a paw and touched Kooper's fur where the topmost tendril of fire reached his neck. Kooper froze, wide-eyed, unable to breathe as the tip of her claw slowly traced the mark through his fur, grazing his skin, up his neck onto his face, stopping where it ended on his cheek. She had no expression on her face, withdrew her paw and asked simply, "Which one of you is blind?"

Unable to speak, Kooper pointed to Boggs and Sharani moved close to him, her face inches from his, staring directly into Boggs' eyes. Her scent filled Boggs' nostrils and he felt her breath ripple his fur as she examined him in deafening silence. Then, abruptly, wordlessly, she turned away, climbed back up the silver maple and continued on until she was out of sight. They all watched her go, the does shaking their heads.

"Sharani's a little different," Jone whispered to no one in particular.

"I'll say," Marissa added.

Spinner broke the awkwardness, "You want us to find you some nuts? I'm tellin' ya, Boggs is an expert."

Jone glanced at her friends who were obviously anxious to leave and answered, "No, we have to go. Good to see you, Spinner....You too, Kooper...Boggs."

The does followed Sharani, speaking low among themselves and soon they were out of sight.

Kooper raised a paw and touched his neck and face where Sharani had traced his black flame.

"Well, you finally met some does," Spinner said with a wink. "That wasn't so bad, was it?"

Boggs said nothing but Kooper asked, "Does don't normally act like that, do they?"

"No, she's a little different, like Jone said. She's an orphan like you two."

"Her mother died? When?"

"When she was just a few months old.

"Who raised her?" Boggs chimed in.

"Two of her aunts."

"Doesn't she have a Grandmother?"

"Yes, Jesska. You've seen her before. She visits Grandma; they're old friends. But, I've heard none of them were very good mothers to Sharani. Her aunts don't get along and Jesska has never gotten over her daughter's death. Jone told me Sharani just acts differently than other squirrels. Jone says she's alone a lot, but sometimes tags along with Jone and the other does their age. The others don't encourage her, but they tolerate her because Jone insists they treat Sharani well. Jone is super nice. Everyone likes her. If it wasn't for Jone, I don't think any does would have anything to do with Sharani."

"She wasn't scared by Boggs," noted Kooper, surprised.

"Doesn't she have cousins?" pressed Boggs.

"Yeah, but they don't spend much time with her, or each other for that matter. Probably because their mothers don't get along."

"Have you ever spoken with Sharani before?" asked Kooper.

"A little. She doesn't say much, but I've never heard her say anything nasty about anybody."

"The others didn't want to have anything to do with us, Spin," groaned Kooper.

"You guys are never going to make other friends, does or bucks, if you don't talk to anyone!"

"I don't care," said Kooper.

Boggs said nothing as he followed Kooper, heading for home. Tempted to follow the does, Spinner hesitated for a moment but eventually followed his cousins, muttering under his breath.

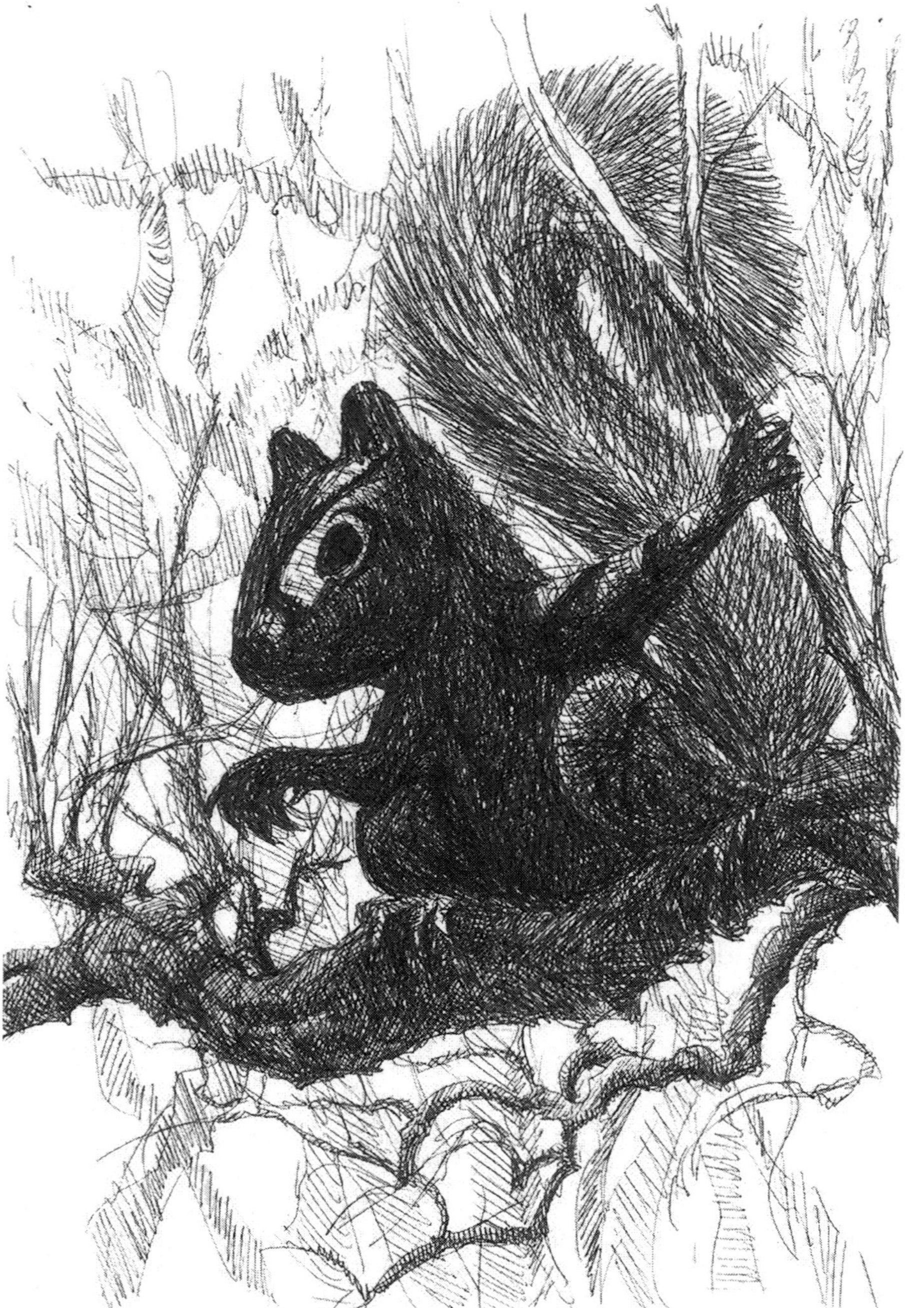

CHAPTER TWELVE

Year 3072 AA
Day 61

WINTER WOULD SOON BE OVER. Snow blanketed the ground beneath the trees, making fallen acorns and nuts more difficult to find. Many in the Tribe had exhausted the food they had stored in their own trees, but the bur acorns and nuts Beka's family had stored were still more than enough for everyone. Visitors usually came in the early morning to avoid Boggs' mid-afternoon visits with Beka. Claryn and Spinner replaced the food that was available to anyone in a good-sized hole not far from Beka's nest. They were often on hand to greet the squirrels that came by, in part to check on their health and encourage any with problems to see Beka.

Impromptu singing often occurred, and Beka's tree was usually filled all morning long with squirrels enjoying each other's company. While a red cardinal or other songbird was a welcome sight, given the constant lack of sunlight, it was the singing that truly brightened Leafensong.

Beka rarely left her nest anymore. She still healed wounds and illnesses but was otherwise content to listen to the singing from her porch, chat and sing with patients and the few old friends who still visited her from time to time, or with Claryn and her grandchildren. Kooper and Spinner visited her every day but rarely brought her food since Boggs did every afternoon, without fail.

The three pups were now almost fully grown, as large as most does. Spinner spent most of his afternoons away with other bucks and does his age who had fully accepted him as a friend. His openness and playful nature made him a favorite of many.

Boggs and Kooper continued to mostly stay away from their grandmother's tree in the mornings. Kooper watched over Boggs almost full-time. Claryn and Spinner rarely looked after Boggs, as Kooper consistently refused their offers to take over for him. Kooper had nearly forgotten about Boggs' Sensing and his own apparent ability to Sense, as Boggs continued to respect Kooper's wishes and not Sense to him. Boggs still had not told Beka or Claryn about it, but every day he Sensed the thoughts and conversations of his family and others. He had gotten much better and could now Sense the thoughts of squirrels from a long way off, even outside Leafensong's border. But he was becoming restless. He wanted more and more to communicate with others by Sensing. He wanted especially to Sense to Beka but was still afraid what she would think.

Would she accept my Sensing? he wondered. *Could she accept it? Would she think it was Ebyn?* These thoughts had consumed him all winter.

***

Beka had trouble concentrating on what her patient was telling her about his injury. Gist was one of the two Sergeants in the Guard that protected Leafensong. He was a middle-aged buck, highly respected as fair and even-tempered. He had fallen from a tree and badly bruised himself the day before. Looking out the entrance of her porch, staring blankly past the bare trees, the brief conversation she'd had with Boggs the previous day popped up in her mind.

What was it exactly that he said to me? It didn't make sense, but I cut him off. I shouldn't have done that…

". . . I mean, I don't normally fall out of trees," said Gist. "But it was icy. And if that clumsy Meese hadn't bumped me . . . Ouch!" he yelped.

"I'm sorry, Gist," Beka said quickly, pulling her thoughts back to the present. *Pay attention, old girl,* she said to herself. She tried to focus more clearly as she massaged Gist's upper back muscles. "Hold your right front leg up. That's right. Now don't let me push it down. Yes, I thought as much. You have some bruising in your upper back and neck…right here…that's causing weakness and pain there, there and here.

"Did I mess myself up permanently?" Gist asked, worried.

"Your muscles are just bruised," she explained. "You'll get over it, but you're lucky you weren't hurt any worse. That must have been quite a fall. You're going to be pretty sore for several weeks. But if you rest these muscles and do as I say, you should heal up faster. I'm going to give you some bark to chew, after I massage your neck and back. I think that's all you need."

With both paws, Beka began to carefully massage Gist's neck

and back for several minutes. He couldn't help but flinch as her paws kneaded the muscle.

"I'm sorry, Gist, I'll try to be more careful. It's this one spot here that's really tender."

"You've got a lot of strength in your paws, Beka," Gist said.

"For an old doe, you mean," Beka replied, smiling. "Well, I've been doing this all my life. Now don't move."

She turned toward the back of her porch. Humming to herself, she sorted through bundles of dried flowers, leaves, roots, bark and packets of dried berries wrapped in leaves she had stored on the shelves. Although she could barely see them in the darkness in the back of the porch, she could easily tell them apart due to their smell and feel. She returned carrying two small bundles of bark tied with thin pieces of vine and handed them to Gist.

"Now, you need to chew a piece of each bark early morning, mid-day and just before sundown. About this much."

She tore off a small piece of each and handed them to Gist.

"You have to chew them until they're soft and swallow the juice they make. Do so until your saliva is free of any juice. Then you can spit the bark out. Go ahead and take your first dose now." Gist didn't notice her sly smile.

He took the two pieces of bark in his paws, sniffed and licked them suspiciously before putting them cautiously in his mouth. He remembered the taste the last time she had treated him for a similar injury. Slowly, he began to chew. As the bitter juice flooded his mouth, his eyes grew wide and his face scrunched up with remembered horror. He spit the bark out into his paws and sputtered, "It's terrible! That's worse than I remember!"

Beka was still smiling, but kindly. She raised her eyes to her grimacing patient.

"This bark is from an old paw paw tree and this is from a young hackberry, each gathered at just the right time. One will help relax those sore muscles and the other will ease your pain. But for them to work, you have to swallow the juice! You'll get used to it soon enough. I've given this to you before."

Gist knew she was correct but he turned the wet pieces of bark over in his paws as he postponed putting them back in his mouth. Finally, closing his eyes with a shudder, he did so and forced himself to chew the awful bark again.

"This bundle should last about two weeks," she said and handed it to him. "By then, your back should be completely healed. But if you don't chew the pieces thoroughly, swallow all the juice and rest your back, you'll be tense from the pain and your muscles won't heal as quickly as they should."

Gist slowly chewed the bark, grimacing each time he swallowed. Finally the bitterness subsided and no more juice came from his chewing.

"Is that enough?" he asked hopefully as he pulled the wet wad from his mouth.

"Yes, that's good."

Thankfully, he went to the porch opening and dropped the bark outside. "It's still awful, but you're the Healer, Beka," he croaked.

Beka smiled gently. "If you chew this each day and don't start to feel better in three days, you come back and see me. And I'll give you a massage every day if you like. Okay?"

"Yes, ma'am."

He carefully stretched his forelegs one at a time and then slowly twisted his back. "That does feel better," he offered tentatively.

"Maybe you should tell Rak you can't go out on patrol for a few days. Spend some time lying on branches, listening to the leaves rustle and squirrels and birds sing. Stop patrolling the border so often. Get some rest for a few days."

"No way! I'm not telling Cap that. I doubt if he'd be too sympathetic over a little bruise like this."

"You'll slow the healing process if you don't rest. I understand the Captain doesn't let up much. The few times I've helped him with bruises and bumps even worse than this, it was hard to convince him to rest."

"He'd have to be in his death-nest to stop patrolling the border. He's one tough nut!"

"Well, at least take some time each day to be still and listen to singing. But the best would be for you to rest and do more singing yourself. I've heard you sing. You've got a fine voice, and singing always helps one heal because it lifts one's spirits."

Gist moved to the edge of Beka's porch, stretching his leg muscles as he went, looked outside and then turned back to face her, "Thank you, Beka. I'll do my best to sing more and enjoy others singing. And I'll chew this awful stuff three times a day as you say and rest when I can." He smiled gamely before turning away. He stopped as Beka spoke up.

"How is Rak these days? I never see him anymore. Tell him he's welcome to come by. If he has any injuries, I don't want him to avoid me." She didn't mention why he would.

"The Captain's fine. He has a lot on his mind these days. He's about to announce who he will name our new Lieutenant. He says we need another officer. We haven't had one since Rak became Captain."

"That will be you or Karmer, won't it? You're our two Sergeants and he's the senior one. I assume Karmer would be his choice."

"Cap hasn't said. Some of our guards think Karmer's too old to be named Lieutenant, but I think he should be. He's earned it."

"Well, I'm sure either of you would make a fine Lieutenant. You've both had plenty of experience."

"I don't know what Cap intends to do. He keeps a lot of his thoughts to himself. Especially of late. I know he's been concerned about stuff."

"Like what? Pack rats?"

Gist hesitated for a moment, but then said, "Yes. I know I can tell you about them. Our guards have seen them across the border now and then. At daybreak or dusk. And lately they've been spotted in pairs."

"That's unusual isn't it?"

"It's unusual to see any pack rat, but especially more than one. We haven't seen two together in years. The Captain's definitely worried."

Alarmed, Beka's eyebrows raised and her eyes widened. "You don't think they're planning…" She didn't finish her sentence.

"We don't know what they're doing or thinking. That's why the Captain is concerned."

Beka didn't want to think about pack rats anymore and said abruptly, "I'm glad we have you and your guards to protect us. I'm sure Rak will make a good decision in naming his Lieutenant, whoever that will be. Either one of you would be a fine choice.

But you take it easy as much as you can. If your muscles don't start feeling better, you come back and see me."

"Yes, ma'am. And thank you!" With that, Gist left.

Beka turned and began sorting through the packets of medicines at the back of her porch, once again making sure each was in its proper place, trying to take her mind off what Gist had told her.

As she worked, Beka's thoughts returned once again to her conversation with Boggs the day before. Now, she recalled what he had told her, "I can hear in my mind...Sense...what others think, Grandma. And I can make others hear what I think."

He had finally told her after considering doing so all winter. But she had dismissed it immediately.

"That's impossible, Boggs. You're only imagining that."

Now she truly considered his statement, *He wouldn't say that unless he really thinks he can do this. And it certainly seems like he understands what I'm thinking sometimes, bringing me a favorite nut just when I've been yearning for one. I've even wondered if he did know my thoughts from time to time. Can he really hear what others think? Is it possible? Clearly he can smell better than anyone else. Maybe being blind or struck by lightning has given him abilities no one else has. And if he can, is he hearing me now?*

Although nervous, her curiosity took over and she decided to try a silent experiment.

Boggs? Are you truly aware of my thoughts? I heard what you told me yesterday. Can you hear what I'm thinking now? If so, can you bring me a hickory nut and a chinkapin acorn? And three silver maple seeds left from last spring. Claryn said there are some remaining in one of the top storage holes. Would you bring me those, too?"

She stopped her sorting and waited, chewing on a bit of the paw paw bark to help her own sore muscles and try to relieve her tension. For a while only silence surrounded her, and she reluctantly went back to work, once again making sure she had every medicine she might need until Spring arrived. Just as hope was almost gone, she heard the familiar sound of claws scraping the bark of her tree. *Is it possible?* she wondered.

"Grandma, it's me, Boggs!" His face appeared at the porch entrance. "I brought you an acorn from a chinkapin, a hickory nut, and three silver maple seeds from storage. You still have a few more left up there. You do want these, don't you?" He held them out in his trembling front paws, his excitement evident on his face.

Beka was stunned. She gazed steadily at Boggs, taking it all in before reaching out to take his offering. Boggs' ability to communicate through thoughts slowly became real to her. Boggs could Sense her thoughts but waited for her to speak aloud. Finally, she spoke, "I don't understand it, but I do believe that you possess this gift of...what did you call it?"

"Sensing," he said eagerly.

"How long have you been able to do this?"

"Several months, I guess. Since last fall sometime."

"Why didn't you tell me you could do this before now?" she asked.

Boggs bowed his head. "Because I wasn't sure how you'd react. I know everyone is afraid of me because they see my blindness as Ebyn. I was afraid you would think this was Ebyn."

"You are not Ebyn! And while I've never known anyone to be able to do this, this...gift you have isn't Ebyn either! You're different, yes, but that's not bad. In fact, you're more special than even I realized, and I cherish who you are!"

Beka reached out to her grandson with a paw and caressed the cheek of his face. She embraced him and felt his muscles relax.

"You've been worried about how I'd react, haven't you?"

"Yes," he said with emotion, almost crying as Beka continued to hold him.

"It's okay. I'm not upset. Do your brothers know?"

"Yes, both Kooper and Spinner do."

"And Claryn?"

Boggs pulled himself apart from her slightly, wiping his eyes with his forepaws.

"I haven't told her, but she may know. Spinner might have told her."

"He has a hard time keeping anything to himself, doesn't he?" replied Beka as they each smiled at one another. But she immediately became serious. "We have to keep this a secret," Beka whispered. "Others won't understand. Only our family can know. You make sure Spinner doesn't tell anyone else!"

Boggs laughed as he sat down in front of her. "I don't think he will, Grandma. Even Spinner is aware how important it is to be quiet about this. He said so himself."

The two of them settled into a comfortable silence while Beka munched on a dried maple seed, enjoying the rare sweet taste. She offered Boggs one and, as he ate, it prompted him to ask, "You gave Gist some paw paw and hackberry bark?"

"Yes. You have to know when to gather the bark and how it's used for it to be effective. Gathered at the wrong time, the bark is too tough to chew and the juice isn't strong enough to work properly." She looked at his eager face. "You want to know about these things, don't you?"

"Yes, ma'am."

"I know that you've been interested in what I do for a long time, asking me question after question about it. And you, of course, realize I've been reluctant to answer you. You want to learn the Healing ways, don't you?"

"Yes, ma'am. I think I can help, Grandma."

"Yes, I think so too. But if I do teach you my ways we cannot let on with anyone outside our family that I'm doing so. Things will go badly for us if the Council finds out you're learning to be a Healer. Only does have been Healers. This must be a secret also."

"I promise I'll keep quiet, Grandma, and so will Koop and Spinner. And I already understand a lot of what you do."

"I'm sure you do," Beka said smiling. "Good. I'll tell your Aunt Claryn."

She stroked the top of his head, then gently scratched his ears, his smile broadening. For just a moment, she thought she could see a resemblance to his mother, Chaska.

"Do I really look like her? Like Mama?" Boggs sat still, waiting with eager anticipation.

Beka was startled by Boggs' reading her thoughts, but quickly smiled again as the reality set in. "Yes, sometimes you do." She answered. "So does your brother. I can see something of her in each of you. Oh, how I miss her! I'm sorry she isn't here now to see how special her sons are. She would be so pleased."

With a sigh and a slight nod, Boggs said, "There's something else you should know, Grandma. I've been Sensing the thoughts of others. I listened to…Sensed…what you told Strap and the

Council about Kooper and me sleeping in the sycamore nest. They still don't like it. They think it's Ebyn."

"Don't you worry about them. If you want to sleep there, go ahead. I can take care of the Council. That tree isn't Ebyn and neither are you. That's just fear of what they don't understand."

"I realize I really am different than anyone else."

"Yes, you are. And that's a good thing, not a bad thing."

Beka turned to the back of her porch and carefully chose several bundles of different bark. Beka realized Boggs had a gift like no other, coupled with an undeniable desire to help and heal like Chaska had. How he would use his strange ability she didn't know, but she believed such a gift should not be wasted. More tears welled up in her eyes. Tears for Chaska and for Boggs. Rubbing them away, she turned to face Boggs, who she found staring straight at her, unseeing, but with a look of profound wonder. She realized he had been Sensing her thoughts. Smiling at him, she said, "You know, I'm sure your mother would have been a Healer. She had the touch, the gift. The desire."

Boggs nodded. "Aunt Claryn told me that, too. Why isn't she a healer like you?"

"She helps me a lot, of course. But it has never been her desire. One has to have an intense calling to be a Healer. I've always had it from when I was your age." Beka paused a moment before continuing. "And apparently you do, too. I do think you should be a Healer if you really want to do so. It's hard work, a lot to remember, and you have to truly want to help others. But..."

Beka paused.

"What is it, Grandma?"

"One aspect of being a Healer can be harder than just about anything. A Healer can't always save a patient. Losing a patient is part of being a Healer."

"You mean Mother?"

"And others."

Boggs felt her sadness, but she quickly pushed it aside.

"But it's also very rewarding. If you want…I'll try to teach you all I know."

Boggs nodded emphatically and Beka heard him Sense, *Yes, Grandma, yes!*

Boggs' intense thoughts startled her for a second but she immediately responded out loud, "Then we can start right now." She turned to pick out four different barks from her shelves and held them out for Boggs to touch and smell, but she could see from his furrowed brow that he had something else to ask her.

"What is it, Boggs? What else do you want to know?"

"I Sensed what you and Sergeant Gist were talking about. The pack rats and all. There was something about which you didn't want to think. Were you trying not to remember something?"

"Yes," Beka replied softly.

"Was it about losing another patient?"

"Yes. More than one. And you're right, it is hard for me to remember. And I don't wish to do so. Not now anyway. Someday maybe I'll tell you what it is." She looked wistfully out the door of her porch. "But not today. Now let's start your lessons. Here are some pieces of paw paw and hackberry bark like I gave Gist, as well as some chinkapin oak and white ash bark. As I have said, each of them must be gathered at just the right time from the right tree, must be used precisely, and you must learn how each of them works and for what purpose. Listen carefully. You must remember all of this, as well as everything else that I am about to teach you. The life of someone could depend on it."

Boggs swallowed hard. He knew he might never be accepted as the Tribe's Healer. But he wanted to learn...and help others if allowed.

"Yes, Grandma, I will. And thank you."

"For what?"

"For believing in me."

Beka smiled. "I've always believed in you, Boggs. And now, even more. I'm happy to share what I know with you, though I'm not certain what will come from it. It may cause more problems for you, but you know that. For now, you'll have to be my secret helper."

"I know, Grandma. I'll do my best to learn well, because someday I want to be a Healer."

Beka didn't answer. She realized Boggs could Sense what she was thinking but couldn't help herself. *I don't know how this will work out. But we might need another Healer soon.*

CHAPTER THIRTEEN

Year 3072 AA
Day 65

IT WAS A MILD, LATE WINTER MORNING IN LEAFENSONG. High in his massive sycamore tree, Rak and his two Sergeants, Karmer and Gist, sat on the wide branch they had used for years overlooking the forest. Their long use had worn away the scraps of loose light-green and gray bark that overlaid only a fragment of the mostly white trunk and limbs so high up. Rak's nest was farther below, where the first large limb angled up from the wide trunk. Like most sycamores, the lower trunk was almost entirely covered with the irregular chips of darker, brown bark. The three were enjoying a breakfast of choice acorns. Small limbs swayed gently in the breeze and songbirds and squirrels sang all around. They were discussing the events of the previous day.

"Cap, some of the guards are surprised you chose Yunkin as your Lieutenant," ventured Karmer.

Gist nodded, "I worry about that too, Cap. He's only been a guard for a year. He's awfully young to be Lieutenant."

Rak smiled. Karmer and Gist had been his closest friends for years, as well as his Sergeants.

"I know this is not what you were expecting," Rak replied. "But I need you to assure our guards that there was a purpose in my choosing Yunkin. He's inquisitive, thinks for himself and he's smarter than any of us."

Rak could see the surprise in their faces. It had never occurred to them that another squirrel could be more intelligent than Rak.

"He's not content to blindly follow orders. He will question even my order if he thinks it's a mistake. Sort of like you, Karmer." Rak winked at Gist as Karmer gasped in mock astonishment. Gist began to laugh and nearly choked on the piece of nut he was eating.

"I know appointing him Lieutenant has its risks, but I trust Yunkin and his instincts. He's made me consider things in a way I hadn't before. It's true that he's young, so you two need to be there for him. I've already told him he needs to listen to you and rely on your experience." Rak smiled at Karmer, adding, "I know you'll have no problem telling him what you think!"

With a guffaw, Gist muttered, "No kidding."

Rak quickly turned to Gist and added, "You need to speak up, too. Don't be silent if Yunk's actions are questionable. He has a lot to learn. All three of us need to bring him along. But he can be a real asset. We need some fresh ideas." He leaned forward and whispered earnestly, "Something's brewing across the border and I'm getting concerned."

"You mean the pack rats, Cap?" Gist knew Rak's answer before he nodded solemnly.

"Pack rats" was the squirrels' derogatory term for bushy tailed wood rats. They were nothing like black rats, who hadn't been seen in the forest for generations. Wood rats were closely related to and looked like white footed mice, usually gray or light brown in color, but were much larger, even longer and more stout than the banded gray squirrels. Unlike mice, their tails were covered with thick fur, though shorter than the hair on the tails of squirrels. The wood rats were competitors for food, and the banded squirrels would not tolerate them in Leafensong. They were bitter, age-old enemies.

"Several guards have seen two together and yesterday Lam saw three," said Karmer.

"Three! That's the first time anyone's seen that many in years!" said Gist. "I saw two myself across the western border a few days ago. It used to be we hardly ever saw even a single pack rat."

"When did you see them?" asked Rak.

"Right at sunup. They've only been seen then or just before dark."

"They sure don't like daytime," added Karmer.

"No, and the fact that they have been seen at all, plus spying more than one together, makes me wonder why. What are they doing? And how many are out there?" questioned Gist.

Rak responded at once, "We can't be surprised by them again. I think we should double our number of patrols. We don't want a situation where our border is breached because we're failing to guard it as thoroughly as we should."

"We'll get that done," promised Gist. "And, Cap, instead of having the same patrols at the same time each day, how about we change them up?"

"Good idea," Rak answered, pleased with Gist's ingenuity. "You and Karmer figure out new patrol schedules. Then you two can tell Yunkin and all the guards. Most importantly, it's your responsibility to make sure everyone follows through. We can't leave the border unguarded." Rak looked into the faces of his trusted friends and was grateful to see their solidarity.

"You bet, Cap," said Gist, the resolve clear in his voice. He looked at Karmer for his assent, but Karmer still had a question.

"Cap, we're at a disadvantage because the pack rats are active at night and we're not. Who knows what they're doing during the nighttime? We're limited 'cause we obviously don't see as well in the dark."

"I know," agreed Rak, his voice full of worry. "We need to continue patrolling from dawn until nightfall. But I've been thinking it's time we have half of our guards sleep in border trees in order to hear if anything is moving around at night and be ready at first light. We must be at the ready for whatever dawn brings. I know the guards are not going to like it, but I think it's become necessary."

"We'll make sure it gets done right away," offered Gist as Karmer nodded. "Do you want to know the change in schedule and who's to be where and when? We can have that figured out this afternoon."

"Yes, let me know after you set it up," Rak answered.

"What about sending patrols outside the border?" persisted Karmer. "It seems like we'll have to do that if we want to find out why we're seeing more pack rats."

"I've thought about that, too," replied Rak. "Let's discuss this some more. We must be careful to have enough guards and also have extra guards along the border ready to assist. It's been a long time since any banded squirrel has gotten into a fight with a pack rat. But we must make sure if they attack again, even if it's across the border when it happens, we realize it as soon as possible and we're ready to counter-attack."

All three of them grew solemn, remembering the Great Battle that happened years before when a large band of wood rats attacked Leafensong. Rak was only a Lieutenant then, and Gist and Karmer were not yet sergeants. In fact, Gist, youngest of the three, had only recently been made a guard. The three of them each still bore scars from that fight. Although the scars on Rak and Gist were mostly hidden by their fur, Karmer had a long, wide ribbon of vividly pink scar tissue across his chest and belly that plainly showed whenever he raised his forelegs.

With his right paw, Karmer absentmindedly touched the crusty edge of the old wound which crossed from his left shoulder to his right hip. He did so whenever he thought of the Great Battle. Suddenly overcome with emotion, his whole body shuddered, and he closed his eyes as the memories flooded back.

Once again Karmer raced across the branch to help his brother, Dram. But once again it was too late. The blood rushed out of Dram's neck from the gaping wound. The two wood rats who had attacked him had moved on to fight another squirrel, but Karmer's attention was on his brother. A moment before, Dram was a young buck, having just been accepted along with Gist into the Tribe's Guard. The older brother, Karmer, was proud and protective of him but now stood helpless as Dram's life ebbed away, his blood drenching their fur. Momentarily oblivious to the cries and screams from squirrels and wood rats who were fighting ferociously, Karmer pressed his paws against Dram's neck, trying to stop the flow of blood.

The wood rats had attacked en masse right at dawn in the middle of summer, when most of the squirrels were still asleep, surprising and quickly killing the few guards along the border. Hidden by the heavily-leafed trees, the wood rats had driven deep into Leafensong before any squirrels had risen the alarm.

The squirrels had never seen such a large number of wood rats. Although smaller groups had attacked the border of Leafensong in the past, always unsuccessfully, the wood rats had never amassed so many at one time. One large wood rat, clearly in charge, urged the others on as they overpowered squirrels, driving them back, wounding or killing them outright until they reached the center of Leafensong, just to the west of the Council Oak.

Though surprised and caught off guard, the squirrels had rallied. Guards rushed in, calling to one another, while other adult squirrels, buck and doe, fought tenaciously. Even though they were outnumbered by the larger wood rats, the squirrels were faster and more nimble. One-on-one, an experienced squirrel guard was equal in battle with a veteran wood rat soldier. Both fought in a similar style, slashing at the other's vitals with powerful jaws and teeth that tore deeply into skin and muscle to crush bone and rip arteries open.

Rak, Daker and other guards had quickly arrived and joined the fray, jumping in front of does and older bucks trying to hold back the wood rats. Gist, a close friend of Dram, fought ferociously with an older wood rat. Although Gist had no real experience in fighting, he was holding his own, parrying the thrusts of the jaws of the larger wood rat with his own, their heads jolted by the clashing of teeth.

Karmer frantically tried to stop the blood gushing from Dram's neck but quickly realized it was hopeless. The wound was too deep, and an artery had been severed. He felt Dram's body go limp as their eyes met. Dram knew he was dying, but a slight smile crossed his face as he looked into the face of his beloved brother. Dram tried to speak, but the blood in his throat merely gurgled. With a final shudder, his eyes clouded over and Karmer pulled him close for a moment before gently laying Dram's body down on the broad limb. Karmer stood up, bright red blood splashed across his chest and dripping from his paws, his eyes manic, looking for the two wood rats who had killed his brother.

They were in the next tree over on a wide branch on either side of Lam, one of the largest squirrel guards and younger than Karmer. Lam was twisting back and forth, desperately trying to keep the two wood rats from slashing his own neck. Karmer realized Lam couldn't hold them off much longer and tore across the branches, aiming for the closest wood rat. In a headlong rush, he bashed his head into the side of the wood rat, breaking a lower rib. The wood rat gasped and hesitated for a moment, allowing Karmer an opening. Karmer aimed for the vulnerable side of the wood rat's neck and slashed with his incisors, opening a wide cut. In shock, the wood rat tried to pull back, but Karmer jabbed his snout deep into the wound and clamped down tight, twisting the skin and muscle held in his teeth. Karmer jerked his head back, tearing out a bloody chunk of muscle and windpipe. A severed artery pumped blood out over both of them. The wood rat reached up with his paws to try and stop the flow of blood, but he was mortally wounded. Karmer shoved him over the side of the branch and lunged past Lam, who was fighting the second wood rat, their teeth clashing.

Karmer dug his foreclaws into the leg of the wood rat, and the wood rat turned to defend himself, expecting Karmer to attack his neck, his most vulnerable spot. But instead Karmer aimed behind the wood rat's knee, clamped his incisors down and yanked back violently, severing muscles and tendons. Unable to hold himself upright with his mangled leg, the wood rat halfway collapsed. But as he fell, he was still able to aim his teeth and reach Karmer's now exposed abdomen. Karmer twisted his body away, preventing the wood rat from cutting him too deeply. Karmer felt his own warm blood spread across his chest and belly, but he ignored his wound, and with his hind legs thrust himself upward with all his might to parry the wood rat's new attack, their front teeth slamming together with a dull thud that jolted the backs of their skulls. Karmer thrust his snout downward, lunging forward at the same time to clamp his jaws around the wood rat's throat, a split second before the wood rat could do the same to him. Karmer jerked backwards and felt the wood rat's neck muscles give way before biting again, deeper. This time Karmer held firm, refusing to let go, closing his eyes tight as the wood rat flailed about Karmer's head with his fore claws. The wood rat tried to cry out but was unable to do so with his windpipe crushed. The wood rat's blood flooded over Karmer and his muscles went limp. Karmer savagely ripped out more of the wood rat's neck and spit out the bloody flesh before pushing him away to fall heavily over the side of the branch.

As the wood rat fell, Karmer looked to see if Lam was all right. Lam was wide-eyed, having watched the unmatched ferocity of Karmer, who was now completely covered with the bright red blood of Dram, the two wood rats he had killed, and his own wound crossing his chest. But Karmer was not done. His fury over the death of his brother drove him on, and he cried out to Lam and others to attack. Lam joined him, and their joint ferocity inspired the other guards to attack the wood rats without restraint.

Rak bit deeply into the neck of the wood rat he was fighting and shook him, dropping the dying wood rat to the ground. Next to him, the smaller, younger Gist did the same with his larger foe. Rak and Gist looked up to see Karmer, Lam and other guards now relentlessly attacking the wood rats. The squirrels had stood their ground.

Finally equal in number to the wood rats, Leafensong's guards were overpowering their foes, who had been unnerved by the sight of the blood-covered Karmer attacking ferociously, with Lam now beside him doing the same. Rak called the guards to press forward, "For Leafensong!" he shouted. Gist, the other guards and then all the squirrels took up the call and surged forward as the wood rats began to retreat. The tide had turned.

Rak searched for Thrane, Captain of the Guard and his superior, and saw him further ahead surrounded by wood rats. Rak spotted Thrane just as the wood rat who was commanding the others savagely sliced Thrane's neck open. The old squirrel fell hard onto the branch where they had been fighting. The eyes of Rak and the wood rat met as the wood rat pushed Thrane over the side to fall to the ground and called to the others to rally around him and retreat. One of the wood rat's ears was a light-colored tan and stood out to the side, making him easily distinguishable from the rest of the wood rats.

Lam was battling a huge wood rat larger than himself, and Rak rushed to his aid. Lam was not giving an inch, and the two rodents clanged their teeth together, each trying to inflict a killing wound to the other's neck while they pulled and clawed at each other's forelegs. Rak slashed the exposed side of the wood rat's neck with his teeth, and as the wood rat twisted to try and protect himself from the new attacker, Lam finished him with a single bite.

Before the wood rat fell, Rak had already jumped off the limb to the ground and rushed forward to the side of Thrane, who hadn't moved since his fall. Rak immediately saw that the cut to Thrane's neck was fatal. Rak cradled Thrane's head with his paws. "We have them on the run, Cap," said Rak softly. "Leafensong is saved."

Thrane looked up into Rak's eyes and in a barely audible voice said, "You're the Captain, now, Rak. Lead the Guard well. For Leafensong."

Rak looked up and saw the squirrels chasing the wood rats north, thirsty for revenge. Rak leaped up the nearest tree and across the branches after them. As solitary wood rats were being cut down and finished off, the main group of wood rats was hastily retreating across the border. The squirrels slowed, uncertain whether to cross the border and continue the chase until Rak bellowed, "No farther! Guards, everyone, rally to me!"

With their Captain lost, Rak took charge as the guards and other squirrels circled, "Guards, stay on the border but spread out!" he ordered. "Be ready to sound the alarm if any more pack rats attack. You others, come with me to help care for the wounded. Turning to find Gist, Rak yelled, "Gist, make sure the guards are spread out across the border and stay put. Don't pursue the pack rats. We don't know what else they might be up to or how many there are. This battle is won, but I want to be ready if they attack again!"

"Yes, Cap! I mean Rak," said Gist sheepishly. "You did well, sir."

"You also, Gist."

Rak now raced back to the site of the main battle, the other squirrels following. He found Beka cradling Thrane's head, her eyes full of tears. She looked up at Rak and shook her head side to side. He was gone. Neither Rak nor Beka could say anything as Beka continued to stroke the head of her old friend. Then she gently laid his head down and got up to help the wounded she could save. Rak looked about and saw Karmer down on the ground, holding his brother, rocking back and forth and speaking softly to Dram, although he could no longer hear. Others were wailing, also cradling their lost loved ones.

As the memory faded, Karmer opened his eyes and shifted his weight from one back leg to the other, causing his old scar to ripple across his chest. Karmer's eyes had misted over and as he looked into the eyes of first Rak and then Gist without saying anything, both knew what Karmer had been re-living.

The courage shown in that battle by the squirrels, and especially the ferocity of Karmer and Lam, was still described by the older guards to young bucks. Rak remembered the wood rat leader with the tan-colored ear pushing dying Thrane off the branch. The death of Dram, Thrane and other friends was something they would never forget.

Rak's face bore a dark shadow. "We were surprised and outnumbered once, and I don't want that to ever happen again. If we begin patrolling past the border, we must be vigilant and shrewd. To do this, we need keen intellect."

"Yunkin is young, but he's certainly no fool. I agree with that," said Gist. "But he can be headstrong, too. Do you think this honor of being named Lieutenant will go to his head?"

"If I thought that would happen, I wouldn't have made him Lieutenant. But as I said, we have to help him. No other guards are more experienced than you two, and I'm depending on you to help him become the Lieutenant we need to keep the Tribe safe. If we help him, and if he listens, he'll be a good officer, hopefully better than us."

Karmer drew himself up. "We'll do everything we can, Cap." Gist stood up holding high the remains of the acorn he was eating. Rak and Karmer touched their acorns to his, and they called out in unison, "For Leafensong!"

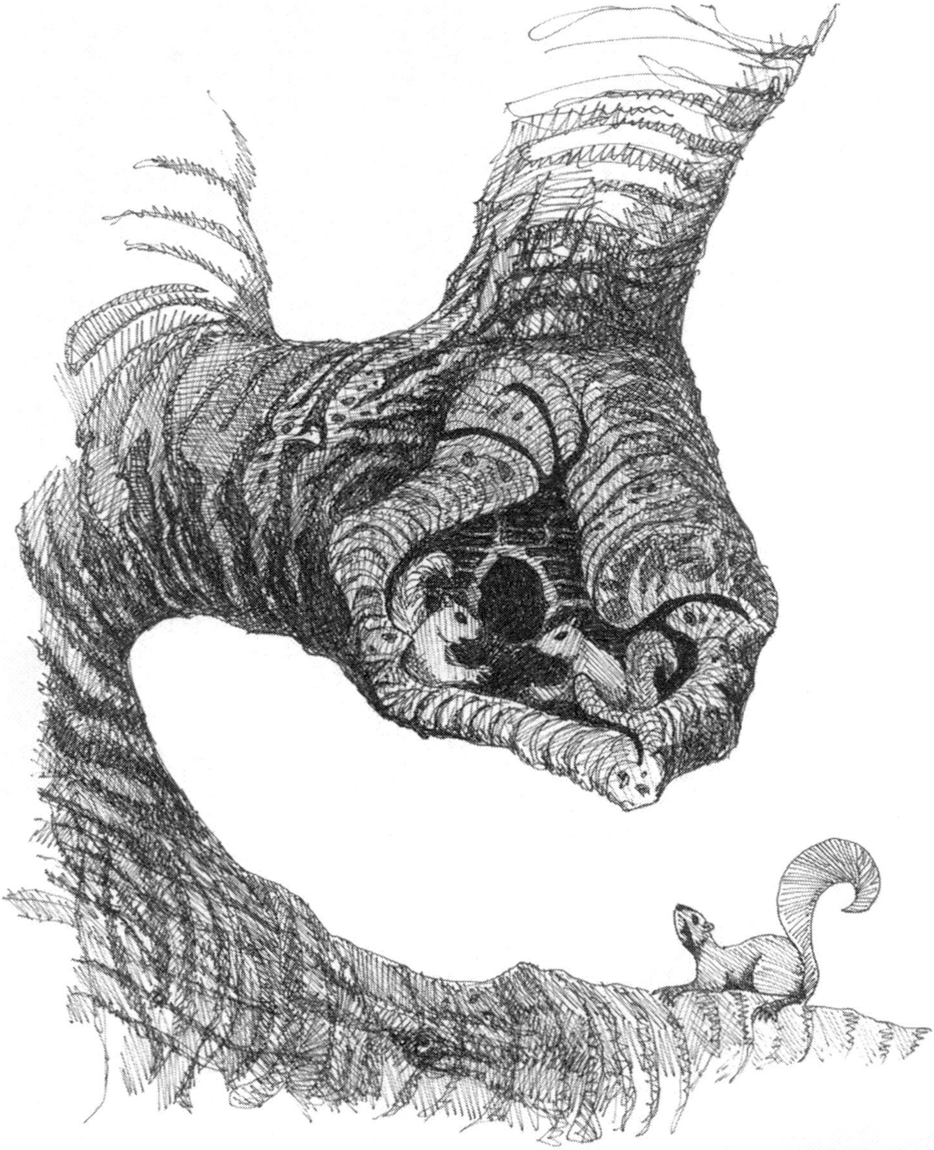

CHAPTER FOURTEEN

Year 3072 AA
Day 66

"YOU'RE SHIVERING! HERE, LET ME WARM YOU UP." Beka reached out her front paws to help her old friend crawl onto her porch. It was still early in the morning and a cold wind blew past the porch's entrance. Beka started massaging Jesska's back and shoulders. "Have you eaten anything today?"

"Oh, I had a couple red oak acorns."

"You need to eat more. Winter's not over yet. You need enough food to keep warm."

"I'm just not hungry, Beka. I haven't felt well. Worse than usual. It's terrible getting old."

"Tell me what's bothering you," Beka said kindly as she handed her a bur acorn.

"I hurt all over." Holding the acorn in her right forepaw, Jesska gingerly rubbed first the back of her right foreleg just below the elbow joint and then reached down to point behind her right knee. "But the pain here is the worst."

"Okay, Dear, let's take a look and see if we can help you feel better. But you eat while I examine you."

Jesska dutifully began to consume the acorn.

"That is good! Your acorns are always the best."

"I'm glad you like it. Now, stretch your leg out. Slowly."

While munching the acorn meat, Jesska did her best to comply despite the pain. She was confused when Beka began to press her own paw gently along Jesska's lower back.

"Why are you feeling my back? That's not where it hurts. Maybe a little, but mainly it's my leg that hurts."

"I know, but sometimes a pain in one place is caused by a problem somewhere else. We have to discover the source of your pain. Now, move your leg forward . . . that's right. Now backwards."

Jesska obeyed. She had learned to trust her old friend's healing methods, even if she didn't understand them.

"It seems this leg muscle has become weak. I think something's getting pinched here in your lower back. Let me massage the muscles there and try to relieve some pressure."

With her front paws, Beka carefully and gently kneaded Jesska's back. "Your muscles are all knotted up." Jesska winced in pain but soon felt the tightness ebb in both her lower back and leg.

"There, I think that will help."

Uncertain, Jesska stretched her leg out carefully, and found that it did feel better.

"Thank you so much. I don't know how you do it."

"I'm glad that helped. But for you to regain the strength in your leg, you need to come back for a massage each day for seven days."

Jesska continued to stretch out and draw her leg back slowly, trying it out. As she did, Beka moved to the opening of her porch and peered out. The grays and browns of the winter forest were muted under the overcast sky. In the distance she could hear several squirrels singing.

"Now, that's some good harmony," Beka said, humming along. Turning back to Jesska, she continued, "I can feel a storm coming. It's making my muscles and joints sore and stiff, too. Probably some of your discomfort is due to that."

"Oh, I don't know. My old body hurts all the time, whether bad weather is coming or not," Jesska grumped. "Maybe if my grandsons cared for me and brought me food every day like that blind grandson of yours does, I'd do better." Beka knew that Boggs' help was unusual for a grandson, but she also knew Jesska's prickly attitude probably made her grandchildren avoid her.

"But your granddaughter brings you food. You've told me that."

"Yes, Sharani does, but not every day, not like your Boggs does."

"I doubt any other buck would be as attentive as Boggs. Kooper and Spinner aren't. How's Sharani doing? I haven't seen her in ages."

Jesska sighed. "Besides bringing me a nut now and then, I don't see her often. I know she hangs out with a few other does on occasion, but she mainly keeps to herself."

"She didn't have a twin like Kooper and Boggs have. That can make a difference."

Jesska nodded. "And she didn't have an aunt like Claryn to take over when her mother died."

"But, your daughters helped out raising her. You've told me so. And they had their own pups so Sharani had cousins to grow up with."

Jesska looked out the doorway of the porch and sighed again, this time more deeply. "Francene and Trellis tried, but they don't have mothering skills like Claryn. Or you. They've never been close to one another and have always squabbled. Their sister was the one who resolved their differences. After Massi died, they even blamed her death on each other. It made no sense, I know, but…her death made her sisters' relationship worse. They've never gotten along like sisters should. They tried to be good mothers for Sharani, but I think she reminded them of Massi's death."

Beka opened her mouth to reply but thought better of it and said nothing.

"I know what you're thinking, Beka. It was probably my fault. I was never the mother or grandmother you were. Like my mother wasn't. And you know I didn't do well after Massi's death, either. I know I neglected Sharani. But it was all too much for me. I should have taken charge of Sharani, but I just couldn't.

"You were in pretty bad shape then," said Beka. "You tried to help but you had your own heartache to deal with. I know it wasn't easy."

"No, it wasn't. Thanks for reaching out to me then. I know I didn't respond well to you or anyone. Her being shuffled back and forth between her aunts was not good for her either. She's got a good heart, but she just isn't normal. She doesn't sing much either, although she's got a decent voice. It's my fault."

Beka looked Jesska in the eye. "No mother should lose a child. It's the worst thing that can happen to us. But it's never too late to try and heal a relationship. I know it's difficult, but maybe you can reach out to Sharani more now. If she's bringing you food now and then, that shows she cares for you. Try to get her to sing with you, just the two of you."

"You're right. You're always right. I'll do that. I will."

"And bring her by sometime. I'd like to see her again."

"I'll do that too."

Jesska stood up on her hind feet, moving gingerly.

"Here, let me get you some more dried redbud and fennel leaves to take with you," said Beka. "That should also help loosen your leg and back muscles."

"Thanks, Beka. I could sure use it." Jesska sat back down on her haunches, carefully flexed her leg and twisted her back ever so slowly.

Beka returned to her shelves at the back of her porch, letting her thoughts about Jesska's family go. She began humming a song to herself as she usually did while she worked, the same one she had heard sung by other squirrels a few moments before. Jesska began to sing the same tune, and Beka smiled, joining in. They had been singing together their whole lives and could harmonize easily.

When their song was done, Beka said, "It seems like I'm out of redbud flowers here. I gave the last out earlier this morning. But I should have some stored high up in my tree."

"You don't have to go get those. That's a ways up there, and I know how tired you've been lately."

"Well, it wouldn't be any easier for you to get them," replied Beka.

Beka was torn between wanting to help Jesska as best she could and accepting the limits of her own frailty and age. Climbing to the top of her tree would be difficult for either of them today. But then it occurred to her that Boggs might be of help. She purposefully thought, *Boggs, can you hear me? Sense my thoughts, as you say? If you can, would you bring me some redbud flowers from my highest storage hole? I can't get to them myself easily and I need them for a patient who's with me now.* She took a deep breath, hoping, then spoke aloud to Jesska. "You know, I just remembered Boggs is supposed to bring me some. I asked him earlier today. And he should be here soon. Let's wait a bit. Okay?"

Jesska hesitated but then said, "Fine with me! Your grandson sure is helpful, even if he is blind. Do your other grandkids bring you medicines, too?"

"Not like Boggs does. They know he brings me food every day so I can ask him to get me medicines, too. But even if he didn't, they probably wouldn't be as attentive. After all, they're young bucks," she said with a grin.

Jesska sighed. "Oh, I know. Most young bucks seem to avoid their elders as much as they can. They're sure they already know everything they need to know. They're ready to be all grown up and join the Guard. I haven't had a really good hickory nut in I don't know how long! My family doesn't sing to me very much either, not like we did to our mothers and grandmothers. No one shows respect to their elders anymore. I'm sure I paid more attention to my grandma."

Beka looked into the distance, trying to remember her faraway youth. "That was so long ago, I'm not sure what we did," she said ruefully.

Jesska thought about that, "Well, maybe I don't remember so well either. We certainly have grown old, haven't we? There are only a few does our age. No one older."

Beka nodded. "And there are even fewer old bucks our age."

Just then they heard a squirrel's claws slowly climbing up the bark outside Beka's nest. Boggs' face appeared at the entrance.

"Grandma, it's me. I brought you the redbud flowers you asked me for. Do you want them now?"

Beka's insides jumped, but she didn't let on how excited she was, trying to behave as though nothing out of the ordinary had happened. She greeted Boggs warmly.

"Yes, in fact I do. Thank you, Boggs! Come on in."

Boggs entered the edge of the porch and reached out with a paw holding a bundle of dried flowers wrapped in leaves. Beka noticed that beneath the package of flowers he also held two hickory nuts. Jesska shifted away from him, unnerved by this closeness to the blind yearling. Boggs Sensed Jesska's unease and moved back to the entrance. "I'll wait outside, Grandma." he offered. "I'll bring you some nuts later. Jesska, here are some hickory nuts for you."

"Why . . . thank you, Boggs," Jesska replied, taking the two small, tan colored nuts. "Hickory nuts are my favorite!" She didn't know what else to say. His unseeing eyes made her uncomfortable, as they did most of the Tribe. Beka realized Boggs had heard what Jesska said about hickory nuts and was now sure that Boggs could Sense not only her thoughts, but the thoughts of others as well. Boggs grinned at her and made his way out of the porch. Beka turned back to her shelves and set about combining some of the redbud flowers with fennel while Jesska moved to the porch entrance. She poked her head out and began peeling the shell off one of the hickory nuts with her teeth, letting the small pieces of broken shell fall to the ground below. She watched as Boggs slowly climbed up the trunk of the old oak, then across a higher branch to where he laid down. Jesska's gaze turned higher and she saw Kooper. He was keeping his usual protective watch over his brother and the skies above through the bare branches. She carried her nutmeat back into the center of the porch where she sat down and began to eat her treat.

"My, what a tasty nut!" Jesska said. "This is a really good one! That youngster certainly knows how to make an old doe feel better!" She munched contentedly. "Your grandson, Kooper, he doesn't have many friends either, does he?"

"No, he pretty much stays at home and watches out for his brother."

"Maybe he and my Sharani would get along. They have similar pasts and are both pretty much loners. They might hit it off as friends."

Beka only half heard Jesska and replied simply, "Hmmm," as she continued to focus upon the bundle of redbud leaves and fennel she was preparing. She wrapped them carefully in long strips of paw paw leaves, tying a small piece of vine around the package, when what Jesska had said finally sunk in. "Sharani, you say? A friend with Kooper? I doubt Kooper will pay her or any doe much attention. He's too focused on watching Boggs."

"That may change as he gets older. It usually does."

"Yes, you're right, but Kooper is different." Beka joined Jesska to look out the porch entrance. Kooper and Boggs hadn't moved. *It might be good for him if he was interested in a doe*, she thought. But, she said nothing further about it.

Jesska was just finishing the last of her nut, so Beka held up the medicine packet. "Here you go," she offered.

Taking the medicine, Jesska smiled. "Thank you! And please thank your grandson for the hickory nuts and for bringing the leaves you needed."

"I will. Don't forget to come back tomorrow for another massage. And bring Sharani. I'd like to see her again. It will give you two something to do together."

"I promise I'll be here. And I'll bring Sharani if she'll come along." The two old friends embraced before Jesska stepped to the porch entrance and peered out once more. Boggs and Kooper hadn't moved since she came inside the nest. Seeing Kooper watching the sky reassured her. She placed the remaining hickory nut in her mouth to carry, holding the bundle of medicine tightly against her chest with one forepaw and slowly crawled out the porch to the top of the stout limb and across to the trunk. She climbed to a different branch and headed south towards her own tree.

Beka watched Jesska to make sure she made her way safely until she was out of sight. Once she could no longer spot her, Beka looked again to find Boggs and Kooper still where she had last seen them. She smiled and thought, *It would be good for Kooper to have a friend, someone other than his family*. But she quickly dismissed the idea with a final thought, *I don't think he'd be interested though. He's too dedicated to Boggs* .

She returned to the back of her porch and adjusted the remaining bundles of fennel and redbud flowers as her thoughts went to what Boggs had done. There was no doubt now that he had read her thoughts. *This could be a real blessing!* she thought. *I'm needing more help.* She gathered her thoughts and now hoped Boggs would Sense them. *I'm getting old, Boggs. If you're going to be my assistant, you need more lessons. It's important for me to share with you how to mix these flowers with fennel. You have to mix them in the correct proportions or else your patient will have terrible diarrhea!*

I hear you, Grandma. Startled, she jumped and her heart thumped. She had heard Boggs' voice clearly inside her own mind for the first time!

"Boggs, was that you I heard?" she asked aloud.

Yes, it is. Beka heard Boggs' voice again in her head. *I'm sorry I startled you.* Beka crossed to the lip of her nest and peered out to make sure Boggs was not anywhere close. She spotted Kooper now in the sycamore and knew Boggs must be fairly close. Following Kooper's line of sight she saw Boggs sitting on a different branch of the bur oak above her, looking down at her. He wasn't close enough for her to have heard his voice clearly if he had spoken out loud. *How long have you known you could make me hear your thoughts like that?*

I wasn't sure I could. I knew Kooper could hear me when I wanted him to. And Spinner, too. I wanted to know if you could as well. I guess you can. Is there anything else I can do for you?

She thought it over. *Well, yes. How about bringing me some leaves from that ash tree just past the burned sycamore? There's a low branch that split last year but is still attached. Can you bring me some of the smaller leaves from that limb?*

How many do you want?

Just a few twigs. Beka replied. *Don't strip the leaves off. Bring me several twigs with the leaves still attached. Small leaves, as small as you can find. I'll show you how to prepare them.*

Before long, there was Boggs at the edge of her nest, carrying ash sprigs with shriveled leaves.

"Thank you," Beka said as she took the twigs and leaves from him and examined them, turning them over in her paws.

"When someone is sick, how do you know what's wrong?" asked Boggs out loud as he settled in on her porch.

"Well, first you ask if they know what's going on and what's painful or uncomfortable. Often they know themselves what's wrong."

"What do you do if they don't know?"

"That's what makes a really good Healer," Beka replied. "It isn't just knowing what medicines treat what problem, but helping a patient to find balance."

"What do you mean, balance?"

"Everything in life is in constant struggle to find the balance that keeps all running smoothly. When someone is sick, you must help them find the way back to wholeness, to balance. Like when a large branch on a tree breaks off in a storm, that tree will change how it grows. Branches will alter the way they grow in order to balance the tree again. Part of that is simply growing toward the sunlight, but all of Nature is trying to regain balance. When we get out of balance, we often get physically ill. A good Healer tries to find the root cause of pain and the best way to restore the natural balance."

"Isn't that hard to do?" Boggs asked doubtfully.

"Sometimes. But the longer you work with this basic principle, the easier it becomes. When you've done this as long as I have, you often can tell when something isn't right and the cause of the problem."

"I've noticed that you touch your patients a lot. Does that help?"

"Oh yes. Were you Sensing what I told Jesska?"

"Yes."

"She didn't realize the muscles in her back were out of balance. She felt pain in her leg, but when I touched her back, I found the real cause of that pain. My massaging helped her back muscles relax and, in turn, her leg."

"Your touching sounds somewhat like my Sensing," Boggs said.

Beka smiled. "If you can Sense what a squirrel's ailments are, you've got a wonderful gift. Just remember to always seek the balance in everything you do, Boggs." She looked at him to make sure he was paying attention. "Not just in healing, but in everything!"

"How do you know when you've found the balance?" Boggs asked eagerly.

Beka delighted in Boggs' desire to learn. She answered with a proud smile. "Well, usually the patient just stops asking for help and ignores me!" she laughed. "But the balance doesn't last forever. Inevitably, change occurs in us just as the forest is constantly changing. We have to make adjustments. Sometimes we get too stressed and forget to seek our own balance."

Beka paused and let Boggs take her words to heart. But soon he had another question for her.

"How do you seek the balance for yourself, Grandma?"

No one had ever asked her such a thing, and she answered eagerly, "I find the best thing is to lie at the opening of my porch or on top of this branch every day, with the wind in my face, to breathe deeply and slowly, and listen to the singing all around me. Unless it's winter, listen to the forest and the leaves, and to the crickets and cicadas in the summer. It's like the forest itself is singing. Listen to the birds and squirrels singing and join in. The music and sounds of the forest calm me and surround me with a sense of well-being. I often prescribe this very thing for healing. Any medicine works better when a patient will both hear and join in the singing.

"And sufficient sleep also helps. Patients who are really ill should sleep and rest a lot, and they should sing or hum to themselves in their mind as they doze off. The music will remain in their thoughts and dreams as they sleep. I know that's what happens to me."

"Why does music help so much?" Boggs asked.

"Beautiful music by itself, just the tune and harmony, is magic. But the combination of words and the tune is even more magical. The meaning of the words and the beauty of the music together joins thoughts and emotions. Every part of our bodies experiences this, not just our minds but our muscles, our guts, our hearts, our inner beings. Songs can intensify all our emotions, from grief and sadness to peace and joy and our whole bodies feel them. Fully experiencing your emotions helps maintain a healthy balance. And I think we're meant to be musical, the same as songbirds. When we're singing, even just in our heads to ourselves, we're at our best. There's nothing like music."

Beka closed her eyes, remembering the song she and Jesska had just sung. It was wrapped in memories of them singing together and with other friends, some now gone, all their long lives washing over her. Boggs Sensed her singing the song to herself, her thoughts and emotions, and realized how strong and meaningful it was for her. He Sensed how her entire body responded, muscles relaxing.

Boggs waited until Beka's inner singing ended and her mind was back to the present. Gently he Sensed to her, *I understand*, and felt her smile in response.

Beka chuckled out loud, "And laughter, Boggs! You can never laugh enough. Laughter is like a song. It's musical. A patient who laughs will always heal faster."

"Too bad Spinner doesn't want to be a Healer. He can make anyone laugh," Boggs said with a grin.

"Yes, your cousin surely can," giggled Beka. "I'm certain he makes many squirrels feel better all the time, but I think one secret apprentice is enough for now."

Beka smiled. She picked up a twig of ash leaves and said, "Now, when you strip the leaves off this twig, be careful. You don't want to tear them."

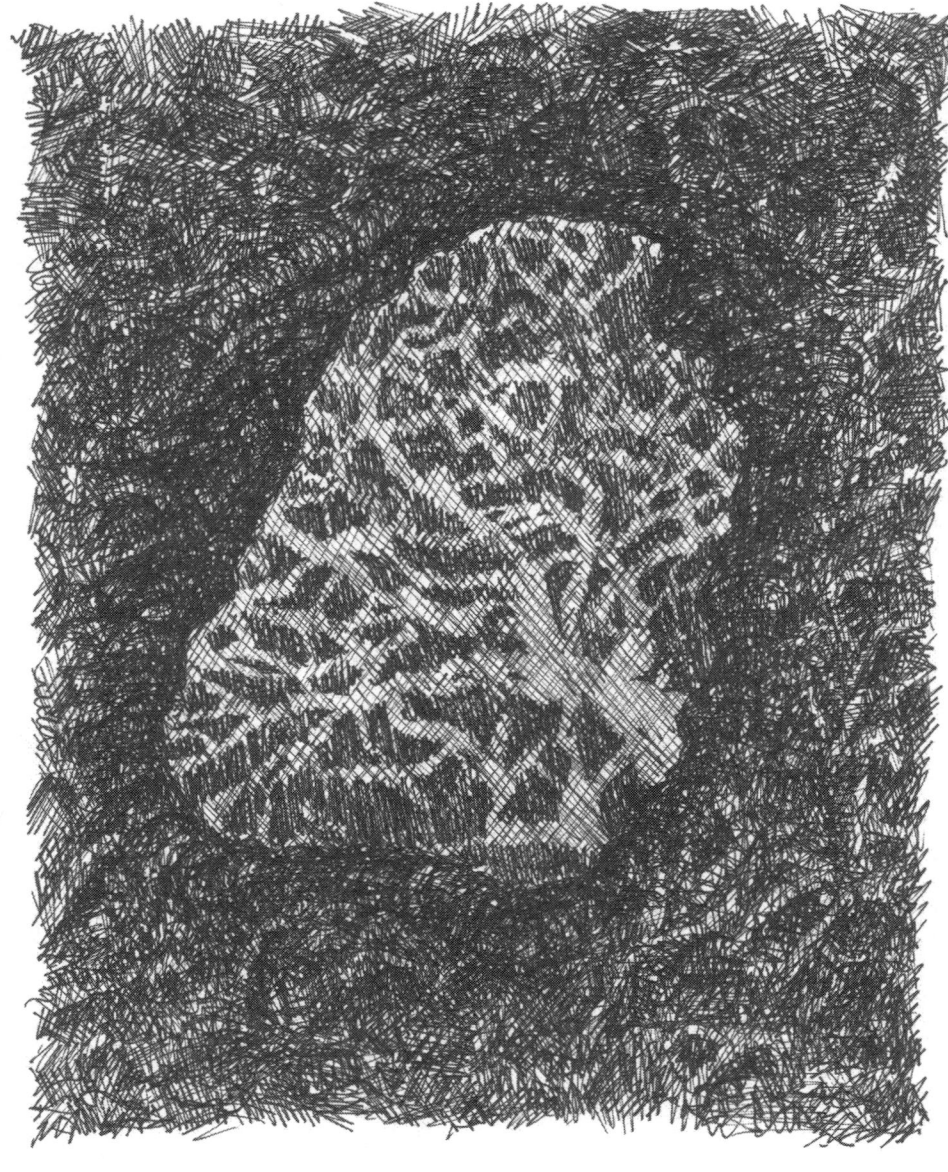

CHAPTER FIFTEEN

Year 3072 AA
Day 66

BOGGS WOKE UP WITH A GASP, HIS NOSTRILS FLARING. He had been dreaming again. It was the middle of the night and Kooper murmured in his own deep sleep. Boggs was now wide awake.

The dream was recurring more and more of late. He had heard voices again. Or at least he thought they were voices. Faint humming sounds, rising and falling, almost like singing but never quite intelligible. Suddenly, Boggs realized he wasn't just remembering his dream. The sounds in his mind, though faint, hadn't stopped with his waking. But as soon as he became aware of this, they ceased. He knew immediately that he had shut them out of his mind himself. He forced himself to breathe deeply and slowly as Beka had taught him, trying to slow down his thumping heart. Very faintly, the humming began again, far off and still unintelligible.

Boggs concentrated on the sounds, keeping himself calm and his mind receptive. They became steadily stronger. His eyes widened in surprise as he thought he heard his own name once, but he wasn't sure. Still, he felt with certainty that the murmurs were meant for him, calling for him. But why?

He raised himself up to the entrance of the nest and listened, his eyes watering from the cold wind in his face, while the voices continued rising, falling, like the wind in the trees. He couldn't see the branches of the sycamore, but could hear them moan and creak. Kooper had described them--pale and barely visible, swaying against the blackness of night. Boggs Sensed the presence of the sycamore and other trees, and knew they heard the voices too. How long he listened he didn't know, but finally the wind and murmuring both lessened and stopped.

Lowering himself back down into the nest, Boggs felt the familiar warmth of Kooper's back against his own once again. Unable to sleep, he waited for dawn.

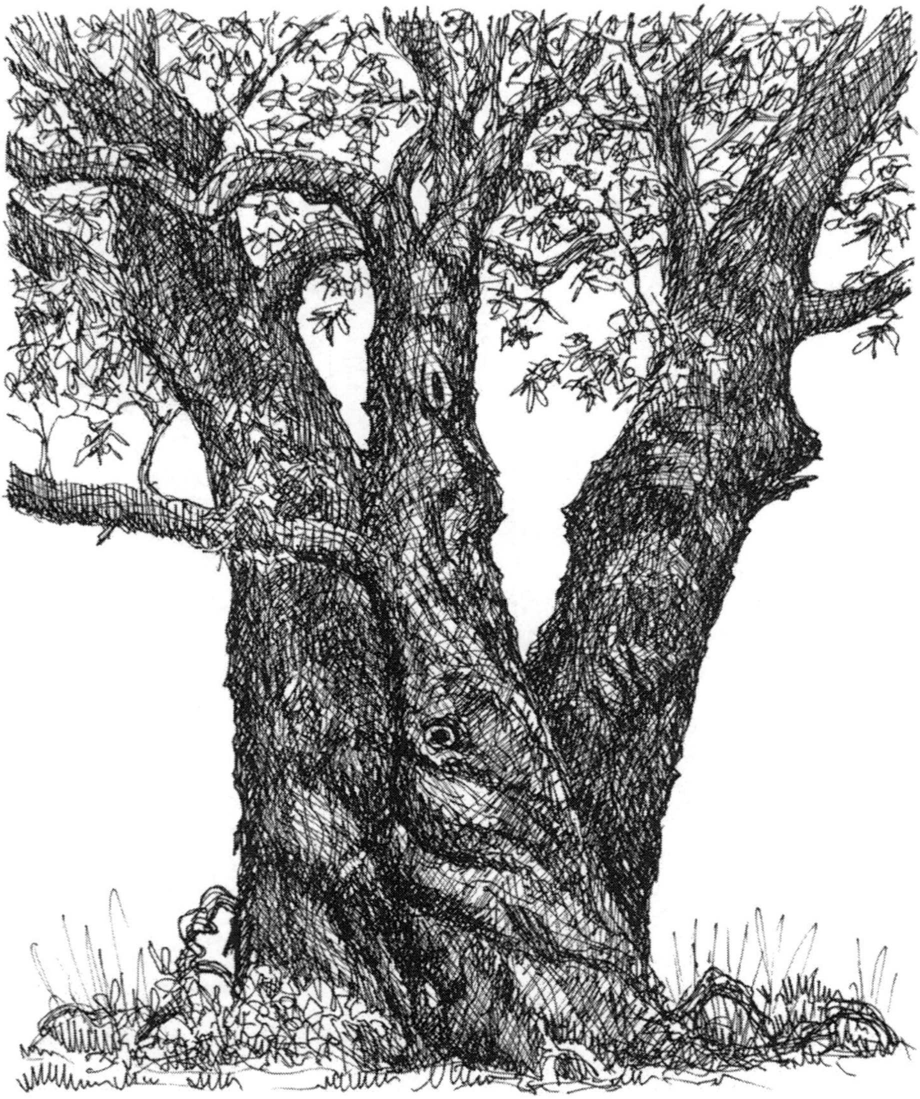

Chapter Sixteen

Year 3072 AA
Day 66

"Hello, Jesska," said Beka. "Who's this with you? Is this Sharani?"

Jesska and her granddaughter climbed onto Beka's porch. It was mid-afternoon.

"Yes, I wanted you to meet her. I don't think you've seen one another since last summer when she was a young pup."

Beka nodded. "I think you're right. Sharani, it's nice to see you again. How are you doing?

"Okay."

Sharani didn't make eye contact with Beka but instead pointed at the shelves at the back of Beka's porch full of bundles of medicine. "What's all that stuff?"

"Those are medicines I use for healing."

Beka expected a follow up question but instead Sharani walked past her and examined the packets, picking them up and smelling them.

"Sharani!" exclaimed Jesska. "Don't be messing with those without asking permission first."

"That's alright," said Beka easily. "Do you have any questions, Sharani?"

"No," replied Sharani simply as she then peered deeply into Beka's inner sleeping nest before returning to the entrance of the porch, walking past Beka and Jesska without saying a word, and looking outside.

Jesska and Beka looked at one another wordlessly and Jesska shrugged. She was used to her granddaughter's impolite ways.

Still looking outside the porch entrance, Sharani said simply, "I met your grandsons once."

Beka moved next to her and looked out the doorway. Boggs was in the sycamore and Kooper in the topmost branches of the silver maple tree on the other side of the sycamore.

Sharani pointed toward Boggs.

"That's the tree your daughter was in when she died," Sharani said with no emotion.

"Yes," answered Beka, waving a front paw at Jesska who Beka realized was about to criticize her granddaughter again.

"I don't think your grandsons are Ebyn," said Sharani as she continued to look outside.

Jesska could no longer help herself and protested, "Sharani!"

"It's okay," said Beka. "No, they're not Ebyn. Boggs is blind, I assume, because of the lightning that killed their mother. But he's not Ebyn. Both he and Kooper are good, kind squirrels."

"I've heard the other one, Kooper, all he does is watch his brother. That's what he's doing now, isn't it?"

"Yes, he is. Anytime Boggs is out of the nest, Kooper watches over him. They're really close to one another, as twins often are."

"Do they have other friends?"

"They have their cousin, Spinner, Claryn's son. She raised them together as brothers. I understand your aunts raised you with your cousins also." Beka waited for an answer but Sharani didn't respond, continuing to watch Kooper. Beka turned back to her shelves and retrieved two packages of dried redbud flowers and fennel, handing them to Jesska.

"Here you go, old girl. How's the back and leg today?

"Much better, thank you."

"Would you like a massage?"

"Not today. Tomorrow maybe."

"I'd be happy to then."

Beka watched Sharani who continued to stare out the porch's entrance.

"Are there any questions you want to ask me?" Beka asked.

"No," was all Sharani said before she turned to Jesska. "I'm ready to go, Jesska."

Surprised to hear Sharani call her grandmother by her first name, Beka turned to see what Jesska's response was, but Jesska just shrugged her shoulders and replied, "Yes, we can go. Thank you, Beka. I'll see you tomorrow."

"That will be fine," said Beka. "Good to meet you again, Sharani. I remember when you were a mere pup. You've grown up to be a fine young doe. I'm glad you're spending time with your grandmother."

Sharani turned her head but stopped just short of looking directly at Beka, held herself there for a moment, then fully turned to look Beka in the eye but said nothing. It felt awkward to Beka but she could tell Sharani didn't realize she was acting in an unusual manner. After another moment Sharani turned, and without looking at Jesska, exited the porch.

Shaking her head slightly from side to side, Jesska said to Beka, "She's just...different."

"Well, it's good you're spending some time with her. You two doing any singing together?"

"No. She's not one for much singing."

"It might be good for her. You, too."

"Yes, I know you're right. I'll try. Maybe I can get her to sing if I start. I am trying, Beka."

"Good for you. Keep trying."

Beka and Jesska hugged quickly and Jesska exited the porch, following Sharani. Beka watched as the two slowly clambered up the trunk of the bur oak and across a higher limb towards the sycamore. For a moment, Beka thought Sharani would go into the sycamore itself but at the last moment she jumped over to a different limb of the oak, then to a smaller branch of the silver maple, avoiding the sycamore. Jesska followed along at a slower pace and Sharani stopped in the maple on a limb directly below Kooper. There she looked up at him, staring for several moments as Beka watched, wondering if Kooper would acknowledge her. He had to realize she was there but he only glanced at Sharani once, otherwise ignoring her. Jesska caught up to Sharani and went past her until she reached the far side of the maple.

"Sharani," Jesska said and Sharani finally took her eyes off

Kooper and followed.

Just then Claryn climbed into Beka's porch handing some dried silver maple seeds to Beka.

"Thank you, daughter!" Beka said as she started munching one of the seeds. She handed the second seed back to Claryn but Claryn waved it off.

"I see Jesska brought her granddaughter, Sharani. She's an odd one."

"Well, we've got some odd ones in our family, too," replied Beka with a smile.

"Her aunts, Francene and Trellis, have spoken to me about her. They say she's a loner, and strange. Their own youngsters don't have much to do with her."

"Her grandmother, Jesska, was pretty much a loner too. I was just about her only friend. Still am, I think."

"We all need friends, even if it's family. I'm sure grateful I've got you."

"Me, too, daughter."

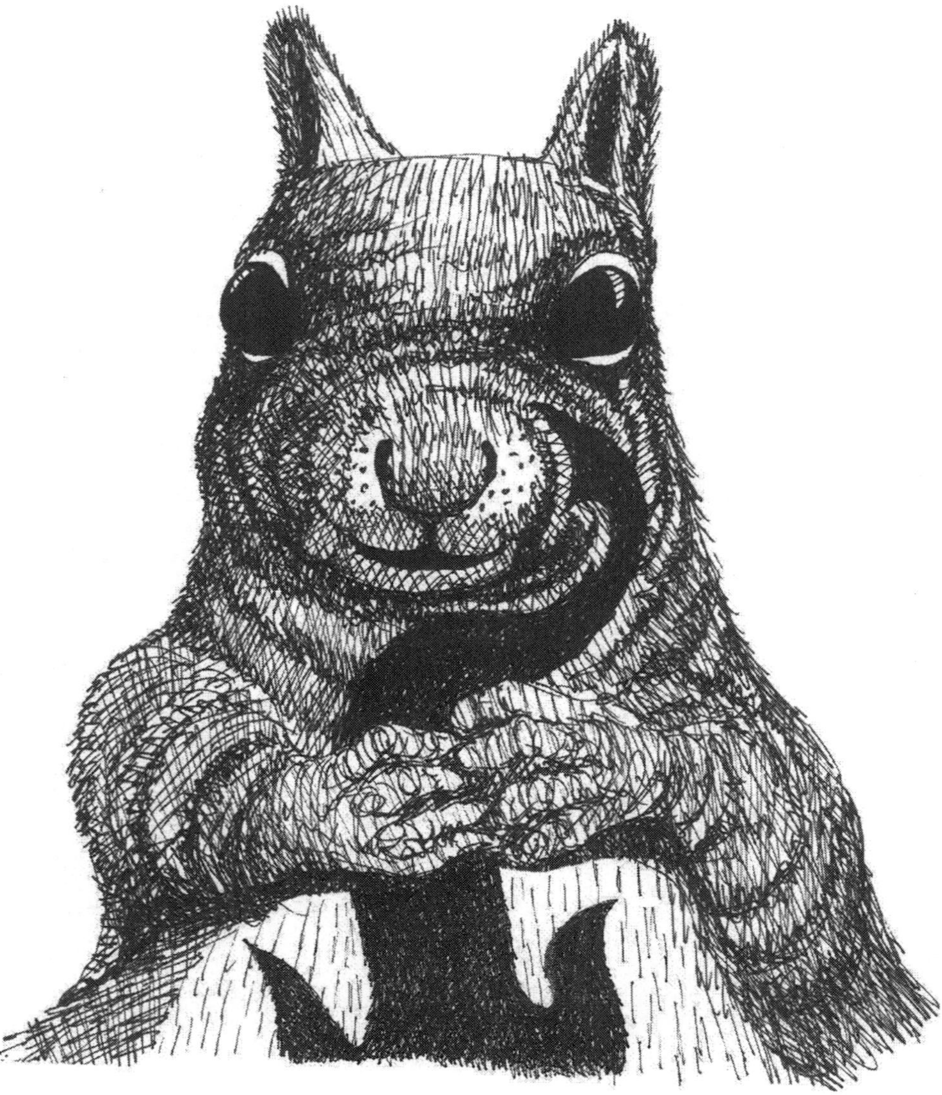

CHAPTER SEVENTEEN

Year 3072 AA
Day 66

LATER IN THE DAY, BEKA HANDED BOGGS A BUNDLE OF DRIED LEAVES TIED WITH A THIN PIECE OF VINE. He held them up to his nose and sniffed deeply, instantly recognizing the sweet smell of black cherry. "As you know, these are used to repel fleas from a nest," Beka explained. "Smaller, new leaves work best, so they should be picked early in the spring. They ought to be replaced every seven days. They'll work for about a year." Beka took back the package and placed it on the proper shelf at the back of her porch.

Her back to Boggs, she continued to sort through her medicines while talking to him. "Sometimes you can find a fallen tree with enough roots still attached to the ground that the tree won't die right away. The leaves will slowly dry up but remain attached. Those are almost always the best leaves for medicine. They're more potent. You can also harvest dried leaves from a branch that has partially broken off a tree but remains attached. They're almost as good."

Beka reached up, took a package of a different type of leaves from another shelf and turned to face Boggs. She opened her mouth to speak but stopped when she realized he wasn't paying attention to her. In the faint light, she could see his detached expression as he faced the porch's entrance. Although he couldn't see the opening, he could feel the faint breeze flowing in. *Have you heard anything I've said?* She wondered. She decided to test him.

"Then you take a really long paw paw root and jam it into your patient's nose, until it comes out the ear." Boggs' face remained unchanged. "And you tie the root in a knot and hang the patient from a tree for a year." Still nothing. Beka shifted noisily and raised her voice. "Listen, young fellow, if you're not going to pay attention, I don't see any reason to continue your lessons today."

Boggs still didn't respond, and Beka sighed. In the silence between them, she nearly shouted, "Boggs!"

Startled out of his reverie, Boggs finally replied sheepishly, "I'm sorry, Grandma. I guess I wasn't listening."

Beka giggled, thinking of what she had just told him. She couldn't be upset with her beloved grandson for long.

"I would say not. But if you heard my last instruction, don't you dare treat patients that way!"

"No, Grandma, I'm afraid I missed it."

"Good. What were you thinking about, anyway?"

Boggs was now totally present. "I...I've been having these dreams. At least I thought they were dreams. Now I don't think so. I Sense voices even when I'm awake. And I think they're calling me."

Beka's brow furrowed, "Whose voices?" she asked.

"I don't know. They're not the voices of anyone I know. And I don't even think they're squirrels. At first I only heard them when I was dreaming. Now I wake up and the voices continue, but I can't understand what they're saying," his shoulders slumped dejectedly.

Beka could see he was haunted by this. She moved closer to him and touched his shoulder gently. Boggs raised his head towards her and smiled, his unseeing eyes directed just to the side of her face. This had unsettled her at first, but she had grown used to it. She knew it simply meant he wasn't completely focused upon her. "How long have you heard these voices?" she asked.

"Almost a full moon now."

"Are you sure its not just some squirrel far away, or a vole perhaps? You told me once you could Sense what mice and voles are thinking, not just squirrels."

"I don't think they're voles or mice. Those I would recognize."

"Maybe they're...pack rats?" Beka shuddered as she said it.

"I don't know!" replied Boggs in frustration. "These voices are different from anything else I've Sensed. I've never Sensed the voice or thoughts of a pack rat that I know of. But I think a pack rat's would be similar to the voice or thoughts of a mouse or a vole."

"You're sure it's more than one voice?"

"Yes. Sometimes it sounds like a chorus."

"Are they singing?"

"Maybe. I'm not sure. The voices are melodic and they rise and fall like music, sorta like the sound of leaves blowing in the wind. But I don't think it's the wind. Sometimes I'm sure I hear words but I can't understand their meaning."

"They're upsetting you, aren't they?"

"Yes. The last few days, the voices have been getting louder, more insistent, like they expect a response from me."

Beka felt Boggs' forehead with her paw. "Well, you don't have a fever. Maybe you're trying too hard to Sense and understand this. Without a guide, it has to be difficult NOT to be confused! You told me it's often hard to understand the meaning the first time you Sense a different kind of animal's thoughts."

"But I've been hearing these voices for a long time now." Boggs responded. "Even though I can't understand what they're saying, I think they're in pain and want me to help them."

"How can you know that if you can't understand them?" Beka asked.

"I just feel it deep inside. I don't know why, but I think the voices want me to..." He hesitated but then continued in a softer voice, "I think they know I can heal whatever's causing them pain."

In the faint light Beka could see the tension and uncertainty in his face. "I wish I could help you, but I don't understand either. I hate to see you so troubled! Can Kooper hear the voices?"

"I don't think he's ever heard them. The only time I spoke to him about it, he said it was just a dream. Of course, he rarely tries to Sense."

Beka had come to fully accept that both her grandsons could Sense and Boggs had the greater ability. But Boggs had never been so confused due to what he had Sensed. Clearly these voices had affected him deeply. "I don't understand what you're hearing, but I believe you. Do you think they're injured or sick?"

"Something like that, yes."

"Do you have an idea where the voices are coming from?"

Boggs hesitated before responding. "From the west, from near the Dark One."

Beka gasped as cold fear gripped her. "No! Don't say that name again, Boggs. That name is Ebyn!"

"I'm sorry, Grandma. I know it's forbidden to mention it but more and more I am convinced that the voices are coming from somewhere near...near that big tree."

"What makes you think that?" Now Beka was truly worried.

Boggs responded quickly, "Because now when I wake up in the morning and hear the voices I crawl out of the nest to listen. If I face west and focus on the voices they don't stop. They get stronger. When I turn away, the voices die out, even if I focus on them."

"Is it only in the morning that you hear them?"

"Yes, unless a storm is approaching. If I hear thunder, then I also hear the voices any time night or day."

Beka shifted herself noisily. "I don't understand any of this. Whoever is the source of these...voices...and if they are far away, how could they possibly know which way you're facing?"

"I don't know." Boggs moaned. "Maybe I'm crazy."

"You are not crazy. I believe you Sense something real. Perhaps they're from somewhere this side of that tree. You have said that distance can affect how clearly you Sense. And there are obviously a lot of animals between here and there."

"I didn't think I could Sense the thoughts of any creature that far away. But now I'm not sure. My Sensing ability has gotten stronger. I know these voices are far off. But when I face and think about...that tree...I can definitely hear the voices more clearly."

Beka covered her mouth with her paw as she listened to keep herself from telling him to stop, letting him continue.

"Grandma, I think I'm getting closer to understanding the voices! I feel that any day now I will be able to do so. Not yet, but soon. If I really concentrate, really focus on the Dark One..."

Beka couldn't keep from breaking in. "Please stop saying that name! It could be dangerous to even mention that tree! Let alone think about it!"

"But I don't believe the Dark One is Ebyn. Everyone thought I was possessed with Darkness, too. I don't think I am, and I don't think it's necessarily true of the Dark One either."

Beka cringed. "Well I don't know for sure about that tree but I do know you're not Ebyn. Your blindness and your ability to Sense another's thoughts certainly make you different, but you and Kooper are not Dark. If anything, you two are filled with more Lucient and goodness than anyone in the Tribe. Kooper would do anything for you. And you help me and others all the time in a way no one else can. It can't be true that you belong to the Dark!"

Beka's words emboldened Boggs and gave him enough resolve to now tell her everything he felt. "I think somebody out there needs my help. Someone who is ill or in pain. And they're calling me...because of my Sensing ability and desire to heal. I think they know I can help them and want me to come there. Our Tribe won't accept me as a healer, so maybe I should go to a place where I might be accepted."

Beka cut him off, her voice shrill. "That's impossible! You would never even get there, Boggs. You'd be killed by a hawk or an owl the day you left Leafensong. And what about your brother? You know Kooper would never let you go by yourself. He'd go with you and die with you, away from your family."

Hearing the panic in her own voice, Beka tried to calm herself. "You need to forget about these voices. If they're from near the Dark One, they could even be dangerous to this Tribe. Maybe they're deceiving you and they want to do you harm. Have you thought of that?"

Boggs answered almost before she stopped talking. "I've thought about it many times. I don't think they're deceiving me. I think the voices are being honest and they're truly in pain. I know it could be dangerous for me to go, but it's something I should do."

Beka realized she was gripping her front paws together so tightly they were hurting. She released them, and her shoulders dropped with resignation. They'd never had this kind of conflict before, and she was confused, worried and emotionally exhausted. She knew Boggs was sincere, but she couldn't accept that his leaving made any sense at all. Abruptly, she said, "I don't want to talk about this anymore, and I don't want to hear about that tree anymore."

He opened his mouth to speak and she cut him off, "No! I have other things to do now. I'll see you tomorrow, Boggs." She turned around to fiddle with her medicines on her shelves.

"Yes, ma'am," Boggs said meekly. He felt badly that he'd upset her.

He scurried off her porch as quickly as he could without saying another word. He crawled on top of the branch above Beka's nest and Sensed for Kooper, who responded out loud, "I'm right here, Boggs. On a lower limb. Are you hungry? Do you want to get some nuts to eat?"

"No," is all Boggs said. He walked along the branch on all fours and climbed up the trunk of the oak until he reached a favorite limb near the top of the tree where he laid down flat on his belly. The wind was picking up and the branch creaked and swayed beneath him. Boggs pointed his nose into the wind. He could smell snowfall approaching. Boggs was confident Kooper hadn't heard or Sensed what he and Beka had discussed. Kooper rarely tried to Sense, not like Boggs did. To himself, Boggs thought, *Maybe I should tell Koop about the voices; maybe he would understand.* But Boggs knew better. *No, he'd be just as upset. And Grandma is right. He wouldn't let me go by myself. And I can't ask him go with me; I can't put him in that danger.*

The wind was now alive, moving in waves that ebbed and flowed. Boggs could hear a gust approach as it whistled through the bare trees. Branches and trunks moaned as they rubbed against one another. Boggs was struck by a cold blast that chilled his skin through his fur, making him shiver all over. The limb beneath him danced in the wind, rising and falling, bouncing with each gust. Boggs floated weightless each time the branch fell, like a great bird held high above the forest by a thermal. The branch twisted, creaking as it bounced around. His shivering stopped as his skin became numb from the cold.

Kooper had watched Boggs as he climbed from Beka's nest to the higher limb. He hadn't heard or Sensed what Boggs and Beka had been discussing but he Sensed just enough to realize that Boggs was upset. Snow began to fall in a light sprinkle, but the flakes quickly became larger, melting as they fell on his warmer nose. Reluctantly, Kooper Sensed into Boggs' mind, "Come on, Boggs. We should get inside."

But Boggs did not hear Kooper's thoughts nor did he feel the snow flakes fall on him. All he could hear was the wind from the west, which he now faced. Wind rising and falling, woven with voices calling his name.

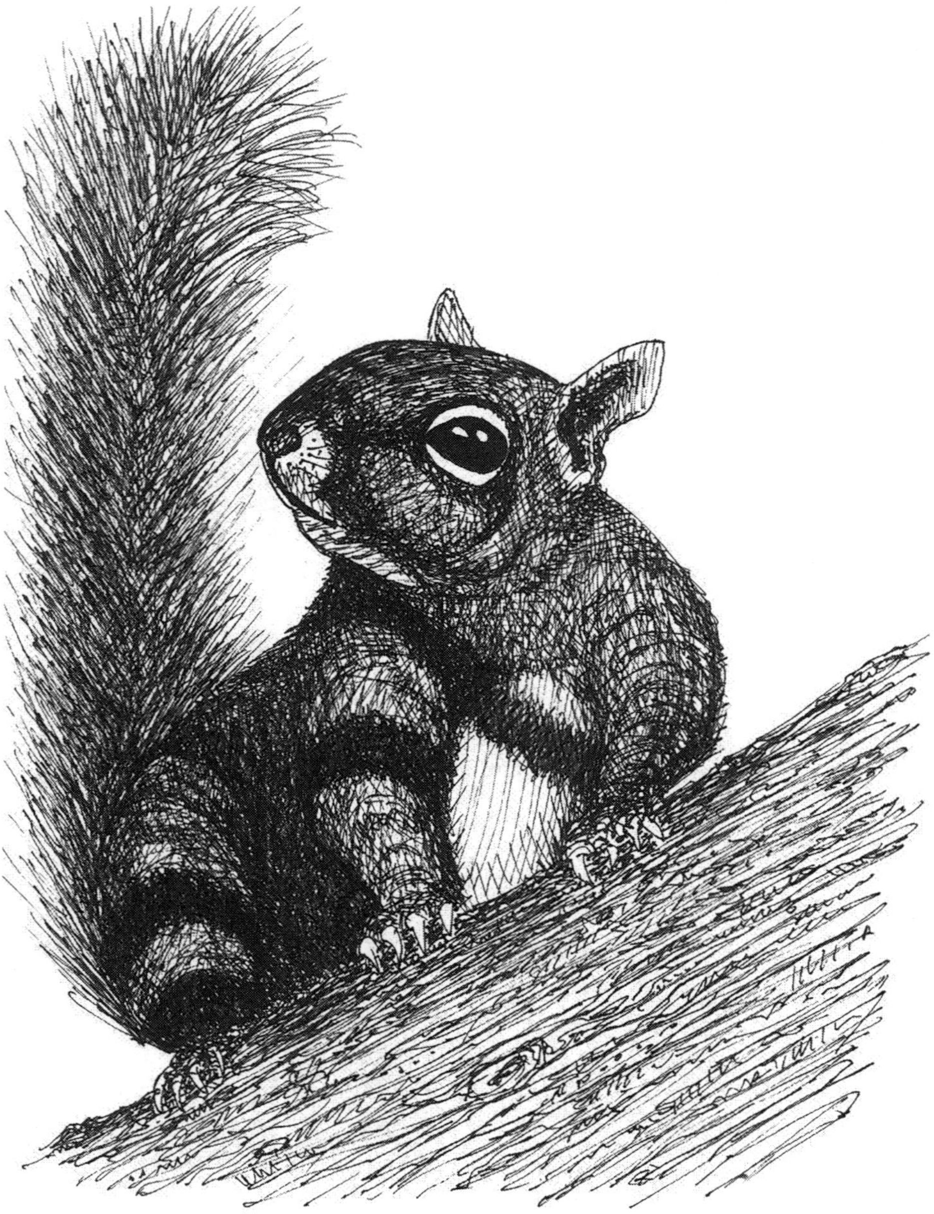

CHAPTER EIGHTEEN

Year 3072 AA
Day 67

YUNKIN AND LAM MOVED SOUTH AT A STEADY PACE. It was just past dawn and they were the first patrol for the day along this section of the eastern border. They followed a trail marked by concentrated urine left on upper branches of the border trees. All guards on patrol left their unique scent to let each other know who had passed through. The pungent odor told them when the urine had been deposited and warned any outliers to stay away. Pack rats and large voles, who competed for the squirrels' food, were prohibited from entering Leafensong, at least during the daytime. The mark also cautioned Tribal members to stay within the safety of the border. Crossing was forbidden with few exceptions.

From the end of a branch in a hackberry, Yunkin and Lam jumped a short distance to the limb of a shagbark hickory and carefully climbed its trunk. They could easily lose their grip if one of the large flakes of bark tore completely loose. As they came to the highest point of the trail, Yunkin stopped. "What is it, Yunk?" asked Lam, his ears twitching nervously as he looked all around. "Did you hear something?"

Yunkin turned his head left, looking eastward through the bare branches swaying in a steady breeze. Narrowing his eyes in thought, he asked, "You ever been outside the border?"

Realizing Yunkin hadn't stopped due to seeing an animal or hawk, Lam relaxed. One of the largest of Leafensong's squirrels, Lam was marked by vivid dark stripes that circled both his well-muscled forelegs and crossed his wide chest. A wicked white scar on his face was usually covered by fur, but was exposed when he twisted his head sideways. Lam seldom spoke of how he had received the scar, but Yunkin had heard the stories from the older guards of the Great Battle. If not for the ferocity and heroism of Karmer and Lam, the pack rats might have prevailed.

"Not often," said Lam softly. "I've only gone a short distance to check out food trees." Yunkin knew that finding trees with food could justify a foray outside Leafensong. "And Gist was right there watching out," Lam added defensively. "I wasn't leaving the border unguarded."

"I've never been outside the border. But there's something I want to check out here," offered Yunkin as he pointed a forepaw to the east, "You wait here. I won't be long. We're a bit ahead of schedule anyway."

I wondered why you were going so fast, Lam thought. He was uneasy about Yunkin leaving the border, but he reminded himself that Yunkin was now Lieutenant of the Guard and had the right to give orders to him. And Lam could tell he was intent on crossing.

"Don't go too far," Lam grumbled. "The Captain wouldn't like that. We'd both be in trouble."

"I'll take responsibility. You're staying and watching the border anyway."

"Why are you going over?" asked Lam.

But Yunkin was off, heading directly east at a fast pace, crossing limbs and vines about half way up the trees. Lam stayed high up in the hickory. He looked all around for movement by any other animals and above the trees for hawks, but also kept turning back to watch Yunkin. *You're about out of my sight!* he thought. *Lieutenant or not, you ought to know better! Where are you going?*

In no time, Yunkin was four large trees past the border. He stopped and forced himself to look around and up above the tree canopy. *Are you sure you should be doing this?* he asked himself. *Be careful! Slow down and don't make any mistakes!* He looked back and could barely see Lam, who hadn't moved. Frightened and excited at the same time, Yunkin's hair stood on end all along his back. He knew guards on patrol had recently seen pack rats at various spots just across the border. But his curiosity was too compelling to keep him from his objective. Guards had told him about a dozen mysterious mounds surrounding Leafensong. The one nearest the border was close by, and he wanted to see it. He moved more slowly and, after passing through two more large trees, stopped in a silver maple that spread its long branches out wide. Yunkin could see through the maple's bare limbs the long mound of earth. It looked just like a fallen log but was much too large for that. The guards had said they assumed they were made of earth, but when he pressed them for details, they admitted they really didn't know as they had never gotten too close. "Those are Ebyn," the guards had told him. "Stay away from them."

But ever since he had heard a guard mention the mounds, Yunkin had wanted to go look at one to see for himself. Naturally inquisitive, Yunkin had explored every square foot of Leafensong where there was nothing like these mounds. He had to visit one. Yunkin looked back. He could no longer see Lam, who was now hidden by the trees between them. Yunkin shivered. He had never been this separated from his fellow squirrels. He nervously glanced up to the sky and all around once again. He did not want to meet up with any pack rats by himself. *I shouldn't have done this without asking Rak,* he thought. *I ought to turn back.* But he knew he wouldn't. Yunkin had become obsessed with understanding all there was to know about the forest, including this mystery he was hoping to unravel. Taking a deep breath, he crossed over to the far side of the maple, dropping down to the lowest branch, directly above the mound.

The last snow had melted off and the mound was covered by a layer of brown and tan leaves, as was all of the forest floor. It looked like he was near the center of the mound. It ran north to south, increasing in height and width to the north where it abruptly ended a good ten feet high and wide and tapered down to the south where it disappeared into the ground. It had to be well over one hundred feet long.

It certainly looked like a fallen tree. The forest floor within Leafensong and without was littered with them. Toppled by storms or old age, some would get caught in standing trees, but all would eventually fall to the ground. After they had lain on the damp soil long enough, a thick bed of dark green moss would grow on top and mushrooms, toadstools, other small plants, even tree saplings, would begin sprouting through.

All that most squirrels knew about fungi was which mushrooms and toadstools were safe to eat and which were more tasty than others. But Yunkin had studied the plants and trees of Leafensong, asking questions of anyone who had answers. He knew which tree species rotted more quickly than others and which types of mushrooms and toadstools grew on different types of decaying logs. He had learned everything a smart squirrel could about the forest within Leafensong.

But there was nothing like this in Leafensong. Not only was the mound gigantic in girth and length, Yunkin noticed that no plants grew out of the leaf litter on top. *This can't be a tree,* Yunkin thought. *But, what is it?* He hesitated for a moment, then jumped down on top of the mound.

He brushed away the thick layer of leaves with his forepaws and found bark, deep maroon in color, perfectly intact without any apparent decay. *It is a tree! How can this be?* Giddy with excitement, Yunkin quickly brushed aside more leaves. The dark bark seemed somehow familiar, yet different than anything he had seen before, marked by an irregular series of raised ridges, sharply edged. He tried to break off a piece with his paws but couldn't. *This is the toughest bark I've ever seen!*

Yunkin rapidly brushed away more leaves and he felt a sharp pang of pain. "Ouch!" he cried out softly as he instinctively pulled his right paw back. Blood began to ooze from the inside and he put it to his mouth, sucking the wound to quench the flow. He carefully moved leaves aside with his other paw and found what had bitten him: a dark red thorn, long as his tail, jutting out from a clump of gray, red and maroon thorns. *This must be a honey locust tree,* he thought.

The forest inside and without Leafensong abounded with them. The squirrels and all rodents enjoyed eating the sweet, stringy insides of their long, dark brown seed pods that dropped each fall. But the squirrels avoided the trees themselves because of their wicked thorns. Tough and stiff, the thorns were needle-sharp and contained a mild poison. A fall from up high onto a honey locust thorn could kill, and wounds caused by them often became infected. Yunkin bent down and smelled the clump of thorns, careful not to touch his tender nose to them. *Yes, they smell somewhat like honey locust,* he thought, *but something more.*

This made no sense. Honey locust were not the tallest of species and no tree, of any type, had bark like this. *This giant tree couldn't have fallen recently or I would have heard about it,* he thought. *But the bark is still intact. Locust wood doesn't rot as fast as many species, but the bark would have started to decay by now, and moss would be growing on top.*

Suddenly Yunkin realized he had been over the border far too long. He jerked his head up and looked west. He wanted to investigate the great log further, but he realized Lam would be worried and angry. If Rak came along, they'd be in real trouble. With one last glance at the bark and thorns, he turned, and as carefully as he could, jumped up into the maple, then raced back to the border, stopping only once to check out the sky and surroundings, his tail twitching nervously.

Lam's anxiousness was evident as Yunkin re-joined him. "Where have you been?" Lam asked in a barely controlled whisper. "I can't believe you were gone that long!" Lam looked all around before continuing. "It's a good thing the Captain hasn't come by. Let's get on with it. We've got to make up some time to reach Alain and Daker! They'll be wondering where we are!" Without waiting for Yunkin to respond, Lam took off to the south with Yunkin following behind, neither speaking. Yunkin tried to focus on patrolling, checking out the sky and surroundings, but he couldn't put what he had discovered out of his mind.

Lam saw that Yunkin was favoring his right front paw and realized it had somehow been injured. But Lam was not sympathetic and neither mentioned the injury. *How can you be our Lieutenant and be this careless?* he wondered. But he soon realized that whatever Yunkin had seen or done had affected him deeply. "Pay attention, Yunk!" Lam said as he grabbed Yunkin to keep him from falling off a high limb. "*What in the world has he been up to?* wondered Lam.

CHAPTER NINETEEN

Year 3072 AA
Day 67

RAK AND GIST SAT HIGH IN AN ASH TREE NEAR THE SOUTHERN END OF THE EASTERN BORDER OF LEAFENSONG, WAITING FOR YUNKIN AND LAM. Rak wanted to check in with Yunkin to see how he was doing on his first full day as Lieutenant. As they came within sight, Gist noticed Yunkin's limp.

"You see that, Cap? Something is bothering Yunkin."

"Yes," responded Rak simply.

Rak and Gist moved in sync to the nearest border tree, and Rak called out as Yunkin and Lam approached,

"Squirrels, you see anything this time out?"

"I didn't see anything, Cap," replied Lam, avoiding eye contact.

"Yunk, what's wrong with your foreleg?" asked Rak.

"It's my paw. A wound from a thorn."

"What kind?"

"A honey locust thorn, I think."

"How in the world did you get that?" asked Rak. All squirrels knew how poisonous locust thorns were and usually were able to avoid them by staying out of locust trees. Rak knew there weren't any in the border trees his guards patrolled.

Oh boy, here I go, thought Yunkin. After a moment's hesitation, he said, "I got it outside the border, Cap. Just a little while ago." Lam continued looking away.

What in the world... wondered Gist.

"Gist, you and Lam carry on the patrol," Rak said sternly but evenly. "Yunk, you stay here and tell me about it."

Lam looked back at Rak and Yunkin as he and Gist continued on to the south. He leaned close and whispered, "Yunkin crossed the border a little ways back, Sarge. I don't know why or how he got hurt. He had me stay on the border. And he sure has something on his mind."

"The Captain will get it out of him."

"So why were you outside the border, Yunk?" asked Rak, deadly serious.

Yunkin let out a sigh. "I'd been thinking about the mounds surrounding Leafensong.

"Mounds?"

Yunkin nodded and replied, "Yes. I'd heard guards talk about them recently. They said they looked like giant fallen trees and the closest one was nearby. So I was curious and went to see it." He watched closely for Rak's response, expecting to be severely criticized or worse.

"I've seen them but I guess I've never given them much thought," said Rak. *Why would you care about those?* he wondered.

Yunkin's nervousness and excitement were both evident as he explained what he had done. "I heard they completely surround Leafensong. I wanted to know what they were 'cause there's nothing like them within the border. It was my decision, Cap, not Lam's. I had him stay in a border tree while I went across. We were ahead of schedule so it wasn't going to make us late. And, Cap, it is a fallen tree!"

Rak jerked his head back in disbelief.

"What? Those can't be trees, Yunk, they're much too big."

"When I saw it, I thought so, too," Yunkin replied. "But the one I looked at sure is. A honey locust with thorns still attached. That's how I got hurt, on a thorn, hidden under the leaves. But, Cap, there's something really strange. It's not decaying like a tree should. The bark is solid and tougher than any living tree I can think of. But it had to have fallen a long time ago or I'm sure there'd be stories about it. I don't understand it."

Normally, this sort of thing would be of no concern to Rak, but it seemed so inexplicable. Now his own curiosity was raised.

"How can that be a tree? There's never been a locust tree that big."

"Not in Leafensong, no, sir. But, there might be one still standing."

Ever so slightly, Rak shook his head sidewise, "No way."

"To the west of us, Cap. The Dark One." said Yunkin, expectantly.

For a moment this didn't register, and Rak frowned until his eyes widened with bewilderment. He felt a stab of fear in his gut. Like all of Leafensong's squirrels, he had grown up hearing how evil the Dark One was.

"It has to be like the Dark One," Yunkin continued excitedly. "It'd be about the same size. I've seen it. It's not a cottonwood. It's not the right shape. But, it could be a locust. That would explain this. I bet the other mounds are fallen giant trees, too. And the Dark One is the last one standing. It's the only explanation that makes any kind of sense. I'd like to investigate another fallen tree, Cap. It wouldn't take much time. And I can make sure the border's still being patrolled while I do it."

"Okay," said Rak, composed again. "But I'm going with you."

Yunkin had assumed Rak would say no. While relieved that Rak was not more angry with him, he was primarily amazed that Rak wanted to look at one of the fallen trees. "Really? When do you want to do that?"

"Right now. There's another one, tree or whatever it is, a bit farther south of here. But first we'll wait until the next patrol comes along so we can tell them where we're going. And I don't want you crossing the border again by yourself. I appreciate you wanting to figure things out, but right now we have to be careful. You know there have been pack rats sighted recently."

"Yes, sir! I've heard that, though I haven't seen any."

"That doesn't mean they haven't seen you. If you go across the border from now on, you go with me or one of the older guards who has fought with pack rats before. Do you understand that? And be on the lookout. We're going as much to check for them as to look for your trees."

"My trees?"

"If that's what they are. You're the one who figured this out. Here's the patrol coming now. We'll tell them what we're doing, and we'll be on our way."

"Yes, sir! And thanks, Cap."

"For what?"

"For taking me seriously."

"That's our job, Yunk. To be serious. We do need to know everything we can about the forest. But we must be careful at all times. Especially now. Something's going on out there."

CHAPTER TWENTY

Year 3072 AA
Day 67

RAK LED YUNKIN AWAY FROM THE BORDER AND SOON THEY COULD SEE THE LARGE END OF THE FALLEN TREE. From a branch just above, they looked for thorns poking through the layer of leaves on top of the mound. Seeing none, Rak dropped down with Yunkin right behind, who immediately began clearing away leaves, exposing the maroon-colored bark.

"It's the same kind of bark, Cap," Yunkin said excitedly. "And there are more thorns! Like the ones on the other tree, they're hard as any thorn I've ever seen!" Yunkin cleared away more leaves. "And see the ridges in the bark? They're like those on any honey locust, but thicker and tougher."

With his claw, Rak tried to pry a piece of the bark off, but it wouldn't break. He reached down to bite it off with his incisor teeth, but it wouldn't budge. He moved over to another ridge that wasn't as thick, finally managing to crack and pry off a small piece. His teeth aching from the effort, he smelled the broken edge and then held it up for Yunkin. "Take a whiff. That doesn't smell like locust. What's that smell like to you?"

Yunkin took the piece of bark and held it to his nose while Rak looked all around through the trees. "It smells like a hedge tree, Cap."

"I thought the same thing. I wonder if that has something to do with this bark not having decayed. Even I know that hedge trees don't decay quickly. They last longer than any other kind of fallen tree."

"But it's clearly a honey locust," Yunkin replied excitedly. "Why would it smell like a hedge?"

Rak shook his head, as mystified as Yunkin.

"Fallen trees always start rotting the fastest where they touch the ground," added Yunkin. "I wonder if this bark is decaying there. Can we check that out?"

"Okay, but we're not staying out here too much longer."

Yunkin dropped over the side of the log to the ground and pulled leaves away to expose the bark where it touched the soil. Once again he was careful as locusts often had thorns on the ground below and around them, although here he found none. "The bark hasn't decayed here either, Cap. It's as solid as on top." Yunkin stood up holding a paw full of dirt, "I've never seen this sort of thing before. Can we check out the stump?"

"No, we need to get back," Rak said, looking off to the east. "What do you smell, Yunk?"

Yunkin held the paw full of dirt up to his nose, "Soil and decayed leaves." He sniffed at the soil again, "And a slight scent of hedge."

"Yunk, get your nose out of the dirt and smell the air."

Yunkin opened his paw and dropped the soil, lifted his snout and breathed in deeply. His eyes widened with alarm. "Pack rats!"

"You should have noticed this scent already, Lieutenant. I was waiting to see if you would smell them. There were two of them, and they had to have been here early this morning or during the night. You can't get so excited about these fallen trees, as interesting as they are to you, and forget that you're Lieutenant of the Guard. You have to be constantly on the alert for danger. If you can't do that, I can't allow you to continue as Lieutenant. Our guards, our Tribe, depend upon you. You must always keep your eyes and your nose open for anything and everything."

Yunkin was mortified. He knew that Rak was right. "Yes, Cap, I understand."

Rak looked Yunkin squarely in the face. "You have to learn from this and never let it happen again. I told you before we came over we were going to look at your tree and also watch out for pack rats. That includes checking for their scent. It's not normal for two pack rats to be together. Something unusual's going on with them. They hate us, and sooner or later I'm afraid they're going to attack us again. For the first time since the Great Battle they're coming close to Leafensong, two at a time." Rak looked out around them, raised his nose and breathed deeply one last time. "Now, let's go."

Rak jumped off the locust log onto the ground and hopped over to the trunk of the bur oak, climbing it quickly to a branch leading back to the border. With a glance at the giant locust, Yunkin followed him close behind. Soon they were back in a border tree.

"Cap, I'm sorry I didn't pay attention and smell the pack rats. I guess I was too excited about the trees."

"Being sorry isn't enough. I made you Lieutenant because you're smarter and more inquisitive than the rest of us," Rak replied. "We need that, but you have to focus your curiosity. You made a mistake out there, and a mistake next time could be fatal to you, our guards or others."

As they headed west away from the border, Yunkin no longer thought about the fallen locusts. He had been astounded to hear Rak's comment about his intelligence and curiosity and hoped Rak was right. But now he was focused solely upon his failure. *I've got to do better*, he thought. *I can't let the Captain down again.*

Meanwhile, Rak was thinking about Yunkin. *Did I make the right decision?* he wondered. *Clearly he's intelligent and open to new ideas. He must know more about our forest than anyone except the Keeper, but can he use his curiosity for what we need? Should I choose another Lieutenant before he hurts someone?*

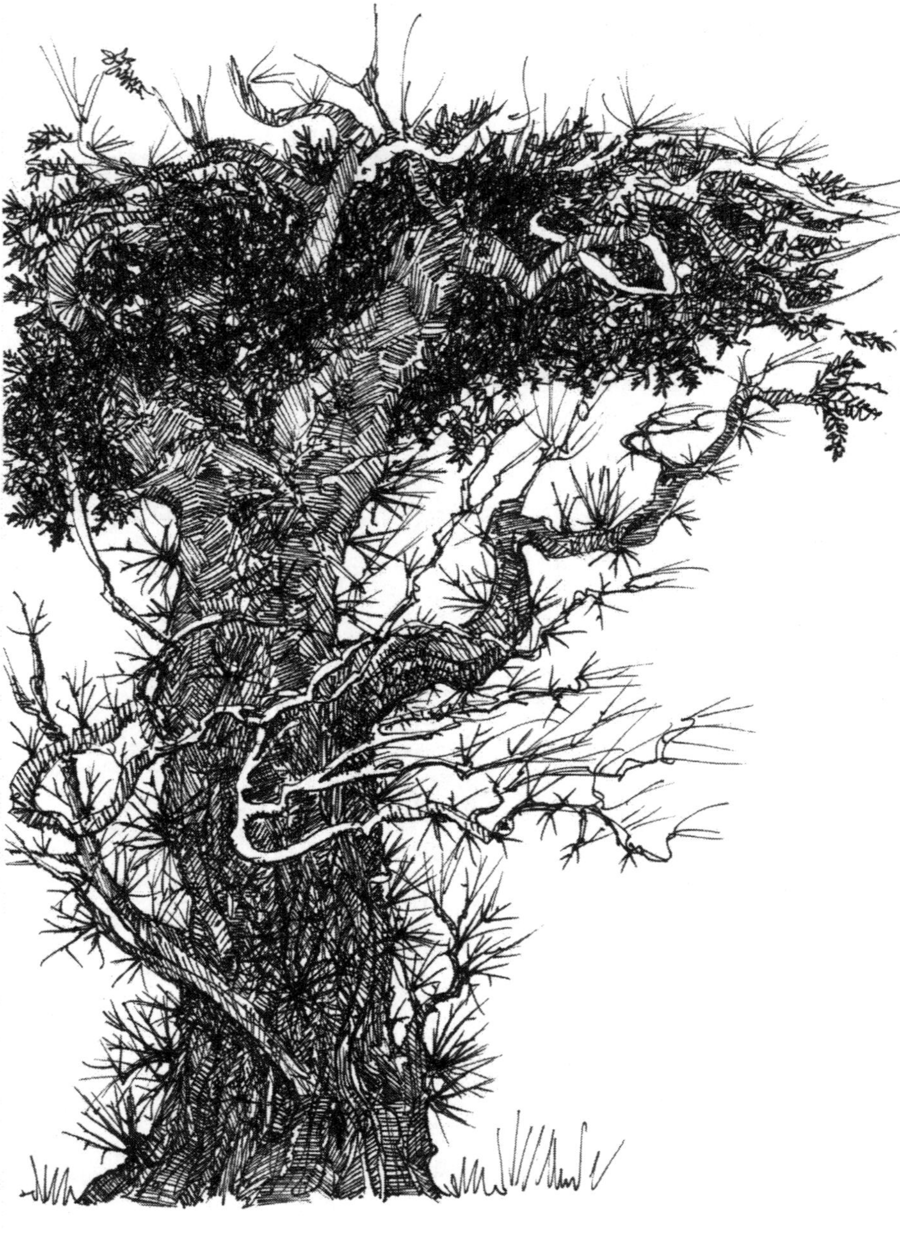

CHAPTER TWENTY-ONE

Year 3072 AA

Day 67

LATE IN THE DAY, YUNKIN ARRIVED AT THE BASE OF RAK'S SYCAMORE EAST OF THE COUNCIL OAK. Rak had told Yunkin to join him, Karmer and Gist from now on every day just before dusk to discuss their concerns and make further plans. The three had done this for years. They had been named Captain and Sergeants of the Guard after the Great Battle with the pack rats, the battle when Thrane was lost. Yunk could hear the three laugh above him.

They've got a right to be laughing about me, he thought. He'd been beating himself up ever since his mistake. *I'm sure Rak's told them about "my trees" and my failure. I know Karmer and Gist think Rak shouldn't have named me Lieutenant. I've heard the guards talk. They say Karmer should have been chosen. I don't have near the experience he or Gist has, and I'm supposed to be their superior?*

Everyone probably thinks I'm not fit to be Lieutenant. They're probably right. I should just resign.

"Yunkin, is that you down there?" called Gist. "Come on up and join us." Trying not to limp noticeably, Yunkin climbed up the imposing trunk past the opening to Rak's nest. Yunkin had never been in Rak's tree. It was huge—a symbol of Rak's strength and status. He took a deep breath and climbed the rest of the way to the branch the three were on.

Before Yunkin could say anything, Gist handed Yunkin a choice hickory nut. The other three were already munching their own. As Yunkin started to eat, Karmer spoke up.

"Cap's been telling us about your trees, Yunk. Doesn't make sense to me. How could there be so many fallen giant trees like that? And you think they're honey locusts?"

Yunkin nodded. "Yes, sir. Obviously, they're different from normal locusts, but yes."

"You don't need to call me sir, Yunk. You're my superior now."

Yunkin stopped before calling him "sir" again and nodded.

"The forest is full of those locust logs, if that's what they are," said Gist. "There's more than just the ones close by. They're on the ground as far out as I've gone."

"Are you sure they're trees? I've never gotten close to 'em," said Karmer.

"They're trees all right," said Rak. "Yunkin is right; they're locusts but different in more ways than just being so big."

"Why aren't there any still standing?" asked Karmer.

"Yunk thinks there's one," said Rak, watching Karmer and Gist closely for their reaction. "The Dark One."

Gist's eyes widened and he looked first at Karmer, then Rak and Yunkin. "You think the Dark One's the same as the trees on the ground, Yunk?" asked Gist almost in a whisper, the fright clear in his face.

"Makes sense to me," Yunkin responded. "The Dark One and the fallen logs are about the same size, I'd say. And from this distance the limbs remaining on the Dark One appear to be similar to a locust."

"Then there's a reason no one has really gotten close to the fallen trees," said Gist. "They really are Ebyn."

But Karmer responded, "We've always been told the Dark One and the fallen trees are Ebyn but maybe they aren't. Either way, what's the big deal? Why should we even care? We've got other things that we have to deal with."

Rak spoke up, "It might not make any difference to us. But I do want to know everything we can about our forest. As long as we're careful—and Yunk's careful—he can explore these fallen trees at least a little more. But I told him he has to take someone with him, someone who has been in a fight with pack rats. And I want extra guards to stay close by in the border ready to come if they're called."

"Seems to me we're taking an unnecessary risk with pack rats about," said Karmer abruptly. "If the pack rats join up and want a fight, whoever goes with Yunk will be in jeopardy along with him. I don't think it's worth the risk."

"It could be dangerous," replied Rak. "But he's not going out there often. Depends on what else he discovers. But now I'm also curious. Yunk, you tell me when you plan on going the next time, and afterward we'll talk about what you discover. Then we'll decide together if and when you go again. But remember you're not going just to look at those fallen trees. Maybe we can also find out what the pack rats are up to."

"That makes sense," said Gist. "But only if we're careful."

"Agreed," said Rak.

"And, Yunk, we're also making some other changes. Starting tomorrow night, I want half of our guards to sleep in border trees or right next to them. We can take turns every other night. Tomorrow Karmer and Gist can tell you how this will work."

Yunkin nodded without saying anything. His thoughts about resigning had evaporated as he realized neither Rak, Karmer nor Gist was asking him to do so. He was now determined to do whatever he could to help and not let Rak down again.

Rak interrupted Yunkin's thoughts.

"Yunk, how's your paw?"

Yunkin held up his paw and all could see the wound was now surrounded by redness and swelling.

"That doesn't look good," said Gist. "You ought to see Beka. She has some medicine that can help with the infection and pain. She really helped my bruised back. I'm feeling much better, but I sure hate the taste of the bark she gave me to chew." He shuddered at the memory.

"Yunk, Gist is right," said Rak. "You don't want that getting any worse. You go see Beka right now and get that taken care of."

"Yes, sir." Yunkin hesitated, uncertain whether he should say something about his failure to detect the pack rat scent across the border, but he didn't know what to say. It was easier to just follow Rak's order, and with a nod to each of the three, he took off towards Beka's tree, trying not to limp.

"I don't know, Cap," said Karmer in a low voice as they watched Yunkin climb down the sycamore and head off. "He might be smart, but he sure is interested in some unusual stuff. I still don't know why we need to pay any attention to those fallen trees."

"The Council would care," added Gist. "They'd start arguing over whether or not the logs are Ebyn."

Karmer snorted, "Some on the Council will argue their own mother's Ebyn! They're a complete waste of time."

Rak didn't respond. He was looking in the opposite direction of Yunkin, at a neighboring honey locust that was covered by thorns. Karmer and Gist both noticed and looked at each other with raised eyebrows.

"Cap, are you getting interested in those locust trees, too?" asked Karmer.

"Maybe so. I'm trying to keep my mind open. Something you should do, too, Sergeant." Rak realized his reply was curt and he turned to face Karmer. "Sorry. I realize Yunkin's interest in those trees may seem strange. He does think differently from us, but that's okay. I want him to know as much as he can about Leafensong, and outside Leafensong. I want him to use all of his brain and not be limited by us. I want him to be creative. He may well come up with ideas we never would, which might make a difference in how to deal with the pack rats. We need to know what's going on."

Karmer got up, noisily brushed pieces of acorn shell off his fur and kicked them over the side of the branch. He stood still for a moment, looking into the distance before turning back to face Rak.

"I don't see how it makes any difference to us if the Dark One is the same as those old logs. Yunkin's wasting his time, and ours, spending energy on that. If Yunkin is as intelligent as you think, you'd better get him to focus on those pack rats. I'm going to my tree. Gist, you coming?" Their trees were right next to one another.

"Yeah, I'm coming," said Gist. "Cap, we'll see you in the morning. We've got a lot to think about."

Rak mumbled, "Okay," but once again was staring at the honey locust. Without saying anything further, Karmer and Gist watched him for a moment and then left.

Rak wasn't observing his sergeants as they left. He was still staring at the locust—one of a crowd of closely growing locusts. Other than it's dark gray color, it did look like the fallen giant he and Yunkin had inspected. Even this far away, the thorns were menacing. Rak grimaced, remembering when he fell from his sycamore the summer before and landed on a loose locust thorn on the ground. The wound in his right flank was deep and had become infected. He knew he should have seen Beka to have it treated, but he didn't want to face her after their confrontation over Boggs. He was lucky the ensuing infection and fever weren't worse. *That was stupid of me,* he told himself. *We need her help, and I'm going to have to talk to her. I've got to use my brain, too.*

The honey locusts were as unique as the banded squirrels. Their thorns and seed pods easily distinguished them from the black locusts, which had neither. While the squirrels avoided the dangerous thorns that were the largest in the forest, they enjoyed eating the pulp inside the seed pods.

The squirrels didn't realize that the seeds weren't needed to grow new trees. Honey locusts more often grew from suckers that shot up from roots of honey locust trees. Groves of the trees were often one tree all grown from the roots of a single locust. Connected under ground, their arteries and veins shared water and food. The locusts sent their roots deep into the earth and were hardier than many trees, able to withstand drought, heat and decay. They leafed out later in the spring and dropped their leaves earlier in the fall, protecting their small leaves from freezing.

A nearby hedge tree now caught Rak's attention. Also called Osage orange, full-grown hedge trees weren't even half the height of locusts or sycamores. This was an old one, its thick trunk covered with narrow ridges of tough, rough bark that criss-crossed at odd angles with deep furrows between them. Large circular, bulbous masses protruded from all sides of the thick trunk. Even though a number of branches had died, they remained attached, and had turned from muted orange and brown in color to a dull gray, and, finally, flat black. Fungi that would have decayed any other dead wood was repulsed by the excessive amount of tannin in the wood. The chemical was so concentrated, it would take decades for the rainwater to leach it out enough for the wood to rot away.

Beneath the hedge, scattered remains of hedge apples littered the ground. Four or five inches in diameter with a light green, dimpled surface when freshly fallen in the fall and early winter, the hedge apples slowly turned darker and soft as they alternately froze and thawed over winter. The squirrels broke open the apples to eat the hundreds of small, nutritious seeds within each one. Only the female trees bore the hedge apples and the small, tough thorns that covered the smaller limbs. From where he sat, Rak could smell the pieces of hedge apples that remained, reminding him of the smell of the giant locust's bark.

Rak shook his head, sighed and slowly climbed down the trunk of the ancient sycamore to his nest, his thoughts a jumble of worry. *Why would bark of the giant locust have the smell of a hedge tree? Yunk's right, it just doesn't make sense.*

But what if Karmer and Gist are right? What if this stuff about the locusts is a waste of time? What are those pack rats up to?

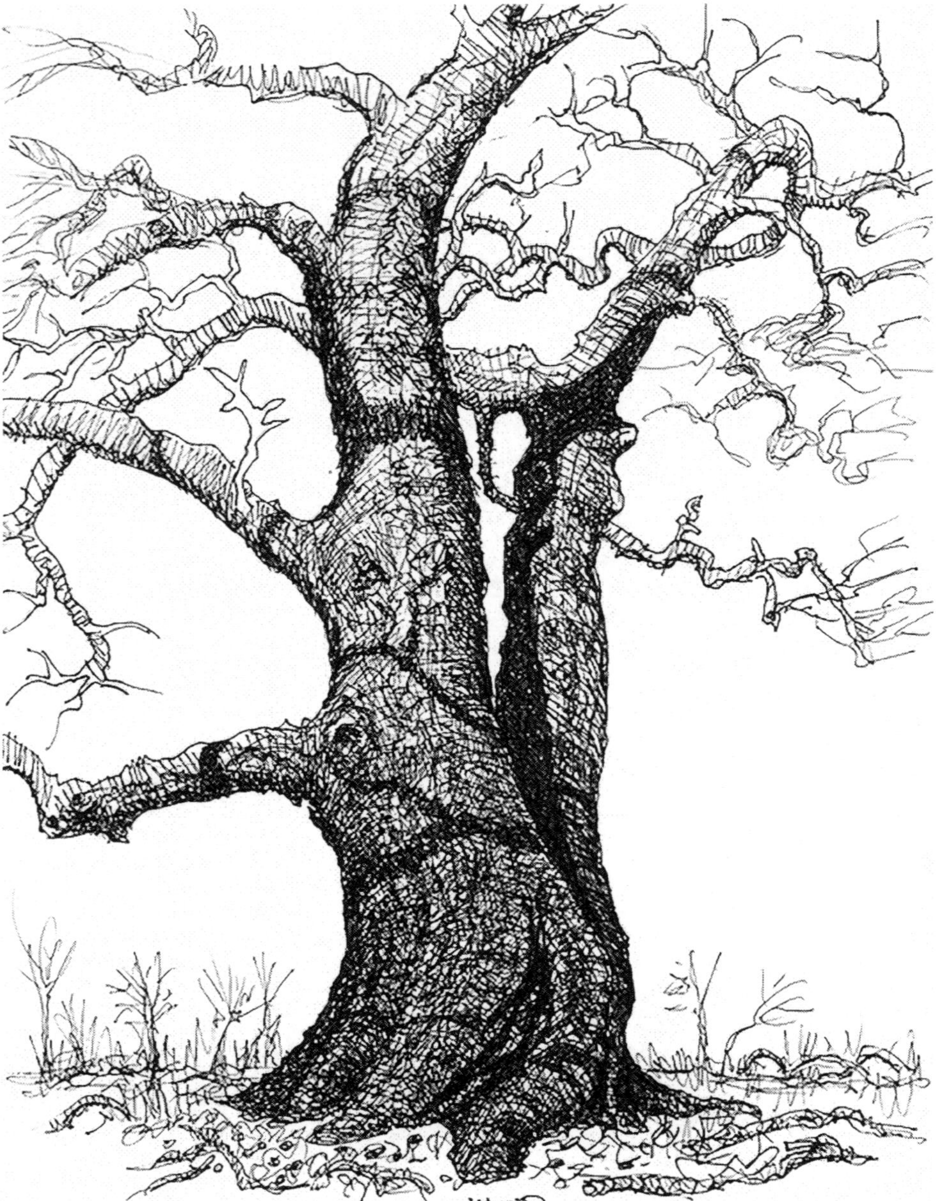

CHAPTER TWENTY-TWO

Year 3072 AA
Day 67

BACK IN HER PORCH AT THE END OF THE DAY, BEKA WAS HUMMING AS USUAL. She was sorting through her bundles of medicine when Yunkin appeared at the porch opening.

"Hello, Beka. May I come in?"

Beka turned and at first didn't recognize him. They had never spoken except in passing. "Why, yes. You're Yunkin, aren't you? I know your mother, and your grandmother was a good friend. Her death was a real loss. How's your mother doing?"

"Fine. I'll tell her you asked."

"Thank you. I'm afraid I haven't kept up with your family lately. I don't leave my nest much anymore. What can I do for you?"

"I've got a wound on my paw." He held out his right paw and opened it, wincing as the cut spread apart. Beka could tell it was a deep gash, and infected. The skin on either side was swollen and red, turning yellow.

"Oh, my. That's not good," said Beka as she reached out with her own paw to hold Yunkin's. "Come over here and sit down. We need to soak that." Beka went to her shelves at the back of her porch and returned with two clumps of dried moss, one bright green and the other gray. She tore a small piece from each and put both in her mouth, chewing and adding saliva until the moss was soaking wet. She pulled the sopping wet moss out of her mouth and gently touched it to the wound, squeezing out the dark green juice. Yunkin flinched, pulling back on his paw.

"I know it hurts, but this will help. The green moss will reduce the infection and the gray moss will lessen the pain." As Beka held the moss against the wound, squeezing small bits of juice out, the pain slowly began to subside and Yunkin relaxed. "This is a nasty infection," she said. "When did you get this? It must be several days old."

"It happened yesterday."

Beka knitted her brows. "I've never seen a wound that recent become infected like this. How did you get it?"

"It's from a honey locust thorn."

"Locust thorns can cause infections if left untreated, but this is especially bad," Beka carefully spread the cut apart looking for any bit of thorn still inside.

"It wasn't just any honey locust," explained Yunkin. "You know those mounds that surround Leafensong? The long humps that look like giant fallen trees?"

Beka shook her head no. She had never been outside the border.

"I heard about them, and I went and looked at one. It's a fallen honey locust but it was a giant of a tree. It would have been taller than even the Singer's Tree. And the trunk is wider than your bur oak's."

Beka frowned.

"I was pulling leaves off the top of the log and didn't see the thorn hidden underneath."

"The wound is deep, but clean. That thorn had powerful poison. Are you sure it's a honey locust?"

"I think so." He recounted his trip with Rak to the fallen log.

"What does it smell like?"

"A hedge tree."

"That doesn't make any sense," Beka replied.

"I know," said Yunkin. "I don't understand it either."

"I'm familiar with both," said Beka. "I use lots of different barks for different purposes and I've never found another tree that smells like hedge. The poison in them can cause infection but not like this. And the thorns aren't long enough to make a cut this deep. I've treated plenty of wounds caused by locust thorns but none like this; it's a good thing you came to see me. If you had let this go, it could have become really serious."

Beka saw the alarm in Yunkin's eyes. "Don't worry. We've caught this in time. It's a nasty wound, but I'm sure it'll be okay."

"It feels better already," Yunkin said as she nodded.

"Good. Here, chew these pieces of moss until they're thoroughly wet."

Yunkin did as she asked, chewing and making saliva but grimacing from the bad taste.

"I'll give you a batch of each type to take with you. You have to soak the wound with equal amounts of saliva from both kinds of moss. Do this four times a day. And you come back and see me every day until this is healed up. There. That should be enough; go ahead and take the moss out. Now hold it against the wound and squeeze the juice out a little at a time. Yes, like that."

Yunkin did as Beka instructed.

"Yes ma'am. And thank you."

"You're welcome."

As she retrieved more moss from her shelves, Beka continued to talk. "You said these locusts were taller than the Singer's Tree? That's hard to believe. I've never seen any tree close to that size."

Yunkin hesitated a moment, unsure, but thought perhaps she would be willing to accept his theory.

"Except the Dark One," he added. "It's about that size."

Beka whirled around, her eyes wide, "You shouldn't say that tree's name so easily, Yunkin. It's Ebyn!"

Chagrinned, Yunkin replied, "Yes, ma'am. I'm sorry. I didn't mean to offend you."

"You didn't offend me. I…I just don't want the darkness to touch you."

Both were quiet for a few moments as Beka continued putting a bundle of moss together before she asked, almost in a whisper, "You really think…that tree…could be another giant locust?"

"Yes, I'm guessing it would be about the same size, and the limbs on it look like a locust's."

"I've never even looked at it except by mistake," she said. "Don't you think it's dangerous to look at it?"

"No. I don't think its Ebyn. I think it's just a tree, a really big tree—the last of it's kind. I'm thinking the forest was full of them at one time. Sergeant Gist says the fallen trees surround Leafensong as far out as he's gone."

Beka wrapped a paw paw leaf around the moss and tied it up with a piece of thin vine.

"There you go. I think you're all set."

"Thank you, Beka."

As Yunkin exited her porch, Beka spoke up again, "One more thing. You tell the Captain thank you. I appreciate his protecting the Tribe. He and I both do that, but in different ways. The whole Tribe appreciates the Guard's work."

"Yes, ma'am. I'll tell him." With that, Yunkin left.

As he left Beka's bur oak, Yunkin saw Boggs higher up in the tree and then Kooper close by. Neither said anything, but he and Kooper each nodded to one another. Like everyone else, Yunkin knew about Boggs' blindness and how Rak tried to banish him to his death when he was a pup. *Hard to believe Rak would do that,* he thought. Yunkin knew Boggs was avoided by the whole Tribe other than his family. *He's lucky to have a brother to watch over him.* For just a moment, Yunkin thought about climbing up to say hello to them but realized it was getting late.

Yunkin decided to visit his mother instead. He knew it might be his last chance to spend time with her, since the guards were to start spending their nights along the border the following day. Like most bucks, Yunkin enjoyed spending time with his mother from time to time and often slept with her in her nest. But just as he started toward her tree, Yunkin abruptly stopped, thinking, *I should spend tonight in the border, start a night earlier than the rest of the guards. But I have to take someone else, like Rak ordered.* Yunkin turned east towards the tree where his cousin and fellow guard, Alain, usually slept, not far from his own nest.

Approaching the nest of Alain, Yunkin called out. "Alain, you there?" It was almost nightfall, and Yunkin was sure he'd be in his sleeping nest already.

Alain popped his head out. He was a lighter colored squirrel with a distinguishing stripe starting at the top of his head going down his back until it spiraled around his tail. "What's up, Yunk?" Their mothers were first cousins, lived close to one another and had raised Yunkin and Alain together. Both were thrilled when each was accepted as a guard two years before. Alain had not been jealous at all when Yunkin was chosen Lieutenant. He told Yunkin then, "I think it's great, Cuz. You'll make a super officer, and I'll be proud to obey your orders."

"How about sleeping in the same nest with me tonight?" asked Yunkin. "The guards are all going to start sleeping in the border trees in twos starting tomorrow. Rak's concerned because pack rats have been seen close to the border. I'd like to start tonight."

Without hesitation, Alain responded, "You bet, Cuz. Where to?"

"Let's go to the western border. That's where the pack rats were last seen. I know a good nest in a tall oak facing west. We should be able to get there before nightfall."

Just before the sky turned completely dark, Yunkin and Alain settled in the nest high in the bur oak. Yunkin filled in his cousin with the day's happenings. Yunkin could scarcely believe all that had transpired, and Alain was the one squirrel Yunkin felt he could be totally open with about his feelings.

"I really screwed up, Cuz. I was so caught up in examining the fallen tree I ignored everything else. As soon as Rak asked me what else I could smell, I smelled the pack rats. I should have caught that immediately."

"The scent must have been pretty faint, though, if they hadn't been there since last night."

"Not that faint. I should have smelled it. I was just too caught up looking at the fallen tree. I'm not sure I should be Lieutenant. "

"Sounds like the Captain still wants you to be."

"I don't know why, but yeah, it seems so."

"He told you why. You're the smartest squirrel in the Tribe. I've always thought so. The Guard needs that, but you've got to pay attention to everything at all times, like the Captain said. You've always gotten lost in your head, like when you decided to examine every dead walnut tree you could find. You didn't pay attention to anything else for days. You can't do that any longer. You've got to focus your smarts for the good of the Guard. For Leafensong."

Yunkin didn't say anything in response. But, the idea that Rak still wanted him was enough. *I must do better,* he thought. *Maybe I can make a difference.* He stayed awake, thinking about the day's events long after Alain fell asleep.

***

Sleep did not come easily for Rak either. The memories of the Great Battle haunted him. He kept seeing the tan-eared pack rat pushing Thrane over the limb as they stared into each other's eyes. Karmer holding his dying brother, Dram. Other dead friends. Families beginning the grief they still carried, all of whom were now his responsibility.

He was mentally exhausted but had to calm his still racing mind. *Sleep, sleep*, he told himself over and over. Finally, he drifted off. He would remain asleep, but tired in the morning after a night of fitful dreams.

*****

Boggs and Kooper were back to back, comforted by the familiar warmth of each other. Boggs kept his thoughts to himself and put a mental barrier up in case Kooper tried to Sense them.

But Kooper wasn't wondering what Boggs was thinking. He was thinking about Sharani. Ever since she had touched his face months before, he had thought about her. He did realize she had stopped and stared at him just days before. *I think she wanted me to speak to her. Why couldn't I at least look back at her? And say something? I'm an idiot. But, she'd be wasting her time with me. I've got no time for her. I've got to focus on Boggs. But, oh, she's so beautiful.*

CHAPTER
TWENTY-THREE

Year 3072 AA
Day 68

SHARANI HAD NOT SLEPT WELL. Awake most of the night, her thoughts were scattered.

Jesska says I need a friend and Kooper might be that friend. Maybe she's right. No one else wants to be my friend—Jone's the only doe who will even talk to me. Her mind blanked out for a minute. Sharani was used to this as it had happened all her life, though normally others didn't notice since her expression remained the same. She waited and presently her thoughts about Kooper resumed. *We do have things in common. Jesska says he's a loner, too. Maybe he would be a friend. But will he even talk to me?*

Finally tired enough, Sharani went to sleep until just before dawn. A bird's song awoke her and she opened her eyes, laying still until she finally stretched. As the sky turned lighter outside, her eyes traced the familiar, dark crevices that slowly appeared in the ceiling of her nest.

Maybe Beka and Claryn can tell me what I should do, she thought. *Beka's the Healer; she ought to know.* Her mind made up, as soon as it was light enough she left for Beka's tree. As she traveled through the forest, moving methodically along limbs and vines, up and down tree trunks, her thoughts were less disjointed than before.

Sharani dropped down to the ground from the ash tree near Beka's oak and saw Claryn sitting on the end of the limb above Beka's nest. From her perch, Claryn saw Sharani approach and dropped down, entering Beka's porch. "Sharani's here, Mother."

"Probably to get Jesska's medicines," replied Beka from inside her sleeping nest. She came out to look out the porch's entrance. "I told her to come for a massage. I wish she'd listen to me more." Beka went to put together Jesska's medicines and Claryn sat down in the middle of the porch.

As Claryn waited, Sharani climbed up the trunk of the great oak from the ground below. She looked about for Kooper and Boggs, but didn't see them.

Probably still asleep, she thought. She didn't want to see Kooper yet anyway, not until she had spoken with Beka and Claryn.

She poked her head around the side of the entrance and hesitated. Claryn was waiting. "Come in, Sharani," she said, her voice friendly and welcoming. Sharani entered as Beka turned around, carrying a packet of bark.

"Well, hello, Sharani. What can we do for you?" asked Beka.

For a few seconds Sharani just stood there, then blurted out, "Would Kooper be my friend?"

Stunned at her directness, Claryn and Beka paused, but Beka quickly recovered. Before either she or Claryn could respond, Sharani walked past them to the back of the porch, picked up a packet of bark, sniffed it and returned it to the shelf. Without turning around, she said, "Jesska says I need a friend. She says Kooper is as weird as me. Do you think we would make good friends?"

Beka and Claryn glanced at one another, both managing to suppress a grin. Beka replied, "Kooper could probably use a good friend, Sharani. Are you really interested in this or is it just your grandmother's idea?"

"I agree I need a friend. I know I'm different: most of the does don't want me around. My cousins don't. Neither do my aunts. I know Kooper's different from others, too. Maybe...maybe he'd be okay with me."

Now Claryn responded. "Kooper is different than others. He is an orphan like you." She left unspoken her thoughts about the difference between the two families. Glancing at Beka, she continued, "Maybe Kooper could be a friend for you. And you for him. But, it's up to him. He's totally absorbed in watching out for Boggs. He's devoted to him and tries not to get distracted. He's done this all his life."

Sharani continued to stare at the shelves at the back of the porch. "I know Boggs is his friend," she said. "But, maybe he'd like another friend. I appreciate that he watches his brother. That's one reason I like him."

Beka spoke up, "We don't know if he's willing to be friends with anyone else or even speak with you. We haven't asked him and he hasn't said anything to us about you. He keeps his thoughts pretty much to himself. If anything, he talks to his brother, Boggs, or his cousin, Spinner."

Sharani didn't reply for some time, sitting on her haunches, still staring at the shelves behind Beka and Claryn. They looked at one another, uncertain whether she intended to reply. Finally, Beka spoke up, "Is there something else you wanted to say, dear?"

Without looking away from the shelves, Sharani replied, "Is the fact that I want to be friends with a buck too weird? No other does my age are friends with bucks. Jesska says it's okay but I can't always tell what is and what's not." She turned back around and looked blankly at them without saying anything further.

Claryn spoke up. "It is a little unusual for a doe your age to be a friend of a buck if he's not a brother or cousin, but it has happened before. What you're feeling is not that unusual." Glancing at her mother, Claryn continued, "I was drawn to a buck at about your age and I let him know it. And we did become friends. More so later on."

Beka raised her eyebrows, but before she could say anything, Claryn responded curtly. "You did the same thing, Mother. Jesska told me all about it." Beka's eyes widened and her mouth popped open before she snapped it shut.

"The other does my age sure talk about bucks but they don't make friends with them."

"Do you care about what they think?" asked Beka.

"No, but Kooper might think it's strange. All I know is I want a friend. Someone I can…try to talk to. I'm not much of a talker, but I…I want to try. And I'd help watch out for Boggs."

"We can talk to him," said Beka.

"Yes," said Claryn. "If he knew you didn't want him to stop watching Boggs, that might make a difference. I think he'd be lucky to have you for a friend. We all need friends."

"Well, not just a friend," said Sharani without the barest hint of a smile. "I think I want more than that later on."

"We know," said Beka. "Remember he's young. And so are you. We'll talk to him today. Why don't you come back tomorrow, and we'll tell you what he says?"

"I'll come back tomorrow morning."

Sharani sat without saying anything further, staring now at Beka and Claryn, back and forth until Beka reached out with her forelegs and hugged her. She felt Sharani stiffen at first but then felt the tenseness in her muscles dissipate. Beka let go and Sharani left without saying anything more.

As Claryn watched her climb back down their oak, she shook her head slightly. "She's got to be lonely. But what if Kooper's not interested in her, Mother? He might not care one bit and tell us she should leave him alone."

"I know. That's the price of opening yourself to another. I guess we've each done that. But she has weathered a lot of disappointment. I think she'll survive, even if he isn't interested."

Boggs was still inside the nest in the scarred sycamore he had shared that night with Kooper, but he wasn't asleep. He had woken up before dawn also, not by tangled thoughts and emotions but distant thunder and voices once again. As soon as he woke, the thunder faded, but not the voices. Boggs had focused upon the voices, which then instantly grew stronger, more urgent. *They must know when I try to hear them,* he thought. *They must be calling for me.* But the meaning of the strange words was still frustratingly beyond his comprehension. *I've come to understand the languages of every rodent I've Sensed,* he thought. *Even the languages of birds I can figure out. Why can't I understand these voices?* Boggs continued to listen, but as singing from birds and squirrels alike filled the new day, the voices faded and were gone by the time he Sensed the thoughts of Sharani as she approached Beka's tree.

Boggs was surprised he had done so, as he wasn't intentionally seeking out anyone's thoughts. He immediately realized that her thought process was completely different than any other squirrel's thoughts he had Sensed. While others usually proceeded from one thought to another with some sense of connection, Sharani's thoughts abruptly changed course, sometimes without any seeming link between them. Fascinated, he continued to Sense her thoughts and heard her say to herself, *If Beka and Claryn will speak with him, maybe Kooper will realize I might be a good friend. He doesn't have to spend ALL his time with his brother.*

Koop deserves that. I'm holding him back. He'd be better off if I wasn't here, Boggs thought glumly.

Boggs' head jerked back when a new feeling overtook him, the feeling that Sharani was listening to his thoughts even though he had not intentionally Sensed them to her. The realization was a bewildering surprise. He immediately put up a mental barrier to prevent her from Sensing any more of his thoughts, if that's what she had done. *Sharani can Sense?* he wondered. *But maybe her mind works so differently I don't understand what she's thinking.* The idea that any other squirrel might be able to Sense like he and Kooper was intriguing but the fact that it was her made it complicated and confusing. Boggs realized Sharani was already a competitor for his brother's affections and time. She felt like both a threat and a possible answer all at once.

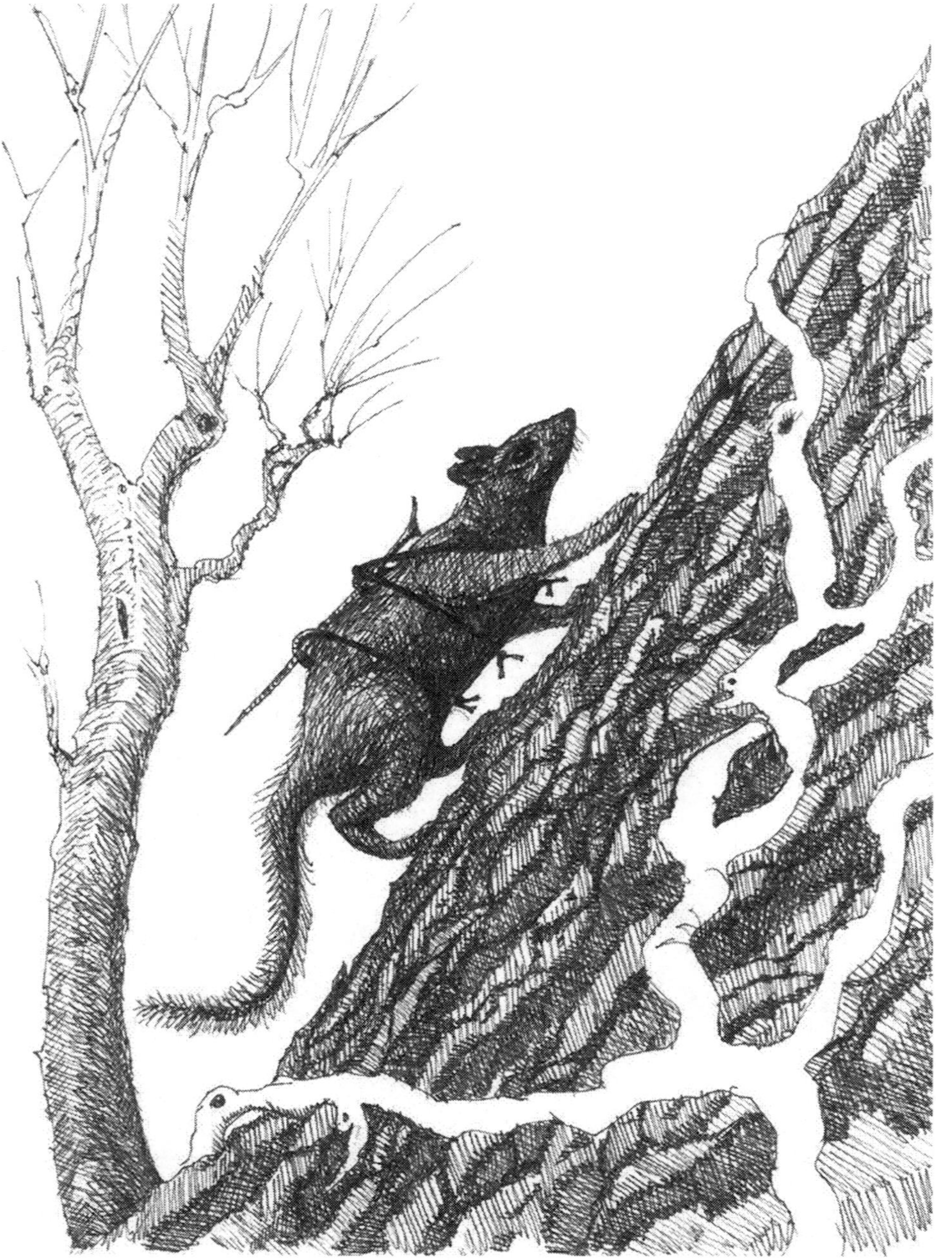

CHAPTER
TWENTY-FOUR

Year 3072 AA
Day 68

**BEFORE DAWN YUNKIN WOKE WITH A START, HIS PAW THROB-
BING.** He felt another squirrel next to him and for a second wondered, *Where am I?*, before he recognized his cousin's scent and
remembered. He stretched and yawned.

Alain moved his face close to Yunkin's and whispered softly,
"Quiet. Somebody's out there moving around. At least two of
them. It's too early and too dark for a squirrel to be up and about."

Careful! Yunkin thought to himself. "We can't be caught
inside this nest," he whispered back to Alain. "We've got to get
out while its still dark, but move slowly, slowly as you can. Stay
low and don't say a word. If they jump us, be ready to sound the
alarm."

"Okay," whispered Alain. He inhaled deeply, let it out and
inch by inch began to move out of the nest entrance into the

darkness, with Yunkin right behind. As they crept along, moving one paw at a time, they heard leaves crunching and stopped. Whoever it was was still there, not more than a couple trees away, just past the border. They moved ahead again, even more slowly, finally reaching a branch opposite the border and hidden from whatever was making the sound. The cousins hung on the rough bark with their front claws, lying flat against the side of the limb, nodded to one another and peeked over the top.

The sky was beginning to lighten behind them and all was silent, until they heard bark scraping. It was obviously more than one creature, climbing a tree just past the border, hidden by thick fog. Yunkin and Alain strained to see as the streams of fog slowly shifted and spied the movement at the same time. Three pack rats were climbing a large oak just two trees away, their outlines visible for a moment as they wound around the tree's trunk.

Neither Yunkin nor Alain had ever seen a pack rat before. Although they had heard that pack rats were bigger than squirrels, the size of the three surprised them. They were longer than any of the banded squirrels other than Lam, Rak and Strap, but noticeably slender. Their tails were just as long as a squirrel's but with much less hair and less than half as thick, and they had longer snouts and larger ears. They looked a lot like huge, white-footed mice.

The pack rats did not speak, but climbed steadily until they stopped on a large branch at the same height as Yunkin and Alain, slowly scanning the trees. For just a moment, they looked directly at the two squirrels, who clung immobile, except for their beating hearts. The pack rats obviously didn't see them and looked away, speaking to one another in a low mumble. Alain and Yunkin couldn't understand what they were saying, but the pack rat in the middle gestured with a forepaw to his left and all three turned in that direction. Without moving their heads, Yunkin and Alain looked the same way and saw two others on a higher branch in the next tree over. Five pack rats!

Yunkin knew he and Alain shouldn't do anything besides watch as long as the pack rats didn't try to cross the border. *What if they do?* he wondered, and his heart raced even faster. Yunkin realized he and Alain were outnumbered, but he wasn't letting any pack rats into Leafensong without confronting them. He knew he couldn't make a mistake, but it was so hard to think about what was best. *Are they planning to attack the patrol? They'll be along shortly*, he thought. *We need a plan. At least they don't know we're here.* His mind racing, Yunkin tried to focus. *They'll be most nervous when they first enter the border tree,* he thought. *That's when we want to startle them. Our alarm will attract the patrol that should be here before long.*

Yunkin moved his right foreleg ever so slowly, touched the leg of Alain and whispered, "Wait." He felt Alain's leg twitch and kept his paw touching Alain's leg as he moved slowly closer to whisper in his ear. "If they enter the border tree, yell as loud as you can but stay put." Yunkin didn't want to explain, as he was afraid the pack rats might hear. He knew they had to maintain their element of surprise.

From the corner of his eye, Yunkin saw one of the two pack rats to the right gesture to the others, then heard him speak. The three to the left began to move and turn. It looked like they were going to come across the border, and he felt Alain's muscles tighten. But instead, the pack rats moved to join the other two. Yunkin again noted how thin the rats were. As they climbed up the tree trunk to a higher branch, Alain and Yunkin saw that the three pack rats all had something attached to them. It looked like a stick, almost as long as its tail, stuck to its back. Yunkin had never seen such a thing before and at first questioned his own eyesight. But the fog had lifted some, it had finally grown light enough to discern clearly, and there was no mistaking what he observed. Each pack rat had pieces of vine tied around its chest and belly holding a long locust thorn strapped to its back, the sharp point facing downward. Yunkin instinctively thought of the wound in his paw which still ached and involuntarily winced. *What does it mean?*

Yunkin and Alain hadn't moved when two of the pack rats turned, yelling, pulling their thorns over their heads and pointed them in the direction of Yunkin and Alain, who froze. The five pack rats huddled together, all with thorns out pointed upward above Yunkin and Alain, who felt the air from the wings of a large owl flying above them, coming from behind, barreling toward the wood rats.

In a second, the owl extended its talons but then quickly pulled them back and with a twist of its wings, veered up and away. The pack rats followed the arc of the owl's path with the points of their thorns. The owl beat its wings rapidly, rose up through the trees and disappeared.

With a bark from their leader, the pack rats slipped the points of their thorns back over their shoulders, between the pieces of vine and their backs, and headed away from the border. The leader of the pack rats turned one last time and Yunkin felt their eyes meet. Yunkin wasn't sure if the pack rat saw him, but he wouldn't forget the icy stare. Then they were gone.

Yunkin and Alain had been frozen from the time the owl had appeared to when he left. They finally breathed.

"I've never seen anything like that," said Yunkin in a hoarse whisper. "Were those locust thorns they carried...and pointed towards the owl?"

"They had to be," replied Alain. "I never would have believed that if I hadn't seen it with my own eyes."

"Same here. Rak has to know about this as soon as possible," said Yunkin.

When the two guards on patrol did appear, Yunkin and Alain quickly filled them in.

"You go with them, Alain, so you have three guards on patrol," ordered Yunkin. "Tell the next guards you meet about the pack rats and owl." With that, ignoring his wounded paw, Yunkin took off to find Rak, moving fast but continually looking about and sniffing the air.

Rak was just emerging from his nest in his sycamore as the last wreaths of fog lifted. Rak saw Yunkin approaching fast. Sensing his urgency, Rak cried out, "What is it, Yunk?"

Yunkin kept quiet until he was in Rak's tree and, in a low but urgent voice, said, "Alain and I spotted five pack rats together just across the western border this morning."

Without hesitation, Rak replied,"Let's go find Karmer and Gist so you can tell this to all three of us. They should still be in their trees. How's your paw? Can you move quickly?"

"Yes sir! It's doing much better."

"Good, let's go."

Karmer's and Gist's nests were in two large cottonwoods next to one another in the center of a grove that stretched across the northern half of Leafensong. Rak and Yunkin advanced rapidly, surprising other squirrels just waking. The two soon caught sight of the Sergeants' trees.

Gist was outside eating his breakfast when he spotted the Captain and Lieutenant. He could tell something was up. "Karmer, it's the Captain!" he yelled over to Karmer's tree. As one of the oldest guards, no one begrudged him his extra sleep. Karmer poked his head out of the nest as Gist, Rak and Yunkin approached. Karmer climbed out to meet them.

"Pack rats," Rak said. "Yunkin, tell us what you saw."

Yunkin's heart was still pounding, but he tried to talk slowly as he told them about spending the night in the bur oak along the border and what had happened.

"Five of them!" said Gist. "That's the most anyone has seen at one time since the Battle."

"Was one leading them?" asked Rak.

"Yes."

"What did he look like?"

"He had a tan-colored ear that stuck out from the side of his head somewhat."

"That's him," said Gist solemnly.

"Who?" asked Yunkin.

"The pack rat who led them when they killed Dram and Thrane," replied Gist.

"And others," added Karmer solemnly.

"And another thing," Yunkin said. "They were carrying thorns."

"Thorns?" said Rak, confused. "What do you mean carrying thorns?"

"They had locust thorns tied to their backs. It looked like they each had pieces of vine tied around their bodies that held the thorns on."

"Why would they do that?" asked Gist.

"For protection. Just as the pack rats were leaving, an owl attacked them. A big one. The five pack rats got close together and they all pulled out the thorns, pointing them at the owl. The owl swerved away at the last minute. It must have seen this before."

Rak, Karmer and Gist each dropped their lower jaws, their mouths agape, unable to speak.

"Then they put the thorns back in the straps on their backs and left, heading west."

"How did they move with the thorns strapped to them?" asked Rak.

"Easily. They seemed to be used to carrying and handling them."

"How long were these thorns?" asked Karmer.

"Almost as long as their tails. About the same length as mine."

"Those had to be honey locust thorns," said Rak.

"That's what we figured."

All four squirrels remained quiet until Gist spoke up. "Five pack rats. Carrying locust thorns to defend themselves. We have to assume they'd use them in a fight with us."

Karmer added, "And who knows how many more pack rats might be out there with thorns?"

Almost as an afterthought, Yunkin added, "They sure were skinny. I thought pack rats were supposed to be stouter than squirrels. They were long—about your height, Cap, but really lean. You'd almost make two of them."

"That's not how I remember them," said Gist.

"No, that's not typical," added Rak. "Perhaps they haven't had enough to eat. Maybe there's a lack of acorns and nuts where they live. Sometimes in a bad year trees in a given area don't put out a lot of nuts."

"You know," said Gist, "no one's told us about finding good nut trees across the border. Usually we hear about at least a few every year. I haven't heard a thing."

Rak added, "Maybe it's a bad year everywhere. Even our bur oaks don't have a lot of acorns this year. Except Beka's tree. Thankfully, her tree always has enough for everyone in the Tribe."

Yunkin spoke up, "Maybe the pack rats want Leafensong because of that."

Rak nodded, "Could be that's why they attacked us years ago."

"They found out we'd fight, all right. They haven't tried that since," said Gist grimly.

"But they might be thinking about it again," said Rak. "Especially if their trees are not producing enough food. We've got to be ready if they do."

"Where are they from anyway?" asked Karmer. "It can't be from anywhere close. I know our guards don't get across the border much, but a few go looking for nut trees, and no one's said anything about spotting pack rat houses. I'm sure a guard would tell us if he saw one, and we'd smell them if they were close by."

"We may have to go find out," said Rak. "I'm thinking these pack rats aren't living apart like they normally do, not when five of them are together like this. Who knows how many there are?"

The thought of an even larger group of pack rats armed with thorns hit them hard. They each knew how dangerous that could be.

"I had Alain join the morning patrol so there'd be three guards together," said Yunkin. "I told him to tell the next guards they met on patrol about the pack rats and for each patrol to use three guards for now. I hope that was all right. I was thinking maybe we should also vary the number of guards in the patrols. If pack rats are watching, that might keep them wondering."

Rak nodded, "Good decision, Yunk."

"You're not limping from that wound as much, are you, Yunk?" asked Karmer. "Did you see Beka?"

"Yes, yesterday," said Yunkin as he held up his paw for the others to see. "It was a good thing I did see her. She said the thorn that cut me must have a more powerful poison than a thorn from a regular locust tree."

Despite the green stain, the others could see it was much better. The swelling had diminished and the yellow tinge was almost gone.

"Good," said Rak, satisfied. "You do what she says, Yunk. We need you healthy."

"And Beka told me to thank you."

"For what?" Rak asked.

"For protecting the Tribe and Leafensong."

Rak immediately thought back to his confrontation with her when he had tried to take Boggs away to his death. It still gnawed at him. From time to time, he intentionally went by her tree simply to see Boggs. He had only spoken to him once in passing, but every time he saw the blind squirrel he had mixed feelings of guilt and relief to see him alive and well. Rak was startled and relieved to hear what Beka had said.

"The next time you see her, you tell her she's welcome!"

A thought suddenly struck Yunkin. "You think maybe the pack rats are carrying thorns from the giant trees? With stronger poison?"

The other three looked at one another with renewed alarm. The idea that the pack rats were carrying the thorns to defend themselves against owls was difficult enough to comprehend. But the idea of fighting pack rats using highly poisoned thorns was staggering.

"We have to assume they are," said Rak. "Think about how this would change a fight. To not just bite with your teeth, but to be able to reach out with a thorn to—stab. A thorn with poison."

"You handled this well, Yunk," Karmer said. "I'm glad you were the one there. I'm not sure I'd have figured this much out."

"But what do we do about this?" asked Gist.

"The first thing is go visit someone," said Rak.

"Who?" asked Karmer.

"The Keeper."

"The Keeper?" replied Karmer, confounded. "Why do you want us to see him?"

"For any information he has about the pack rats. He knows more about everything than anybody. And maybe we can find out more about the honey locusts. Now that we know the pack rats are using thorns, those trees may be important to us all."

"Who's the Keeper?" asked Yunkin, wondering why he'd not heard about this squirrel before.

"The Keeper of the Lore," explained Rak. "He's in charge of remembering the history of Leafensong, although the Council doesn't pay much attention to him these days. The Keeper knows more than anyone else about the history of our Tribe, Leafensong and the surrounding forest."

"I've never heard of him."

"He keeps pretty much to himself," explained Rak. "Although he's a member of the Council, he hasn't attended any meetings in years. Everyone knew him when he used to be the Tribe's teacher, telling the Tribe, mostly pups, stories about our Lore. But he hasn't done that in a long time. He became bitter because Strap and the Council don't want to hear anything historical."

Karmer snorted, "They'd rather just argue without knowing the facts."

Rak continued, "Unfortunately, Karmer is right. But the Keeper might be able to help us understand what's happening with the pack rats. Let's go."

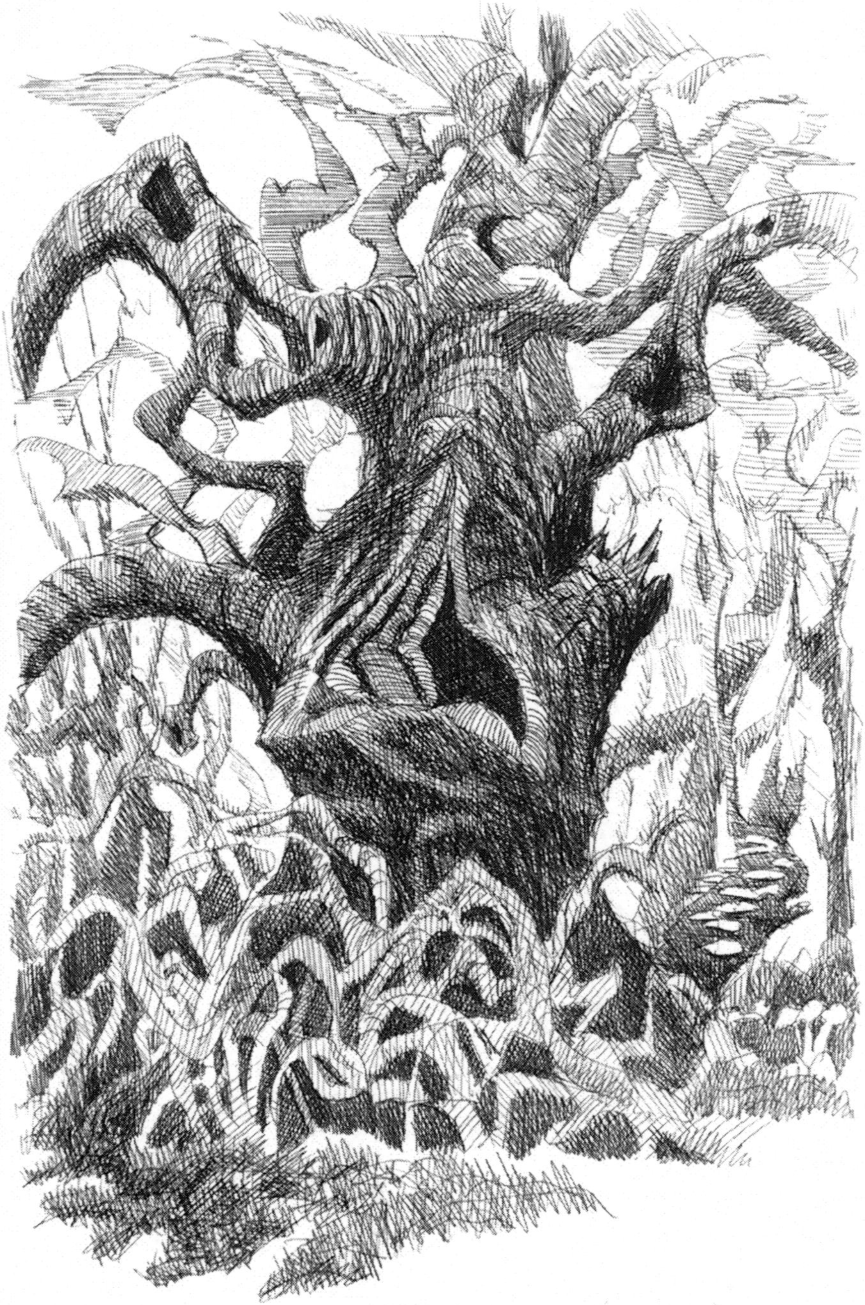

CHAPTER TWENTY-FIVE

Year 3072 AA
Day 68

THE FOUR HEADED EAST THROUGH THE GROVE OF COTTON-WOODS PAST THE COUNCIL OAK AND THEN VEERED NORTH. Rak stopped to point out an ancient, squat ash tree with the top partially broken off.

"That isn't much of a tree," said Yunkin.

"Not anymore," replied Rak before he moved on. "This has always been the Keeper's Tree—including the Keepers before him. He's one of the oldest squirrels in Leafensong. The oldest buck for sure."

As they crossed onto vines and fallen branches jumbled together at the base of the old ash, Rak called out, "Keeper, are you home?"

They didn't hear anything and Rak led them to the large triangular-shaped hole in the center of the stout trunk.

"Keeper, are you there?" Rak asked again.

A gravelly voice responded gruffly from inside, "Who's asking?"

"It's Rak, Captain of the Guard, with Lieutenant Yunkin and Sergeants Karmer and Gist. We're here to ask you some questions. We need your knowledge of the Lore." After a moment's quiet, the four heard shuffling and mumbling inside the nest and finally an ancient, grizzled squirrel with long, gray hairs bristling out over his eyes stuck his head out and looked at them suspiciously. Yunkin had seen him once or twice before but Yunkin had never paid him any attention.

After glancing at them, one by one, the old buck pulled his head back in, muttering as he went, "Well, come on in if you have to."

Rak led, followed by the others. Yunkin's eyes slowly adjusted to the dark. The inside of the nest was huge but filthy. Old cobwebs coated with dust hung from the high ceiling, and the walls of the nest were covered with mildew and mold. Yunkin had never seen such a mess of a nest. He was astonished at how much room there was. A number of squirrels could fit inside, but obviously few had entered in ages.

The Keeper had gone clear to the back of the nest, beyond where light from above illuminated the level floor. Broken shells from nuts blanketed the floor on either side of the path he took. The Keeper sat down on a flattened pile of leaves with a groan, dust rising from the crumbling debris.

As he and the others followed the Keeper, Yunkin felt dampness in the wood beneath him and looked down. The center of the floor was mushy where rot had set in with white speckles and streaks of fungi. Yunkin raised his snout and saw that there was a gap in the ceiling where the sky showed through.

After brushing aside pieces of broken shells, Rak sat down with Yunkin on his left and Karmer and Gist to his right, all facing the Keeper.

"So what do you want to know?" asked the Keeper gruffly. "Where the best trees with food are? I don't know that stuff. All I know about are things no one is interested in. Old things. Like me." He lowered his head, half way laying down.

"No, we're after information only you know, Keeper," Rak replied. "We need to know some history. The Lore."

The Keeper raised his snout and looked suspiciously at Rak and each of the others in turn before lowering his face and replying, "No one's asked me about our Lore in a long time."

"We want to know about the locust logs that surround Leafensong," said Rak as he motioned to Yunkin to explain.

Yunkin spoke up eagerly, "Yes, the giant honey locusts. At least I assume that's what they are. I've only checked out two. Their wood smells like hedge but they're covered with bark and thorns like honey locusts. They had to be the largest trees ever." Yunkin was now getting excited. "Are they the same kind as the Dark One?"

At the mention of the Dark One, the demeanor of the Keeper immediately stiffened. He was still suspicious but now fully alert. "Just what is it you think you've figured out, youngster?" he asked.

"I think there were a lot of these giant locusts surrounding Leafensong at one time. And they've all died and fallen. All but the Dark One. It must be one of these, too, isn't it? But why aren't there any inside Leafensong? And their wood doesn't decay like other species. Does that have something to do with the wood smelling like hedge? Are they locust or hedge or something different?"

Rak hadn't heard this from Yunkin before. He stopped Yunkin from speaking further by touching his foreleg.

"You've asked him a lot of questions, Yunk," said Rak. "What about it, Keeper? What do you know about these fallen trees?"

The Keeper eyed each of them through squinted eyes before looking away, seemingly through the wall of his nest. "No one has asked me anything for a long time. Why do you care about this?"

Yunkin was eager to respond but Rak held up a paw, halting him. "It may not be important. We don't really know. Pack rats have been sighted recently just outside the border. I'm concerned about them, too, and have additional questions for you. But, I thought you could also answer Yunkin's questions about the trees. You used to go to the Council meetings. I remember your talks but I don't recall you ever talking about these giant logs. What do you know about them?"

The Keeper continued to look away but replied, "I thought all my knowledge was a waste. That I would never use it again."

Rak explained to Yunkin, "The Tribe has always had a Keeper of the Lore. The Keeper's job is to learn the Lore, our history, from the previous Keeper. To know all we know and have ever known about the Tribe, Leafensong, the forest. To never forget it. And to be a part of the Council so that whenever they want to know something of the Lore, the Keeper can recite it to them."

The Keeper spit. "The Council! They don't want to hear or learn anything about our history! They just want to argue with each other! To hear themselves talk! The last time anyone on the

Council asked me anything, they didn't like what I told them. I told them what I knew about the fallen locusts. They told me I was wrong. Fools! They only want to hear what they already think, even if it's nonsense! Now, they don't even acknowledge that there is a Keeper. I'm just an old inconvenience to them. So I stay away."

The anger the Keeper felt towards the Council surprised Yunkin. He didn't know much about how it operated. As a yearling he had attended a few meetings but found them boring and he had avoided them since.

Rak spoke up, "The Keeper is right. The Council members mainly like to argue about Lucient and Ebyn. But most of them don't really want to understand what anyone else thinks."

Yunkin spoke up, "But, Rak, you're a member of the Council."

The Keeper interrupted, "Yes, and so am I. But, I haven't been there for years! They don't want me there, and I don't want to be there! It's a waste of time. Your Captain has to be there because he's Captain of the Guard. But he doesn't take part in those stupid arguments. At least not the last time I was at the Council." The Keeper looked at Rak questioningly.

"No, I usually ignore them," conceded Rak.

"What about Strap, the Leader?" asked Yunkin. "Isn't he interested in the Lore?"

"No," responded Rak. "Strap's more interested in staying in power than anything else and treats the council mainly as a game. He lets the others argue among themselves and watches to see who can sway the others. Their debates don't really concern him. He's pretty much able to persuade them to do anything he wants."

"That's all he cares to do," said the Keeper contemptuously.

"He doesn't care about the Lore. He's a bully! A *smart* bully, but a bully."

"He cares for the Tribe, but I agree he's too interested in his own power," acknowledged Rak.

"Until he respects our history, he'll never be a good Leader!" barked the Keeper.

Rak changed the subject. "What can you tell us about the giant trees, Keeper? Is the Dark One the last of a number of giant trees that used to grow around Leafensong? That's certainly not what the Council thinks."

The Keeper sat up, his feet crunching against the crushed leaves, and began to explain.

"Yes, that is the Lore. Before our Tribe settled here, we traveled far and wide. The forest used to be full of the giant trees. They were everywhere. And they were all honey locusts, though obviously far larger than the honey locusts that grow here now. Leafensong was settled here for two reasons. One, this just happened to be a spot where none of the giant locusts had fallen. None of the trees had grown right here, so there weren't any logs. And the closest ones had fallen pointing away. It was surrounded by the logs but none lay here. It was a place of rest because we didn't have to climb over the logs or worry about the thorns. They're poisonous and dangerous, always injuring someone."

"It still is dangerous outside the border. Yunkin found that out," said Gist.

The Keeper continued, "And also because of the bur oak acorns, it was paradise." The Keeper's face softened and his voice grew wistful, "Long, long ago, the Lore tells us, our Tribe didn't belong to any one place. The other squirrels didn't like us because of our bands, our markings. We kept to ourselves and moved constantly, year after year, looking for a tree with a good crop of nuts. We'd settle in the fall and stay for one year, moving at the end of summer when the new pups were old enough. We had done this for generations."

"But when our Tribe came across this place, this wonderful place where bur oak acorns, our favorite, were so abundant, and the locust logs were absent, our does decided to stay. It had been a difficult time before they came here. We had been forced to move twice that year; food was scarce everywhere and we were starving. Pups and elders alike had died. We needed to rest and recuperate. Finally everyone was able to eat well and heal. A few bucks wanted to leave again the following year, but the does refused to go. They said they'd only leave if Leafensong stopped producing acorns, but it never did."

Yunkin broke in. "Leafensong? You mean if the nuts in all the bur oaks here stopped producing?"

"No, no, no," said the Keeper, shaking his head. "Leafensong wasn't always the name of this place. Leafensong was the name our does gave to the one tree they wouldn't leave. The bur oak that produced so many acorns. Where all the does had nests and gave birth to their pups that first year. Where all of our ancestors were born. The Mothers' Tree! The Healing Tree! What we now call Beka's tree! That's the true meaning of Leafensong."

"Why Leafensong"? asked Gist.

"You probably think that the Tribe has always sung," replied Keeper. "Well, not before we came here. That tree was what the does first sang about! It inspired us. And we never stopped singing. The name later came to be used for the entire homeland inside the fallen trees. But Beka's tree is the real Leafensong!"

"I've never heard this," said Gist.

Karmer nodded slowly. "I've heard this before, but I'd forgotten it. I think I heard it right here as a young pup."

"Yes, I used to teach all the pups our Lore in this nest. That's why this nest is so large. But the Council said it was a mistake to hear the Lore. They said I was wrong and no one should listen to me. Eventually no one would come. You probably were among the last to hear it. And now you're the first to hear any of the Lore in years."

"What a loss," said Yunkin. "I don't understand why anyone wouldn't want to know the truth…about everything!"

Rak was no longer listening. He was remembering trying to take Boggs from Claryn, from Beka's tree, from Leafensong, and the does' heated response. *How many does know this history?* he wondered. *Was their anger due to their knowledge of this?*

Almost as an afterthought, the Keeper added. "Of course, we weren't the first ones here. The acorns of that bur oak were prized by those here before us. They didn't like us taking over. We just had more numbers and drove them out. They were here long before we came, generations of them. I'm sure they've never forgotten it or forgiven us."

"Who?" asked Gist. "Another tribe of squirrels?"

"No, no, no. Pack rats! This was their home. They had lots of middens surrounding Leafensong—Beka's tree. Far more than normal. They prized that tree and its acorns just like we do. But we drove them away and demolished their homes. Couldn't stand the sight or smell of them. We outnumbered them, and they figured we'd leave in a year like we always did, so they didn't put up much of a fight. But after the Tribe stayed, they were furious. And they fought to win it back. A lot of squirrels have died to keep Leafensong ours."

"You mean there were battles long ago with pack rats?" asked Gist.

"Yes! Every few generations the pack rats would try to expel us again. Huge battles. Many have died on both sides. You think that fight a few years ago you were in was the first? Heck no! That was just one of many. And probably not the last! This was their home, and I'm sure they still want it back."

"It sounds like you were here all this time," said Yunkin.

"Our history is etched in my brain, taught to me by our last Keeper. I know what he and the Keepers before him knew just as well as they did. We've always had a Keeper of the Lore. But I don't know if we'll have another Keeper after me. I don't see Strap or the Council trying to keep it going!"

With that, the Keeper slumped down once again. "I'm sorry, but I'm tired. Old and tired. I'm happy you were interested enough to ask. Thank you, but you need to go now and let me rest."

"One more thing," said Yunkin. "Do you know why the giant locusts smell like hedge?"

"No. I'm sorry but I don't."

With that the Keeper pulled himself up straight one more time, his face now lit by the light from the ceiling, his eyes brimming with tears. "Thank you, thank you for asking about the Lore. I didn't think anyone would ever ask me anything again. If you want to hear more, please come back. Please. I'd appreciate that. But now I've got to rest." With that he laid back down on his bed of leaves.

Without saying anything further, Rak motioned for the

others to follow him out of the nest. But as they exited, Yunkin, the last to leave, lingered inside the opening. Instead of filing out with the others, he returned across the floor of the cavernous nest and approached the Keeper, who opened his eyes.

"Keeper, I will be back. I do have more questions for you."

"It will be good to talk to you, Yunkin," replied the Keeper and he closed his tired eyes once more.

Yunkin now joined the others who were waiting for him outside. Yunkin looked up at the ash tree's trunk and saw the gash high up on the trunk where snow and rainwater had been entering.

"Its too bad water gets in there," he said. "That's why the floor in the Keeper's nest is getting soft. Ash wood decays quickly."

"Nothing we can do about that," replied Rak. "But, we do have things we need to accomplish. Yunkin, you go tell Beka about the pack rats carrying thorns and that they might be thorns from the giant locusts with the stronger poison. Tell her about seeing five pack rats, and that she might have to treat more thorn wounds like yours. Ask her if she has enough medicine for this and if not, ask her if she can get more. And Gist, you go spread the word. I want every guard not on patrol to meet up at my tree at noon today. And tell them to immediately start using three guards on every patrol."

"They'll want to know why," replied Gist.

"Go ahead and tell them, and to be on the alert. But encourage them to keep this quiet. That's enough. No reason yet to alarm the whole Tribe. And then come to Karmer's tree—we need to talk about this some more."

"Yunk," Gist spoke up as he began to leave. "You did well.

Good job, Lieutenant." For the first time ever, Gist had called him by his title.

After Yunkin and Gist left, Karmer and Rak stood together for a moment before they traveled back to Karmer's cottonwood, "You're right, Cap. Yunk is smart and curious. It's a good thing you made him Lieutenant. He's lucky, too. Even though he was hurt by the locust thorn, he found out about the poison that way. And he was in the right place to see the five pack rats across the border use the thorns against the owl."

Rak nodded. "Sometimes it's better to be lucky than smart. Fortunately, he seems to be both. I just hope the good luck continues and we can figure out what to do about the pack rats. I hope he is smart enough," added Rak looking back at the Keeper's ash tree, "because I'm not sure I am."

Karmer, too, looked back at the Keeper's tree. "That tree won't last forever. It's old and breaking down. Like the Keeper. He needs to find a replacement, a new Keeper he can teach."

"That's something we need, but the Council may not see it that way," replied Rak, dejectedly.

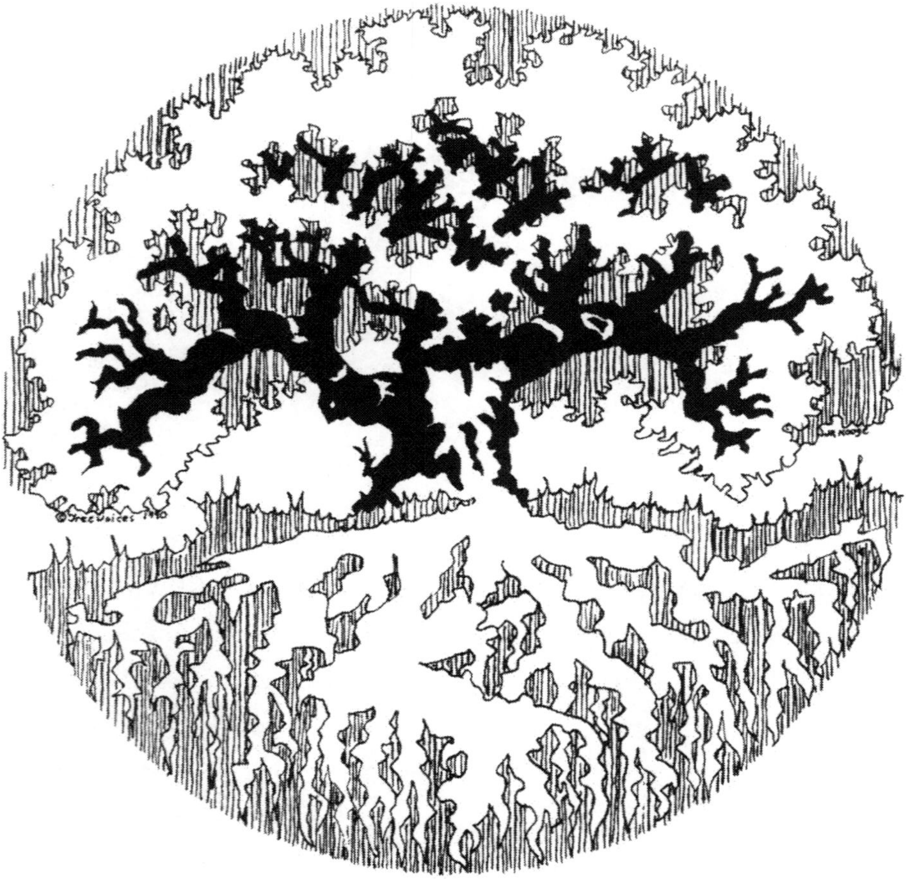
©Tree Voices 1990

CHAPTER
TWENTY-SIX

Year 2602 AA

Day 316

BEKA'S TREE WAS NOT ALWAYS THE LARGEST OAK IN LEAFEN-SONG. For its first fifty years it was stunted, never gaining more than ten feet in height or over an inch in girth. The canopy of leaves from the trees overhead had kept it in shadow. Without the sunlight to photosynthesize enough food, it survived by feeding off of the same trees that kept it in shade. Clumps of fungi and bacteria attached to the tips of the tree's roots and millions of feathery strands of hyphae reached out through the soil. The web of fungi also connected to the roots of surrounding trees, taking sugars they generated and feeding them to the young bur oak. It had received just enough food to survive.

The bur oak's cells were smaller and its wood more dense because of the slow growth. The growth rings which most trees developed—due to alternating speeds of maturation in summer and winter—were absent. But a genetic abnormality also created unique characteristics. The veins and arteries crossed over and around one another. Instead of running in straight vertical rows, they were tangled and interlocked, similar to southern live oaks that grew far to the south. And like live oaks, as a result, the wood was far stronger than most bur oaks. It was more flexible, resistant to splitting, and able to withstand storms that whipped the branches back and forth. The interlocking grain survived the penetration of damaging fungi and prevented decay. When a limb from a neighboring tree fell and damaged the oak's bark, it was able to grow new wood and bark to heal over the wounds. Year after year in near total shade it had managed to survive and grow increasingly stronger, waiting for its chance to reach for the sunlight.

It was mid-autumn and the leaves were still thick on most of the trees. An early cold spell arrived, and the frosty air sent squirrels and voles scurrying into their nests, sad to see the warm weather end. The sap in the trees slowed as the temperature stayed well below freezing for several days. Then the trade winds shifted and a warm front rushed in from the south. The balmy, humid air rose over the frigid layer of air underneath, then cooled to the point that it could no longer hold ample water vapor and rain fell heavily.

The rain froze as it fell through the lower layer of chill. Huge flakes of heavy, wet snow piled up quickly on the leaves and limbs. The snow turned to freezing rain, building up a thick, heavy crust of ice on top of the snow-covered leaves and branches, which began to break under the weight. The sharp crack of splitting wood resounded throughout the forest as branches fell to the ground with a thud. Limbs hung suspended, wedged between closely growing trees or dangling upside down, still attached to the trunks where the split wood had not completely broken free. Whole trees fell over, their roots ripped from the soil. Eventually, the ice and snow would melt and quench the forest, but in the freezing air, it maimed and killed. The small bur oak was lucky to avoid the falling timber, while other small trees were pummeled and split apart, damaged beyond the ability to survive.

The following spring, sunlight flooded much of the forest floor, no longer shielded by the trees that had tumbled or lost limbs. Acorns and nuts sprouted, and tiny saplings sprang upwards where the sun now warmed the ground.

Finally able to capture the newly found sunlight, the bur oak shot up and out, leaves multiplying and producing quantities of sugar to feed its growth. By the time the neighboring trees had lengthened their broken branches not torn off by the storm, the bur oak had captured enough of the canopy that it would not be shaded again. Its leaves grew thick, and in a few years they blocked most of the sunlight from reaching the forest floor. Many of the new trees beneath it died, but a few survived, also fed sugars by the bur oak and other trees through the web of fungi that linked them all, hoping for their turn in the light.

Over the next four hundred years, the bur oak thrived and grew taller in the full sunlight, fed from the decay of toppled trees, fallen branches, discarded twigs and the annual crop of leaves. Its trunk grew broad at the ground to support its heavy weight. Fierce storms tore off the ends of the longest limbs, leaving ragged holes. But its remaining branches were stout and healthy, setting forth more leaves each spring. The interlocking grain of the wood kept out the diseases to which other trees succumbed. Most holes caused by the loss of branches closed up with new wood and bark. Where too much had been torn out, fungi managed to soften just enough inner heartwood, allowing squirrels and birds to make nests within the trunk and limbs. But the bark remained healthy and mostly intact, protecting the layer of living wood just beneath that transported sugars throughout the tree and drew up water from the roots. The strands of symbiotic fungi attached to the ends of the roots spread throughout the soil, collecting and feeding the nutrient-filled water to the roots while the bur oak sent its sugars to feed the fungi and any neighboring tree in need. The oak produced an abundant crop of hairy-topped acorns, larger and sweeter tasting than any other species'.

A small Tribe of gray squirrels discovered the great oak as they traveled through the forest late one summer. It had been a hard year for them, having to move twice, driven away by squirrels that didn't like the unique markings in their fur. When they found the oak and its multitude of acorns, they decided to make the tree their home that year.

The bur oak and surrounding woods were already inhabited by wood rats, who also prized the sweet tasting acorns and had lived there for generations. Their middens—homes composed of small pieces of branches piled on the ground reaching several feet in height—surrounded the oak in far greater numbers than the solitary wood rats normally allowed. The middens protected the various chambers used by the wood rats for sleeping, eating, food storage and relieving themselves. The wood rats urinated on the middens themselves, crystalizing the outer layer of the wood and preventing fungi spores from attaching to it and causing decay.

The squirrels detested the smell of wood rats and their middens. They were natural enemies, as they competed for the same food. The more numerous squirrels drove the wood rats away and tore apart the middens, scattering the stinking wood on the forest floor, away from the bur oak. The wood rats decided to wait the squirrels out and reclaim their tree when the squirrels moved on the next year.

The banded squirrels stored the tree's abundant acorns in the cavities of the tree's trunk and limbs, and in the surrounding trees as well. All the does nested in the bur oak, feeding on the stored acorns, easily surviving the cold of winter. In the spring they gave birth to the largest number of pups the Tribe had ever known. The does decided their new home deserved thanks and composed a poem to the tree that became a song. The young squirrels scampered through the oak's leafy branches that spring and summer, learning to harmonize, encouraged by their mothers, who composed additional songs about their blessed home.

The great oak had again put out an abundant crop of its large acorns. For the first time in generations, the banded squirrels did not move on at the end of summer. The does said the oak had welcomed them, and they refused to leave, singing their praise to the great tree they named Leafensong.

The bur oak relished the singing that filled its branches, further strengthening its will to endure and its resistance to decay. Although the Tribe of squirrels couldn't hear its slow, subdued voice, murmuring in contentment, in their hearts they knew their tree sang along with them in harmony. This tree was meant to be theirs.

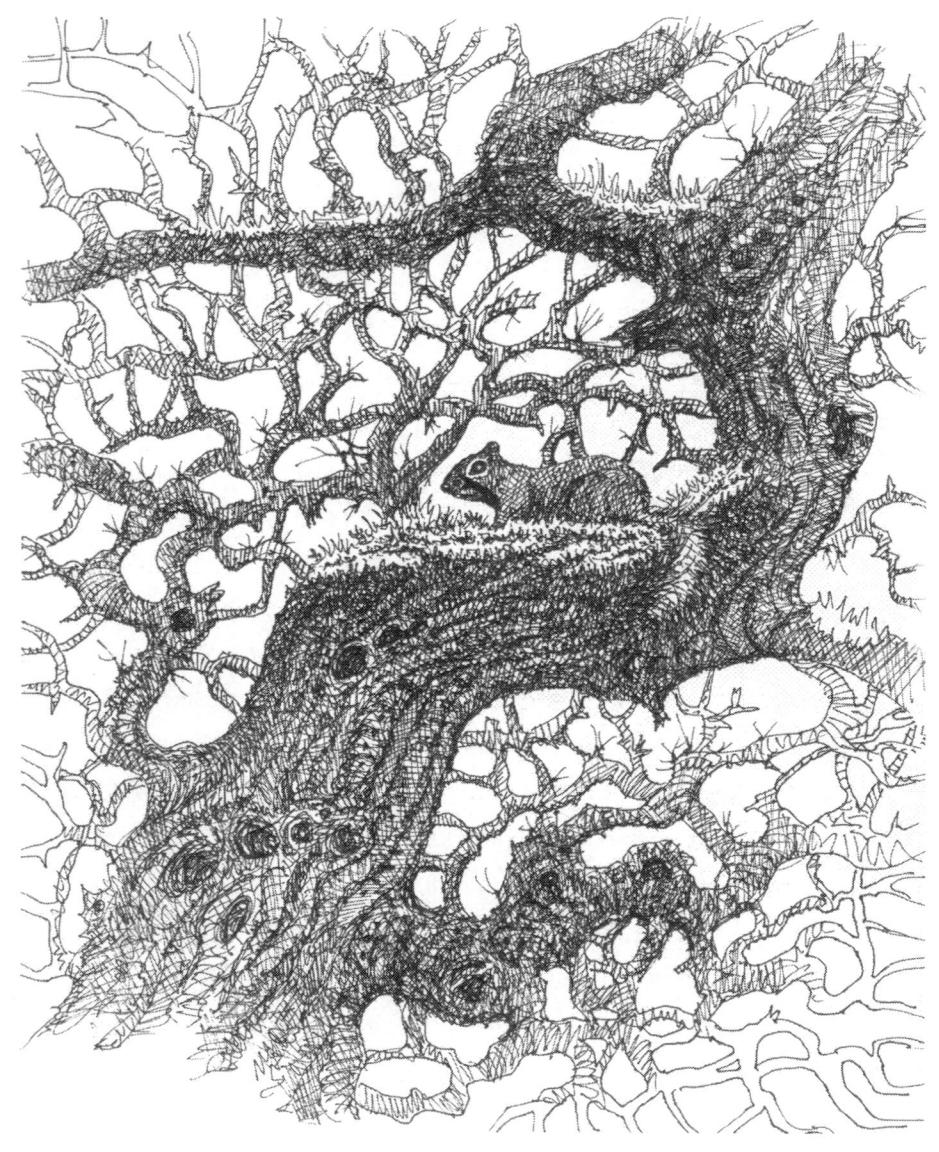

CHAPTER
TWENTY-SEVEN

Year 3072 AA

Day 68

"I KNOW WE TOLD SHARANI WE'D TALK TO KOOPER FOR HER, BUT I'M NOT SURE IT'S A GOOD IDEA," CLARYN SAID TO BEKA AFTER GOING BACK AND FORTH ABOUT IT ALL DAY. "He might get angry with us. And maybe a friendship with her wouldn't be a good idea for him. Different than others but not like she is. I've never seen anyone like her."

"I have. Somewhat anyway. A doe my age who died long ago. Her name was Asia."

"Did she have friends?"

"No. Several of us tried but got frustrated with her and finally gave up. Me too, I'm afraid. She was similar to Sharani in some ways but even more strange."

"Was she an orphan?"

"Eventually, but her problems started long before her mother died. Her mother had even worse problems and finally did herself in."

"She killed herself?"

"Everyone thought that's what happened. She was found beneath the Singer's tree. She'd fallen and it was obviously a very long fall. She had to have climbed nearly to the top. There was no reason for her to be up there unless..."

"I've never heard of a squirrel doing that."

"That's the only time I know of. She was a tortured soul. Her mind wasn't right and she couldn't be a good mother. It really messed up Asia."

"In what way?"

"Well, for one thing, Asia just about never spoke. If you tried to talk to her, usually she'd just stare at you. The way Sharani does. I got the feeling Asia was trying to speak but couldn't."

"Was there something wrong with her mouth? Her tongue?"

"No, I don't mean she couldn't speak. She could, but, her words usually didn't make sense. Some squirrels made fun of her. Eventually, she just gave up talking."

"They made fun of her? That's terrible!"

"Yes. Not often, as a few of us reprimanded anyone who did. But it happened."

"And she never got past it, was never able to speak normally?"

"No. It was very sad. She died young. Not like her mother, but when she was about your age. I think she just gave up wanting to live."

"She ever have pups?"

"No."

"At least Jesska is trying to help Sharani."

"Yes, I'm happy that Jesska is doing this now."

"It took her a long time."

"Remember what Jesska's been through. She didn't have anyone to help her after her daughter's death. You and I have had each other."

"Yes, you're right," agreed Claryn, reaching out her front legs to hug Beka who whispered, "I don't know how I would have survived without you, Daughter."

"And the pups. What a joy they've been to us, even with Boggs' blindness."

"It's partly why he has other abilities," said Beka. "His ability to Sense, to smell so well. He can hear really well, too. I'm not sure he'd give them all up to see."

Claryn nodded. "And he's had his brother and the rest of his family. Poor Jesska and Sharani," Claryn said. "They've not really even had each other. I agree, Sharani could use a friend. But do you think Kooper should be that friend? Would a friendship with Sharani even be right for him? We don't want him mixed up as a result."

"No, but it could be good for him. What do you think Spinner thinks of her? He knows her some. Let's ask him. Is he around?"

"I think so." Claryn looked out the porch entrance. 'Spinner's with Kooper. I'll go tell him you want to see him."

Claryn left and returned with Spinner. Beka and Claryn quickly filled him in .

"Do you know her, Spinner?" asked Claryn.

"Yes, but not real well," replied Spinner. "Sharani doesn't hang out much with other does, let alone bucks. But, I like her; I've never heard her say anything negative about anybody. I think she's kind. And smart, too. Just different. Mainly in how she speaks and looks at you. The other does don't want to hang out with her. I thought that was okay with her but maybe not. She's so different, I can't tell. But Kooper's not your typical squirrel either. They just might hit it off. They both could probably use a friend," Spinner said with a twinkle in his eye. "He met her once, late last year. I told you about it, Mother. When Boggs and Koop and I were up north one day, Sharani, Jone and some other does came by. Most squirrels are afraid of their flames, probably because of how Aunt Chaska died, but she sure wasn't frightened."

Claryn didn't say anything but her heart stopped for a moment thinking once again of her sister's death.

"Do you know Yunkin, Spinner?" asked Beka, changing the subject. "He's the one I treated for the bad locust wound. He told me Rak feels bad for trying to banish Boggs."

"He should," said Claryn.

"Yunkin also told me Rak comes by now and then to see if Boggs is okay."

Claryn raised her eyebrows. "I didn't know that."

"I don't know Yunkin well," said Spinner. "I know the guards were surprised Rak named him Lieutenant because he's so young. But, the word is he's really smart and that's why Rak chose him."

"He certainly is curious," said Beka. "Yunkin told me about these huge logs across the border. He went to look at a large mound and discovered it was actually a giant, fallen tree. Rak went with him to look at a second one. Apparently they're all around Leafensong."

"I hadn't heard about this," replied Spinner.

"It just happened two days ago. And clearly he's intelligent. I noticed he was admiring you, Claryn," said Beka with a smile and a raised eyebrow.

"He must be really smart then," said Spinner with a wide grin.

"Well he's never said much to me," responded Claryn.

"Lots of bucks think you're beautiful, mother. You're so good looking they're too intimidated to say anything to you."

Claryn flushed. "Well, I don't know about that." A slight smile crept across her face and she looked down to hide it, quickly changing the subject. "If Kooper would only let us watch Boggs, he'd have time to spend with Sharani."

"He's never paid any interest to any does," said Spinner doubtfully. "I don't think he has a clue how they think."

"Oh, so you're the big expert on does?" teased Claryn.

"Absolutely!" responded Spinner. "It's because I'm so…sensitive."

Claryn snorted and she and Beka both laughed.

"You're just funny," said Beka giggling. "And that goes a long way with does. Keep doing that and you won't have any trouble getting one interested in you. Probably too many of them."

"Should we tell Boggs about this?" asked Claryn. "How would he react?"

Spinner responded, "I don't know. He's been more quiet lately."

Beka nodded. "He has." But she didn't mention what Boggs had told her about the voices. "You know, Boggs told me about Sharani touching Kooper's face," continued Beka. "He didn't see it, of course, but he could tell what was happening and he and Kooper talked about it later. Boggs said he Senses that she's got a good heart."

"Well, he'd know that better than anyone," said Claryn. "And if he thinks that, I guess I'm okay with telling Kooper what she wants. See if he'll at least speak with her."

"Yes. Let's get it over with before the day is done," replied Beka with equal certainty. "Spinner, can you tell Kooper we want to talk to him?"

"Sure."

But before he left the porch, Beka added, "Spinner, don't you tease Kooper about Sharani. That would not be helpful."

"Yes, ma'am."

Claryn and Beka looked out the porch entrance to watch, but couldn't see Spinner, Kooper or Boggs. They heard Spinner's claws catch in the bur oak bark and realized he had gone higher up in the oak. After only a minute, Beka heard the scraping of claws on the bark again, just before Kooper popped his face down over the top of the porch entrance, upside down, and jumped on to the porch. From the blank look on his face, Beka and Claryn could tell Kooper had no idea what they wished to discuss with him.

"Is Spinner watching Boggs?" asked Beka.

"Yes," said Kooper. He looked back and forth between his grandmother and aunt. "He said you both want to talk to me. What about? Is it something about Boggs?"

"No," replied Beka. "Sharani."

"Sharani?" responded Kooper, bewildered. "What about Sharani?"

"She's asked us to talk to you about her. She'd like to be your friend."

"My friend?"

"Yes. She said her grandmother, Jesska, told her she thought you two might get along."

"She's lonely, Kooper," added Claryn. "She wants someone to talk to."

"She told you this?"

"Yes. This morning. She knows she's different. The other young does aren't interested in being friends with her."

Kooper thought, *She is different, but so am I.* "So is Boggs," he said. "Jesska didn't suggest Boggs be her friend?"

"I don't know," replied Claryn. "But Sharani asked about you."

"Maybe if you became her friend, Boggs could too," suggested Beka. "Sharani said she doesn't mind you watching him."

"Mind me watching him?" Now he was offended. "Of course I'm going to watch him."

"I didn't put that right," corrected Beka. "Sharani told us she likes that you watch him. That you're so loyal to him. She admires you for that."

"And she said she'd even help you watch Boggs," added Claryn.

"I don't need anyone to help me watch Boggs," Kooper said firmly. "That's my job and that's not changing."

"No one wants you to stop doing that. But, we, Spinner too, could help watch Boggs now and then so you could spend a little time off. You don't need to be the only one who watches him."

"Grandma, you're too busy with your patients."

"Yes, she is," agreed Claryn. "But Spinner and I can watch Boggs more often."

"No. I don't want to watch Boggs any less. This is my job, not yours or Spinner's."

"Why is that?" asked Beka. "Why do you have to be the sole watcher of Boggs? Seriously, I don't understand."

"Neither do I," said Claryn. "Spinner and I can take turns. It doesn't have to be you all the time."

Kooper shouted back, "Yes, it does! If it wasn't for me, Boggs wouldn't be blind!"

Claryn and Beka's eyes grew wide. Neither spoke until Beka asked softly, "Why do you say that? Boggs was born blind because of the storm and the lightning. You didn't cause that."

"Yes, I did. If I hadn't been born first, he wouldn't be blind."

"Oh, no, Kooper," Claryn said as she reached out and held his forepaws. "You weren't the cause of his blindness. It could just as easily have happened to you. We'll never know why he's blind and you're not. But it's not your fault. You can't blame yourself for that."

"You didn't choose to be born first, Grandson. It's just the way it worked out."

"Let us help watch Boggs," continued Claryn. "He's our family, too. You can have other friends besides Boggs and Spinner."

"Boggs doesn't."

"We know," said Beka. "But that doesn't mean you shouldn't. Spinner likes Sharani. And she likes you! She wants to spend some time with you, to be friends. We think it would be a good idea, Kooper."

"I don't need any more friends. Boggs and Spinner are my friends. And you two."

"Most squirrels your age, any age, have more friends than just family," replied Beka. "Boggs' blindness has prevented that."

"And our flames on our chests. Squirrels don't like me either."

"I know," agreed Beka sadly. "But mainly its Boggs' blindness."

Kooper didn't respond.

"Spinner says he likes her," Beka added. "And Boggs says she's got a good heart."

"I don't care," said Kooper but Claryn and Beka both saw a glimmer of something more in Kooper's eyes.

"I know our family keeps to ourselves a lot and we do pretty well that way, but I think it'd be good for you to have another friend," urged Beka mildly.

"I do too, Koop," added Claryn. "Just talk to her. You can't have too many good friends. It's a privilege that she wants to get to know you. It would be good for you to talk to a doe, to interact with a doe, someone other than your aunt and grandmother."

"And she does seem lonely. She's reaching out. Just try talking to her."

Kooper didn't respond at first but finally said, "I guess I could do that."

"So if she comes by you'll speak to her? Not ignore her?"

"I don't ignore her. I nod at her when I see her…sometimes at least."

"We've seen you look the other way when she's close by," said Claryn. "It's as though you're pretending she's not there."

"I'm busy watching Boggs," said Kooper defensively. "He's my responsibility. I don't have time to jabber with Sharani or anyone."

"Yes, you do," said Beka.

"Okay, yes, I won't ignore her."

"Thank you, Kooper," said Beka. "You know her grand-mother, Jesska, is one of my oldest friends. She's been worried about Sharani for a long time. Maybe Jesska's right that you two could get along.

"I said I'll talk to her. I can't promise anything else."

"That's all we ask," said Beka, relieved. "She'll probably be here sometime tomorrow morning. Just say hello."

Kooper nodded and left Beka's porch and climbed onto the top of the thick limb holding her nest, then to where it joined the trunk of the old tree. Out of range of hearing Beka or Claryn he stopped, looking around for Boggs. Kooper couldn't see him but did see Spinner higher above who waved when Kooper looked at him. Kooper climbed to join him but didn't say anything as he sat down. Spinner was watching Boggs who was farther below, on the opposite side of the bur oak from Beka's nest.

"They talk to you about Sharani?" asked Spinner.

"Yeah. You know about this, too?"

"Yeah. And I'll be happy to watch Boggs more. He'll be okay. Mom and I will both help watch him."

Kooper didn't reply, his thoughts a jumble. He knew he should appreciate their assistance in watching Boggs, but he felt guilty even thinking about taking time off.

"You don't need to spend every minute with Boggs, Cuz. It's not every doe that wants to be friends with a young buck. I know Sharani's a little weird but she's nice, too. And smart and good looking. Consider yourself lucky she's interested in you. Just talk to her. It's not that hard, and it'll be good for you."

"I'll try."

Thunder rumbled in the distance.

"How about if I sleep with you two tonight?" asked Spinner. "The three of us haven't done that in a while."

Kooper nodded but didn't respond, his thoughts focused now on Sharani.

All of this was Sensed by Boggs. *Koop's too focused on my wel-fare. Sharani could be a good friend for him and he deserves something more than just watching me. I'm holding Koop back.*

He moved higher into the old oak, above Kooper to a spot which had become his favorite place to lie down and think, where moss grew thick on a gentle crook of a limb. It made for a soft, comfortable bed to lie on and he flexed his paws as the tendrils of moss reached between his toes. He was careful not to damage the tender strands of moss—separate but also part of a whole. The thunder rolled in the distance, slowly, barely audible, and the voices came to him once again. But instead of listening, Boggs now Sensed his own question back. *Are you my friends?*

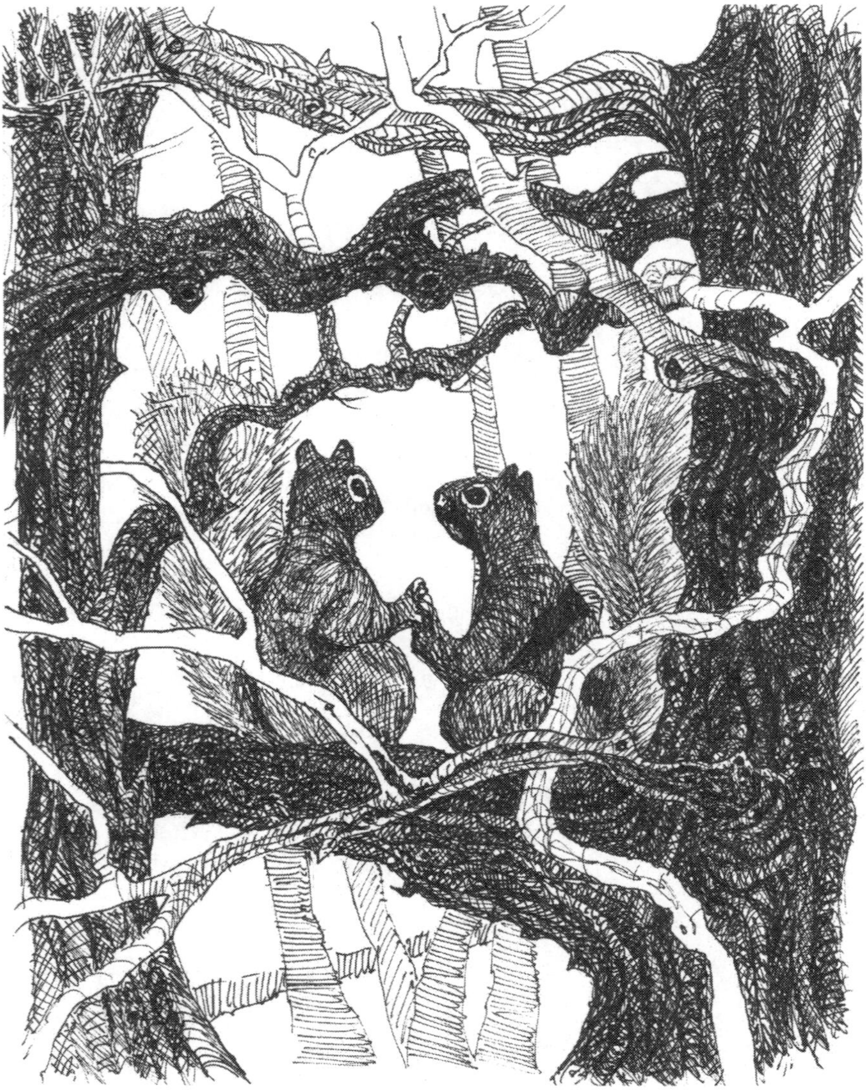

CHAPTER TWENTY-EIGHT

Year 3072 AA
Day 69

EARLY THE NEXT MORNING, SHARANI RETURNED TO SEE IF BEKA AND CLARYN HAD SPOKEN WITH KOOPER. Although nervous, she was determined to see this through. She entered the ash tree on the other side of the sycamore from Beka's tree where she saw Kooper, Boggs, and Spinner sitting together. This time Kooper didn't turn away when their eyes met. She looked up at Beka's nest to see Beka and Claryn watching and raised her front paw. *They talked to him!* she realized before turning back to look again at Kooper, her paw still held up but not moving.

"Go on," urged Spinner. "I'll stay with Boggs."

Kooper's heart was pounding as he crossed over into the ash tree and approached Sharani who had lowered her front paw, waiting.

"Claryn and Beka. They spoke with you?" asked Sharani.

"Yes," said Kooper, looking sideways at her. After a short, uncomfortable silence, he looked directly at her. "I'm sorry I ignored you before, Sharani. But I'm usually busy watching my brother."

"I like that you watch him."

"Spinner's watching him now. You have breakfast yet? Spinner said there's a silver maple with fresh buds to eat that's not far from here. You want to go check it out?"

Sharani didn't respond at first. Two questions in a row had jumbled her thought process, but she realized he was waiting for an answer. "Yes," was all she could manage.

Claryn and Beka watched as Sharani and Kooper headed north together.

"Well, we'll see what comes of this," said Claryn. "He's never talked to another doe as far as I know, and she won't be an easy one to talk to."

"He needs to learn to do different things. That's what makes squirrels special, our ability to change, to learn new things, to become more than we are. It's why we're able to create, to make up new songs, new lyrics. If he's willing, he can do this."

Kooper and Sharani silently crossed limbs and vines, both looking straight ahead, Sharani following Kooper. They hadn't gone far when Kooper stopped, turned around and blurted out, "I'm not used to talking to does or anyone other than my family. No one else has ever wanted to talk to me."

"Why?"

No response could have surprised Kooper more.

"Because I've got this flame on my chest."

"And on your face," Sharani added, raising a front paw to point at it.

Kooper thought she was going to touch his face again and froze, waiting, but Sharani only traced the tip of the flame in the air and said simply, "I like it."

Kooper managed a smile and muttered, "Thank you." He turned and started walking again with Sharani following. They didn't go far before Kooper stopped once more and turned back to face her.

"I'm sorry you lost your mother."

Sharani, expressionless, didn't respond. Kooper reminded himself that she didn't act like others. "You lost her when you were a new pup, like I did, right?"

Sharani nodded. She realized Kooper was inviting more from her and she should say something else, but couldn't think what until she managed, "I don't remember my mother. You?"

"I don't think so," replied Kooper. "But, my grandma and aunt Claryn have told me so much about her it seems like I do. Has Jesska told you about your mom?"

"Not much."

"Have your aunts?"

"No."

Once again, Sharani thought she should continue but the words failed her. "I'm not used to talking."

"That's okay. Do you like to sing?"

"I don't know."

"Don't you sing with Jesska?"

"No. She's asked but I never have."

"Want to sing with me?"

"Do you sing with Beka and Claryn?"

"Sure. And with Boggs and Spinner, too. We all sing together.

A lot. How about if I start a song and you just join in?"

Sharani didn't reply. Kooper began an old song Beka and Claryn had taught him about one's love for their mother.

Sharani sat, listening to Kooper's beautiful voice, trying to focus on his words. She concentrated and the meaning slowly came to her. Without warning, a wave of emotion came over her, a feeling she'd never experienced before. She covered her face with her front paws.

"Are you okay," asked Kooper, worried. "Did I say something wrong?"

"No," Sharani sputtered as she lowered her paws and realized her eyes were wet. She raised a paw again to feel the strange moisture.

Kooper was quiet for a moment.

"I've cried for my mother," Kooper offered quietly. 'I've often wondered what she was really like. And what it would have been like to have her."

"Me, too," Sharani managed to say.

"Want to try and sing that song with me?" he asked finally.

"I don't think I can."

"How about trying it. I'll start again and you try to follow along."

"I'll...I'll try."

Kooper began singing the same song again. After a short time, Sharani joined in. Haltingly at first, she stumbled as she repeated Kooper's words as best she could, but Kooper sang slowly, patiently repeating phrases for her.

"You've got a nice voice, Sharani," he said, his eyes sparkling. Sharani's whiskers twitched. Once again she was overwhelmed with emotion. "I think we sound good together."

"Me too," replied Sharani. She had never thought she would sing with anyone else. Or that anyone would encourage her to sing.

"Let's do that verse again," said Kooper. "Then we can see if we can find that maple tree."

"Okay."

Beka and Claryn perched at the entrance to Beka's nest as they listened to Kooper and Sharani sing. They could tell how kind and encouraging he was. As the two young squirrels sang the song a second time, Claryn added, "Sharani's not used to singing. But she's got a good voice."

"They sound fine together," said Beka. "But then Kooper's had a lot of practice."

"Yes. That's one thing we've taught him well."

Spinner and Boggs also listened to Kooper and Sharani sing. Spinner could tell from Boggs' face and his demeanor that he was troubled.

Boggs had Sensed everything Sharani had said to Claryn and Beka, and now Kooper. And what Kooper had said to each of them. His own thoughts were scrambled.

"I should be happy for Kooper, Spin, but…"

"It's okay, Boggs," said Spinner. "Having another friend is something you haven't experienced. And a *doe*. I can understand why you'd be sad. You can be happy for him and sad at the same time."

Boggs didn't respond but knew part of his sadness came from realizing this might be his way to leave Leafensong without Kooper, to find the source of the voices. The idea of saying goodbye to his family was almost too much to bear. Fear and sadness mixed together in his mind and he turned from Spinner, clenching his fists in worry. *Where would I be going? Who are the source of the voices? Would you be my friends or something else?*

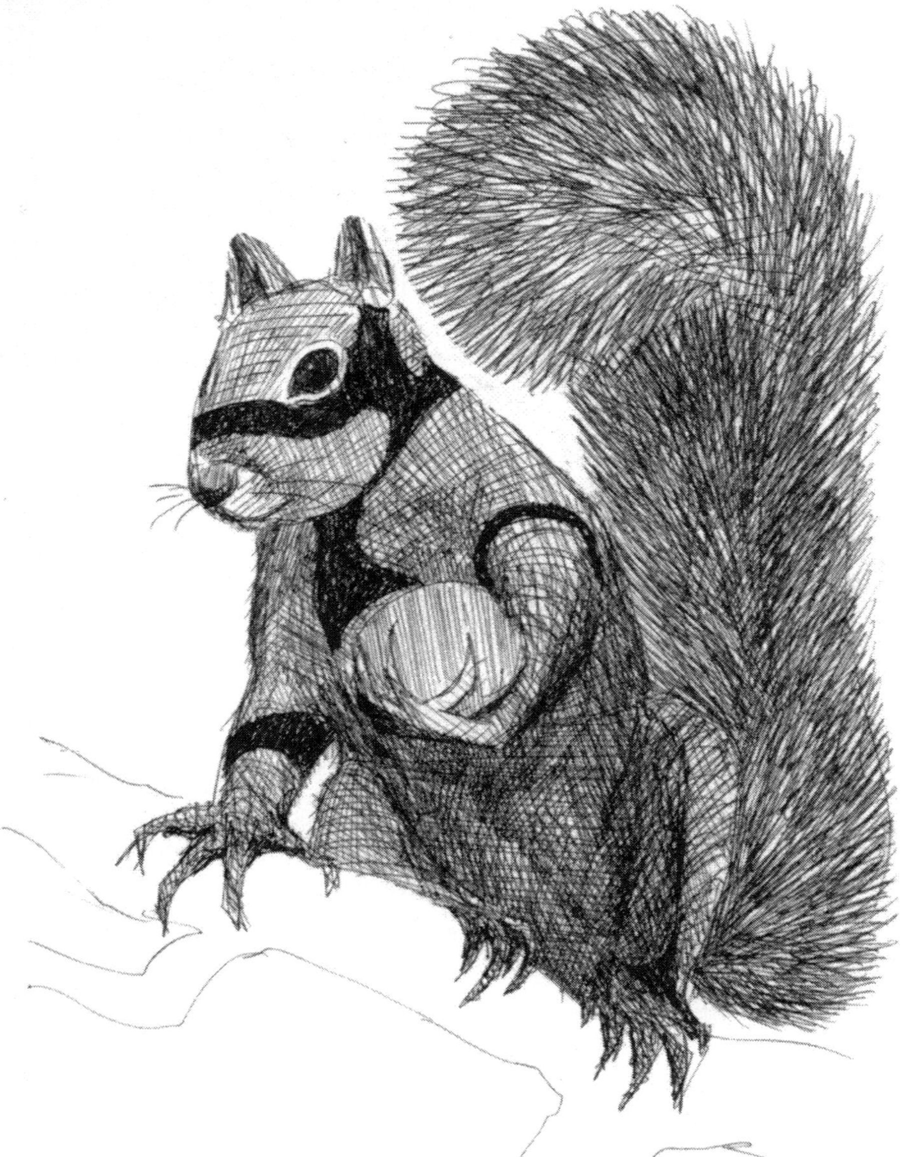

CHAPTER
TWENTY-NINE

Year AA 3072
Day 69

LAM HAD AGREED TO MEET YUNKIN AND ALAIN AT DAYBREAK, BUT HE WAS NOWHERE TO BE SEEN. Songbirds were already singing, and Yunkin was anxious to get going.

"Maybe he meant a different cottonwood," suggested Alain. He could see Yunkin's irritation as the two scanned the trees in the early morning light.

Without looking at his cousin, Yunkin said, "You heard him. He said right here, in the tallest cottonwood along the northern boundary. At dawn."

Alain knew Yunkin was right. But he also knew that Rak had ordered Yunkin not to cross over the border without Lam or another of the older guards who had been in a fight with pack rats. "Don't you even think about us going over without him," warned Alain. Yunkin didn't respond.

They both saw Lam at the same time. He was east of them, headed their way and easily identified due to his large size and slow, steady gait. They watched as he closed the distance and finally crossed onto their branch, his weight making it bob up and down. Without a word he sat on his haunches looking across the border.

Yunkin couldn't remain quiet any longer, "We wondered if you were coming."

Lam's words didn't mask his own irritation. Still looking northward, he said, "I was here before dawn. I woke up the patrol to the east of here and told them what we're doing. And Daker, Matson, Kuel and Eljo should be here soon. They'll remain here while we're across. We can leave as soon as they arrive."

Yunkin now remembered that Rak had said to have other guards on the border when crossing. "Thanks for doing that," Yunkin said, chagrinned.

Lam turned and looked directly into Yunkin's eyes. "I know you two have seen pack rats, but you haven't fought them. I have. And had friends killed by them. Lieutenant or not, Yunk, we're not going over the border unless we get some things straight right now. If you don't like it, we'll go find the Captain and get this worked out with him." Lam's words now became a command. "If anyone sees a pack rat, let the others know immediately. If you've seen one, there may be more, and they've probably already spotted you. They move in shadows and can be hard to notice. They also move more quietly than we do. Pack rats may seem to move slowly, but that's deceiving. They can be as quick as many squirrels, and their teeth are just as strong and sharp. In the battle we had with them, they killed some of us just like we killed some of them." Lam halted for a moment before continuing, his steady gaze now changing to a frown. "These thorns you saw them carry worry me. I don't know how they'd use them."

Yunkin and Alain nodded without saying anything. They each remembered the sight of the owl that knew better than to attack pack rats holding thorns. Lam continued, the tone of his voice no longer stern. "Now, which of these downed trees do you want to look at? Does it make a difference?"

Yunkin said, "No," but as soon as he said it, he wondered if Lam really questioned whether it made sense to look at them at all.

"Here they come," said Alain as he pointed east. The other guards were in sight. Daker was in the lead with the others behind. With a raised forepaw Lam acknowledged them as they approached.

"Let's go," said Lam. "And be as quiet as possible." He headed north, crossing the nearest branch with Yunkin and Alain right behind. The day was warming up quickly for late winter, and most of the snow would melt before the day was done. As they moved through the trees, each of them looked up through the bare branches at the gray clouds overhead. Once Lam stopped for a more thorough scan of the sky and forest. He whispered before they moved on, "You always see more when you are still yourself."

The three soon came upon the downed giant at the same time. It lay mostly east to west, with the larger end to the east, closer to the border. The dark bark on the side facing them stood out starkly between the thin layer of snow on top and the snow on the ground. Lam stopped once more in the hickory closest to the fallen tree. After once again scanning the forest, he turned to look at Yunkin and nodded, waiting for Yunkin to lead. Yunkin wanted to look at the stump where the tree had broken off and headed that way until he was on the lowest branch of the hickory directly above the large end. "Be careful," Yunkin said, pointing out thorns that pierced the snow on top of the log. "Those are thorns with poison."

Yunkin dropped down onto the log and moved carefully to the end, watching and feeling for thorns among the snow and leaves. He brushed aside the wet snow which had already started to melt. "It's another honey locust, all right," he whispered. He looked over the end to the snow-covered ground. No thorns poked through the snow where he would land, but he hesitated. There could be thorns hidden and he was taking a risk jumping down. *We should have started at the thinner end*, he told himself. Holding his breath, Yunkin dropped down onto the snow and, feeling no thorns, finally breathed. He motioned to Alain to drop down right next to him.

"I'll stay up here," said Lam.

Alain joined Yunkin and together they pushed apart the snow and leaves. They found no thorns and quickly met the edge of the massive stump just below the surface of the ground. The bark on the outside edge was as thick as the length of his tail but soft and mushy. Yunkin uncovered more of the stump inside of the bark, revealing dagger-like spikes where the wood had ripped loose when the treetop fell. But these sharp edges and points were also rotten and collapsed when touched. The frayed edges poked out of a thick layer of white and gray fungi that covered most of the stump. Alain leaned over and smelled the wood. "It does smell like locust and hedge, Yunk, just like you said."

Yunkin sniffed the stump himself and nodded. He began digging in the half-frozen dirt along the outside edge, telling

Alain, "I want to look at the roots." Alain joined him, while Lam watched the forest and sky above, every now and then glancing down to see what the two were doing.

Yunkin and Alain's sharp claws quickly dug into the ground and soon they found a root not far beneath the surface. The root was as thick as the length of two squirrels, covered by the same bark as the fallen trunk, with thorns attached, which they were careful not to touch.

"I've never seen a locust root with thorns or bark like this," noted Yunkin. "It looks like a branch, not a root." Yunkin's knowledge didn't surprise Alain, who knew his cousin was constantly inspecting everything in the forest. Yunk was the most curious squirrel he knew.

"Let's dig deeper," said Yunkin. "Maybe it's only the roots at the very top that are like this. But be careful of the thorns." He dug carefully down on one side of the root, but stopped when he realized the thorns prevented digging deeper. Alain assumed they were done digging but after hesitating a moment, Yunkin reached down with his mouth and grabbed a thorn, almost as long as his tail, between his front teeth. Alain jerked back in horror.

"What are you doing, Yunk?!" Lam saw what Yunkin was doing and was equally frightened but didn't say anything, choosing to focus on the forest around them and the sky above.

The thorn was soft and flexible. With a quick yank Yunkin easily pulled it loose and spit it out over the side of the hole. Before Alain could say anything, Yunkin said excitedly, "It pulled right out. Maybe they're all like this." Alain held his breath as Yunkin grabbed a second and then a third thorn and spit them outside the hole next to the others. "They're all like this, Cuz."

Remembering Yunkin's swollen, festering wound, Alain asked, "Are you sure it's safe to pull these out with your teeth?" he asked.

Yunkin responded, "Yes. Beka said the poison only acts in a sore or wound where it can get in your blood. As long as you don't have an open sore in your mouth, you can even swallow it and not be hurt."

Yunkin continued to easily yank out other thorns. Fearful, but not wanting to let Yunkin down, Alain exhaled, forced himself to push his face forward, closed his eyes at the last minute and nervously gripped the thorns before him with his teeth. Encrusted with dirt, these thorns were also soft. With a quick yank they came loose easily. Alain raised his nose and spit them out over the side of the hole. He looked at the thorns distastefully as he continued to spit out crumbs of dirt and moldy pieces of leaf. Although soft and flexible, these thorns didn't look any different than those on a normal-sized honey locust tree. *That wasn't so bad.* He told himself. *If you're up to this, Cuz, I guess I am too.*

Before returning to the bottom of the hole to dig, Alain glanced up and saw Lam, who remained on the top edge of the log almost directly above. Lam's eyes darted all around and up through the bare branches.

This is too dangerous! thought Lam, his nose clogged with the must of fungi and mold released from the newly excavated soil. *If there was a pack rat close by, I couldn't even smell him.* But he realized what Yunkin and Alain were finding was unexpected and he refrained from saying anything.

A pile of the soft thorns now lay on top of the ground on either side of the hole as Yunkin and Alain continued to dig. Soon they were at the bottom on either side of the root. Alain could see

Yunkin through the open space beneath and realized that Yunkin was not stopping. He had widened his hole and was digging deeper, pushing the dirt up and over the edge. Alain returned to digging himself and quickly discovered another root below the first one.

"Here's another, and it has the same bark. Thorns also," Yunkin said.

But both immediately saw that this one was different. Another root had wrapped itself around it in a tight spiral.

"I've never seen anything like this," said Yunkin. "Look how these are twisted around each other. You can't even get a paw between them."

"And thorns from one root are piercing the other," replied Alain. "They couldn't have always been this soft."

Both kept digging and pulling out thorns, having to move the growing piles further to the side and discovering more roots below, which also were twisted around one another.

Lam whispered just loud enough to get their attention. "Stop digging!"

Yunkin and Alain looked up as Lam dropped off the end of the log onto the ground between them, crouching low. They each stayed in their respective holes, peering over the edge in the same direction that Lam was looking, to the north. From their low vantage point they couldn't see anything.

Lam pulled himself up, stood erect on his hind paws and said out loud, "They've seen us. Pack rats! Stand up with me." Yunkin and Alain climbed out of the holes to stand on either side of Lam and followed his line of sight.

Five pack rats were standing side by side atop another giant log to the north, about 100 paces away, their brown fur clearly visible against the snow. They were close enough that Yunkin could see their dark brown eyes. These pack rats were also slender, and their faces looked gaunt. *Are these the same pack rats we saw yesterday?* he wondered. Just as he thought this, one of the pack rats in the middle reached over his shoulder with his foreleg and, in one swift movement, pulled out a locust thorn. It was the pack rat with the tan ear, the one Rak had asked about. The one who had killed Thrane. He was older, his brown hair tinged with gray. The other pack rats followed suit and all pointed the sharp ends of their thorns directly at the squirrels, holding them with both forepaws.

Yunkin and Alain froze until Lam barked loudly three times. Immediately, three muffled barks were heard to the south and west.

It's Daker and the others, but they're too far away! thought Yunkin.

The tan-eared pack rat said something, and all five pack rats jumped off the fallen log onto the ground and took a step forward, their thorns still held out in front, menacingly. Then a second step. Without taking his eyes off the pack rats, Lam stated evenly, "Get ready."

Eyeing the thorns held by the pack rats, Yunkin thought of the thorns he and Alain had pulled off the roots, and took two quick steps to grab two of the thorns that were lying close by. "Here, take one," he said, holding one out to Lam and another to Alain. Do what I do!" he commanded. As he picked up a third thorn, he held it in both paws like the pack rats with the point held forward and took two steps forward. Lam and Alain followed suit. *I just hope they don't realize these are soft and useless,* Yunkin thought, careful not to shake the thorn he held, which might cause it to wobble.

The tan-eared pack rat jabbed his thorn up into the air and the pack rats stopped advancing, the others jabbering at each other. They obviously hadn't expected this. Lam barked three times again, and they all heard three barks in response, this time louder. *Help is on the way,* Yunkin thought.

The pack rats continued to look back and forth at one another, the one on the end speaking more loudly, motioning with his thorn, clearly agitated. The tan-eared one in the middle gruffly responded with an angry bark, still holding his thorn out in front, but after a moment more he abruptly jabbed his thorn straight up in the air and uttered a short command. The other four immediately turned, raised their thorns over their shoulders, re-inserted them between their straps and quickly climbed back up onto the fallen log behind them. The tan-eared leader did the same and followed them more slowly up on to the log as the others jumped off to the north and out of sight. The leader once more pulled out his thorn and held it steady, pointing it first at Yunkin and then at Lam, not saying anything, before finally turning away, jumping off the log and disappearing along with the others.

Alain dropped his thorn and climbed quickly to the top of the giant log next to them. "I don't see them," he said, remaining in place as he looked northward, scanning the entire log the pack rats had crossed and the ground at either end through the trees.

Finally, they heard the four other Leafensong guards scurrying through the trees and Daker's voice calling out.

Lam answered, "Over here. Watch out, we just saw pack rats." When they arrived, Lam explained to Daker and the others what had happened, and they tried to absorb it all, looking around nervously. Eljo climbed to the top of the great log to be on the look-out with Alain.

"We need to take some of these thorns with us to show Rak," said Yunkin, still holding on to a thorn.

"These would have been worthless if they had attacked us," said Alain from atop the log. "We should remove some good ones, too."

Confused, Daker asked, "What's he mean, 'these are worth-less'?"

As the others crowded around them, Yunkin held his thorn, then without any effort, quickly bent it over. Lam's eyes widened. He examined the thorn he held and found it also bent easily.

"What's wrong with these thorns?"

"I'm guessing they've been weakened by being buried in the ground," responded Yunkin.

"But these wouldn't have done us any good. Those pack rats…."

"They didn't know that. At least I assume they didn't know that," said Yunkin with a slight grin.

Lam sighed, the tension visibly leaving his face. "Good job, Lieutenant. That was quick thinking."

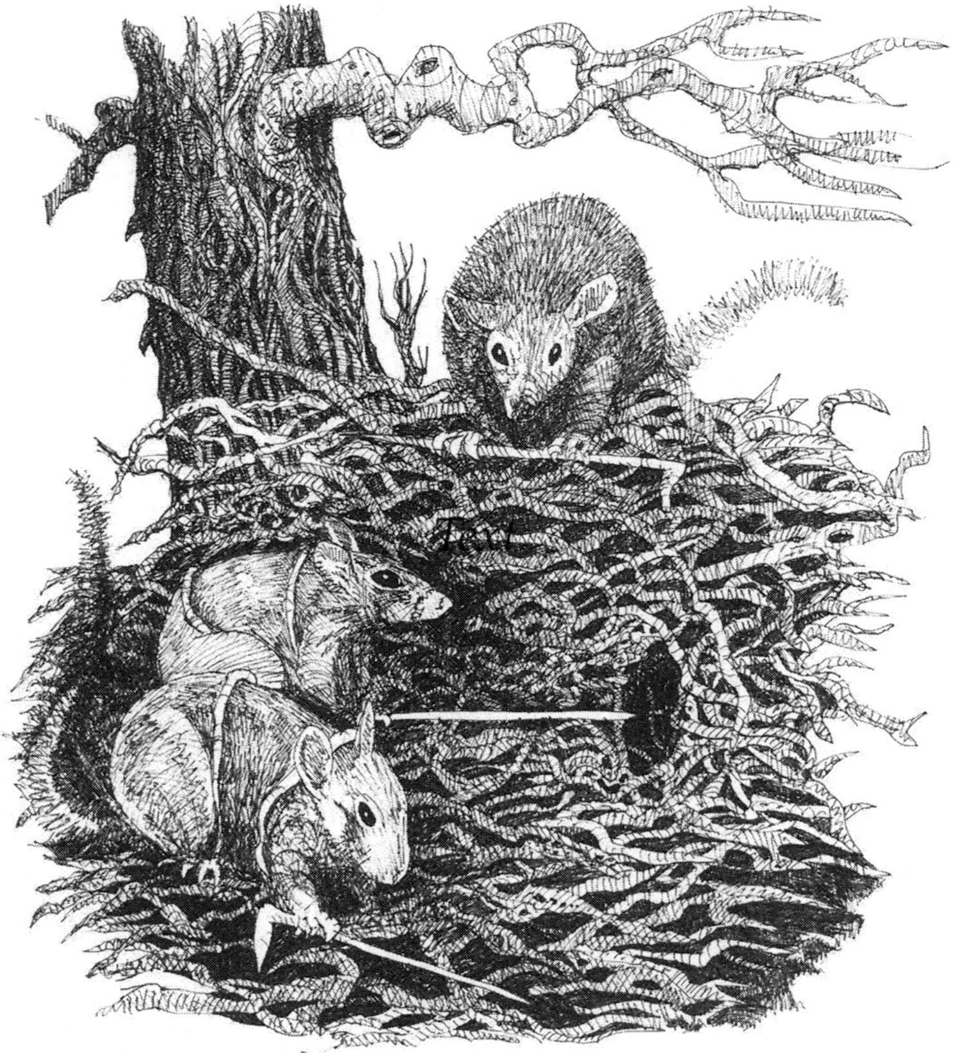

CHAPTER THIRTY

Year 3072
Day 69

RAGNAR, CAPTAIN OF THE WOOD RAT SCOUTS, WAS MYSTIFIED. *How long have the squirrels used thorns as weapons?* he wondered. *Why haven't we seen them carry thorns before now? The one time we approach them with thorns is the first time they have thorns? How could that be?* But he was also angry with himself. *You shouldn't have confronted them! Now they've seen our thorns. Skag said not to allow that. He'll be furious if he finds out.*

Ragnar sat atop the midden of sticks he had hurriedly thrown together when he and his four Scouts had arrived only a few months before. Built at the base of a medium-sized hedge tree, his midden was close to his Scouts'—he could see them from where he now sat. They were a good distance north of Leafensong, past where the squirrel Guards might come out looking for good nut trees. None of the trees outside Leafensong had a good crop the previous fall and the squirrels had not been seen anywhere outside Leafensong's border since Ragnar and his Scouts had arrived.

Ragnar was in the beginning of his senior years and had been Skag's right hand until quite recently. Skag had demoted him from being his top General when Ragnar started objecting to some of Skag's actions. Skag said being named Captain of the Scouts wasn't a demotion, but Ragnar knew better. Skag wanted him away from the Pack and Ragnar was happy to oblige.

Ragnar had been one of the Pack's most formidable soldiers in his younger years. He was naturally athletic and larger than all of the wood rats besides Skag. Ragnar's ferocity in the Great Battle was legendary and his slaying of the squirrels' Captain was still bragged about by the older wood rat soldiers. But the wood rats' retreat from that battle still gnawed at him. He told Skag before they attacked that they didn't have enough soldiers, but Skag sent them in anyway, not wanting to risk any more wood rats. Skag had apologized to Ragnar afterwards, saying Ragnar had been right and Skag wouldn't make that mistake again. But he had never forgiven Skag, or himself, for the loss of the Battle or so many of his soldiers. Their deaths still haunted him daily.

In his early years, Ragnar's mother had instilled in him a deep hatred for the banded squirrels. She told him the story that had been passed down for generations of wood rats.

"Those squirrels stole our Mother Oak, Ragnar! That tree had never let us down. We had never gone hungry and it should still be ours, surrounded by middens, not infested by striped squirrels! Promise me you'll do all you can to reclaim our tree and home from those thieves!" He had promised her, and his failure to win back their ancient home before she died brought unrelenting pain to his heart.

Years before the Battle, Skag and Ragnar were each leaders of the wood rats that lived close to them. But Skag was more driven to be in charge and was the better fighter. He was brilliant and charismatic, larger than life, a natural commander. He had been able to convince the wood rats to band together and form an army to take back their Mother Oak. Ragnar and the others bought into Skag's noble vision, to join together and form the Pack, a community living in caverns below ground far to the west of Leafensong, and there to build an army of soldiers to take back the Mother Oak.

After the disastrous Battle, Skag discovered how to use honey locust thorns as weapons, and Skag's mastery over the Pack was complete. The members of the Pack had agreed to change their ways and had sacrificed dearly by enlarging the caverns and bearing and rearing more young to increase their numbers of soldiers, all trained and armed with thorns. For years Ragnar had been his General, his right hand in transforming the Pack with the single aim of taking back the Mother Oak from the hated squirrels.

But over the last years Skag had changed. At first his bouts of anger were sporadic, but recently they had become more frequent. Even pregnant does who dared to complain about giving up their pups to the commune were subject to his anger. He could explode in unpredictable fits of rage and injure whomever was closest to him. Twice he had killed soldiers over seemingly petty offenses.

Skag had demanded that the caverns be enlarged to house more and more soldiers, forcing does to have children more often, removing them from their mothers to become blindly obedient to the cause. Ragnar had remained committed to Skag's vision and his Sergeants had kept their soldiers in near-constant training, to be ready to march and fight with their thorns when Skag ordered it. When not training, the soldiers continued to enlarge their caverns, digging out the soil and carving away roots, or went further and further out to find food to feed their growing numbers. But the forest had been stripped clean for food and the wood rats were suffering, barely eating enough to survive. Perpetually hungry, Skag kept them subdued with his exhortations and threats. The soldiers were now more frightened than inspired.

Ragnar had started to object to Skag's increasingly violent ways, and the two had come close to blows before Skag announced he was almost ready to attack. A day had been chosen, Skag told Ragnar, and that day was fast approaching. Ragnar knew they would lose soldiers again, but it would be worth it to recover the Mother Oak.

Skag named Ragnar Captain of the Scouts and sent them to watch the squirrels and report back to Skag of developments. And he commanded them to keep their thorns hidden from the squirrels. "Our thorns must be a surprise," Skag had told him. "When we invade, those squirrels will have no chance against us!"

Ragnar was happy to get away from Skag and his increasingly erratic behavior. Seeing how the Pack had changed had become unbearable, but Ragnar was committed to fulfilling his promise to his mother and win back their oak.

Until today there had been nothing to report. Ragnar had been shocked to see the squirrels brandishing thorns. The way they handled the thorns, the same way the wood rats did, indicated the squirrels knew how to use them.

Ragnar knew he had failed to follow his orders. His hatred for the squirrels had gotten the better of him. But doing so had at least caused the squirrels to show their own use of thorns. *We now know the squirrels have armed themselves,* he thought. *We needed to know this so we wouldn't be surprised. Skag has to be told about this.*

"Treak and Drum, come here!" ordered Ragnar. The two Scouts scurried over, eager to see what he wanted. "I need you to return home and report to Skag what we saw this morning, that the squirrels are also armed with thorns. Tell him that they handled their thorns like we do. Explain only that. Don't tell him the squirrels saw our thorns. Ask what his instructions are for us now, and if the invasion will still take place on the day planned."

Ragnar could see the fear in their eyes. They each knew the trip was dangerous and the information would upset Skag.

"You watch yourself," Ragnar added. "Stay out of Skag's reach if he gets violent. Tell him I'm awaiting your return with his instructions and I need to know when the invasion will start. That should keep you safe. Then get back here as soon as you can. Be safe, but hurry!"

Ragnar watched the two wood rats as they ran off across the forest floor through the underbrush, the thorns fastened to their backs bobbing along. He felt guilty. He knew they were in danger of hawks and owls. And telling Skag that they needed to return to Ragnar might not keep them safe. But Skag had to hear this.

*Should I have gone instead? No, I'm too old and slow. That would have taken too long. Should I have told them to tell Skag the squirrels saw our thorns? No, that might drive Skag to…*Ragnar refused to let himself think any further about what Skag might do. He knew anything was possible.

Ragnar retreated to his sleeping chamber lined with dry grass in his midden. He thought again of his promise to his mother. *Soon, Mother, soon,* he thought, *our army will retake our Blessed Oak, and the Pack can be made whole again.*

Ragnar tried to sleep but too many thoughts roiled him. *What will Skag do to Treak and Drum? Will Skag call off the invasion? Did confronting the squirrels warn them that something was up? Have I hurt our chances for a successful invasion? What have I done?*

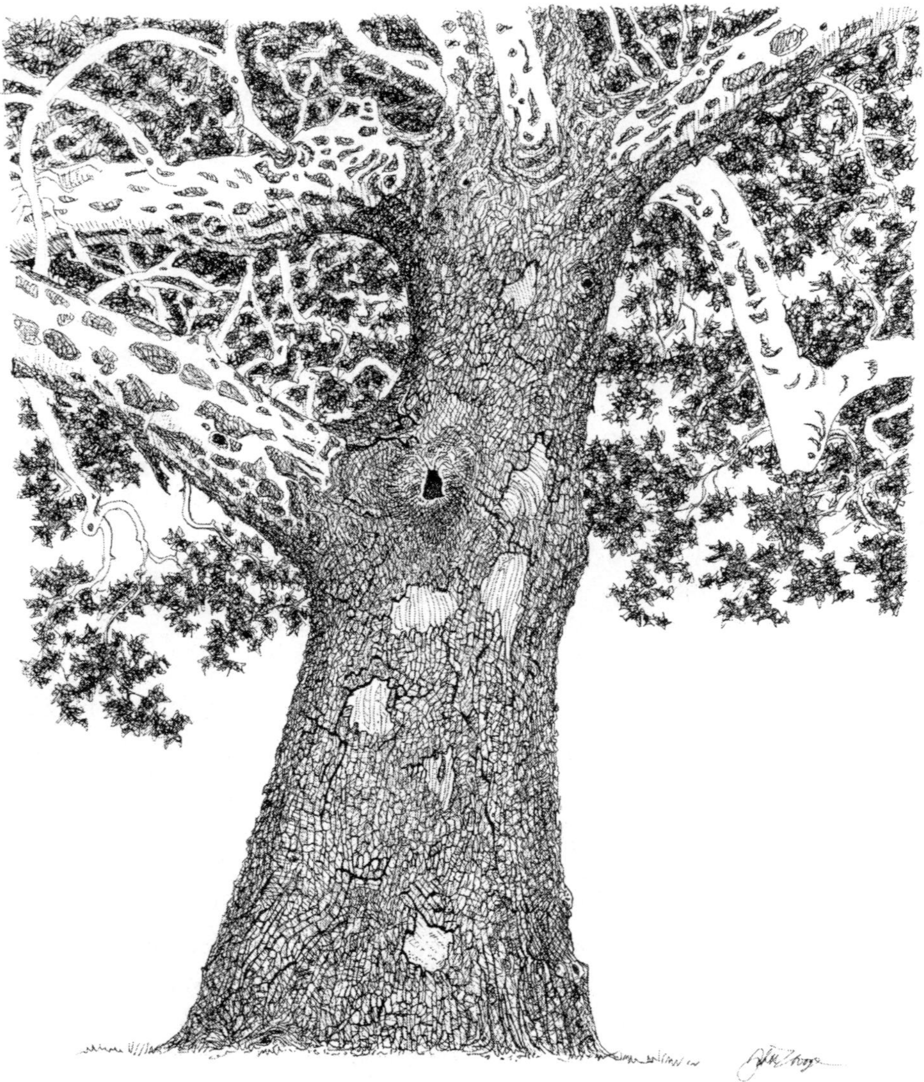

CHAPTER THIRTY-ONE

Year 3072

Day 69

LAM, YUNKIN AND ALAIN CLIMBED THE WIDE TRUNK OF RAK'S SYCAMORE TREE, EACH HOLDING TWO THORNS IN HIS TEETH FROM THE GIANT LOCUST THEY HAD VISITED, A LIMP ONE AND ANOTHER CUT FROM THE LOG They found Karmer and Gist with Rak, anxiously awaiting them on a large branch high above Rak's nest. Daker had already relayed the details of their encounter with the pack rats. After examining the thorns, Rak asked, "Was the tan-eared one with them?"

"Yes," said Yunkin. "He was leading them."

"When they left, he was the last to leave," said Alain. "He stood for a moment pointing his thorn at Yunkin and then at Lam. He looked pretty serious."

Rak seethed with anger and determination, and they all felt the gravity of the danger at hand.

"All I know is without Yunk, some of us might not be here," said Lam.

"That was quick thinking and a smart move," said Rak. "Good going, Lieutenant. He could see that Yunkin wanted to say something more. "What is it, Yunk?"

"I think we ought to use thorns ourselves. At least some of our guards on patrol could carry thorns like the pack rats. And I think we could figure out how to use them in a fight. The pack rats have obviously done that. If they attacked us with thorns, we'd be at a disadvantage. But if they see our guards carrying thorns strapped to our backs like they do, they might think we know how to use them. If they're thinking about attacking Leafensong, they might think again."

Alain spoke up, "The pack rats are obviously used to moving about with them. It looks like they're strapped on with two pieces of vine tied around their chest and belly. That keeps their forelegs free plus they can pull the thorns out easily. I bet we could figure all this out."

Lam nodded, "I think it's a good idea."

"And we don't have to carry poisoned thorns," said Yunkin. "We can get thorns off regular locust trees, like that one there." Yunkin pointed to a honey locust tree close by. "They look the same as the poisoned thorns. Pack rats shouldn't know the difference."

"Maybe they don't know about the poisoned ones from the big logs," suggested Karmer. "The thorns they carry might be regular locust thorns."

"Maybe, but we can't count on that," replied Rak. "We have to assume the worst, that they do know and are carrying the poisonous thorns. But now I want to hear more about these roots you were digging around. That's what you were doing when the pack rats showed up, right?"

"Yes!" said Yunkin excitedly. "The roots on that stump are as different as the logs themselves! We didn't dig down that far…"

"The heck we didn't!" said Alain. "I've never dug a hole so deep."

"So what'd you find?" asked Rak.

"The roots aren't like any other roots I've ever seen," explained Yunkin, and he went on to describe just what they found.

"You ever see thorns from one locust pierce another locust or any other tree?" Rak asked Yunkin.

"No. Never. Do you want us to inspect the fallen logs or their stumps some more?" Yunkin hoped Rak would say yes, but Karmer, Gist and Lam were clearly against it.

Rak paused before responding. "I think you're done inspecting these roots at least for now. You may have saved some of your lives with them, and you've figured out some things that are really important, but if you hadn't done this you wouldn't have been in jeopardy. Now you've got something else to figure out—how to carry and use these thorns. Having our guards on patrol carry them just might keep pack rats from attacking Leafensong. We have to assume they're out there watching the patrols. We're seeing more and more of them, and at least some of them are obviously itching for a fight, probably with these." Rak held up the thorn in both paws like Lam had showed him. "We need to keep them at bay while we figure how to use these things in an attack."

Gist responded, "We'll do it, Cap. We might not know how to use them as well as the pack rats yet, but by Lucient, we'll figure it out. Our guards are brave. If the pack rats want a war, we'll give it to them."

"I know our guards are brave. But these might help us avoid a war as well as win one," Rak said sternly. "No one should go to war unless it's absolutely necessary. Leaders who haven't done all they can to avoid war aren't fit to be leaders. It's our job to balance protecting the lives of our Guards with keeping Leafensong and everyone here safe. But if the pack rats do attack, I want to win that fight."

Lam added, "With Yunk to help figure it out, I think we can."

"I hope you're right," said Karmer. He turned to face Yunkin. "Lieutenant, we need you to continue to make good decisions. The Guard and the whole Tribe is at stake. What we're facing is beyond my understanding. But, I'm ready to follow you and the Captain into anything."

Yunkin couldn't respond.

Gist lifted the point of the thorn he held up in the air. "Here's to Yunkin. Our smart Lieutenant we're lucky to have. And here's to Leafensong." The others each lifted a thorn and touched the points together as they cried forth in unison, "For Leafensong!"

CHAPTER THIRTY-TWO

Year 3072 AA
Day 69

THE KEEPER COUGHED AND HIS WHOLE BODY CONVULSED, WAK-
ING HIM FROM HIS LATE AFTERNOON NAP. His eyes still closed,
he wiped the spittle from his mouth with his forepaw. Grunting
as his old muscles complained, he shifted his body to move the
pain throbbing deep in his hip. *One of Beka's massages would sure
feel good*, he thought. *Or maybe I could get some redbud and fennel.*
He opened his eyes and realized it was almost dark. Muted light
came in the entrance and barely lit the inside of his nest, the re-
cesses dark in shadow. He realized it was too late in the day to
travel to Beka's tree. He sat up on his haunches, flinched from a
spike of pain and sat still. He knew he wouldn't be going back to
sleep any time soon; he was awake most nights anymore.

His thoughts shifted to the meeting with Rak and his guards
two days before, and a smile crossed his face. *That was almost a real*

Telling, he thought with satisfaction. *A few still have an interest in the Lore. That Yunkin is certainly a curious fellow. No one's ever asked me about the giant locusts, at least not that I can remember. I wonder if Rak will bring his guards back for more Lore.*

Doubt then struck the Keeper and his eyebrow twitched. *What if I can't remember all of it?* This had been a fear his entire life. Until recently, he had kept the concern at bay. But he had become preoccupied with doubt. His entire self-worth was based upon his knowledge of the Tribe's history and his ability to recite it. Lately he had begun to believe it didn't matter, as no one had asked him anything in so long. But the questions of Yunkin and the others now gave him hope.

He closed his eyes, slowed his breath and centered himself. *Well, it's time for my exercises at least.* "Before Leafensong was the wandering…" Once again, the Keeper began reciting out loud the Tribe's history as he had done each day for months. But his recitation was interrupted by other thoughts. *Maybe they'll be back and ask more questions. Maybe there will be another Keeper. And I can teach him. Maybe I'm not useless after all. Now, where was I…*

***

Yunkin hadn't fallen asleep yet. He and Alain were in the large oak tree on the western border once again, their backs against each other. Alain had fallen asleep quickly and hadn't budged. Yunkin had tried but was unable to sleep, his mind whirling. He recalled the pack rats holding their thorns, their tan-eared leader angry, ready to attack. He wondered if pack rats were near them right now, out in the dark, and recalled what the Keeper had told him—that the banded squirrels had driven them from

Leafensong. *No wonder they want this place back*, he thought. *It was their home first. Beka's tree is a special tree. Leafensong. There's no other tree like it with its acorns that never fail. Are the pack rats hungry? Are they starving? I'd be angry at us too and would want the tree back. We're really to blame. Why do we get to keep this place and keep them out? Does being here so long justify this? How long had they been here before us? Should that make a difference?*

These questions had bothered him ever since the meeting with the Keeper, but Yunkin hadn't mentioned them to anyone. *Rak would be disgusted with me if he knew I felt...guilty.*

Just thinking of the word bothered him. He did feel guilty that his Tribe had stolen this place, that it had caused so much death to squirrels and pack rats ever since. But he also felt wrong even thinking this way. *No! I can't afford to feel guilty about taking Leafensong. I've got a job to do. I can't care about the pack rats; I have to care about my own kind! How do we use the thorns? That's all I need to figure out right now!*

***

Rak did not feel guilty. He, too, was unable to sleep, but his thoughts were solely about whether he was smart enough to lead his guards and protect the Tribe. And he wondered if Yunkin would make good decisions. The idea that they needed to use thorns to combat the pack rats was overwhelming. He had no idea how the thorns should be used. *Yunkin seems to think he can figure out how to use them. Lam and Alain believe in him. I'm glad he saw the pack rats handle them. If anyone can figure this out, he can. And he is gaining the confidence needed to lead others; not many are willing to take on such responsibility. I'm glad I chose him...so far anyway. If only he makes good decisions about these thorns. What on earth will tomorrow bring?*

***

Beka slept but intermittently. The day had been long. Claryn had finally left to sleep with Spinner as usual. Sometimes Claryn and Spinner would sleep with Beka in her nest, but they both enjoyed being alone now and then. She awoke with a start from the pain in her paws and forelegs. She sighed and got up, sat still for a moment while she gathered her thoughts and flexed her aching paws. She knew she needed some pain medicine so she could sleep—the massages she had given her patients for years caused her own discomfort every night. Once she was clear-headed, she moved slowly in the dark, feeling her way by scent and paw through the doorway from the sleeping nest out onto her porch. She reached up, but hesitated, unsure whether to get redbud flowers and fennel or the stronger bark she used for pain.

This isn't so bad; I'll just take some flowers, she thought. But a new spasm rushed in and she decided on the bark instead. She felt with her paws for the nearest bundle, picked it up and sniffed to confirm she'd grabbed the right one. Then, she bit off a chunk.

The vision came to her of Sergeant Gist's screwed up face, his eyes widening, as he first tasted the medicine. She smiled. *That was funny*, she mused. *All good things come with some bad. Part of the balance.*

Her thoughts shifted to Kooper and Sharani, and again she smiled. *I bet their adolescent minds are going crazy. Young love. You were that way once, too*, she told herself. The image of a youthful Thrane came to mind. He was so handsome, so strong. He had such a nice smile, and he was funny! He had been her greatest, though not her first love. *I wonder how the Keeper is doing*, she thought. *I haven't seen him in years. I should go visit him. I know he's upset by how the Council has ignored him.* Beka sighed as she chewed her bark. The Keeper too had once been young and virile, and Beka had prized him for his quick mind and wit. But the last time she had seen him, he had changed. He had aged greatly and grown bitter, and she had seen fear in his eyes. *Our time is coming to an end, Keeper*, she thought. *We're getting old, and there's only so much we can do for the Tribe, for our families, for the young ones.*

Beka moved to the porch entrance and spit out the bark, then returned to her inner nest to try and sleep.

***

Sharani was wide awake, thinking of singing with Kooper. She still wore the smile she'd had since their walk together. She was tired and would soon sleep, content. *I'll be good for him. Make him happy. Help him watch Boggs. Maybe help Beka with her healing? The family is all so...interesting. Kooper's cute. And I think he does like me. A little. He sings so well! Do I really sing okay?*

***

Boggs could have Sensed the thoughts of Sharani, but he purposefully blocked her thoughts, and Kooper's. He had Sensed their thoughts earlier when they had gone on their walk, and, for a moment, as he settled in the nest, he had Sensed Kooper's thoughts but stopped when he realized Kooper was thinking about her. He was glad for their happiness. But it increased his own feeling of being alone, separate from the others, even though he and Kooper were now back to back, sharing the same nest. *He deserves time away from me. I shouldn't be his concern.*

Boggs blinked his unseeing eyes and realized tears had emerged. He reached up a paw to wipe them away. *Sharani can help Beka and Claryn to keep you here, Koop,* Boggs thought without letting Kooper Sense his thoughts. *Spinner, too. You must stay for your own good and for the family. But I must go.*

The voices had returned. They did now most nights. They no longer stunned him, and he readily listened. Once again, they sounded like they were in pain, pain that had existed for ages. *I hear you,* he Sensed back. *I'm coming. Soon.* But then he blocked them. He had made his decision and knew in his heart it was final. Turning around, Boggs gripped his brother tightly around his chest and felt Kooper's shallow breathing. Kooper placed his own forepaw over Boggs' but neither said anything. The tears returned to Boggs' eyes and he let them fall onto the warm oak wood beneath them. To himself, he thought, *Don't be angry, Koop. I'm sorry.*

***

Kooper wasn't trying to Sense Boggs' thoughts. He was still wide awake, thinking about Sharani. It had been wonderful to walk with her to the silver maple where they found new spring buds to eat. At first he'd been nervous, his heart thumping, but as their time together continued, and as he convinced her to sing, he had become more comfortable. *She is smart and funny,* he thought. *And she doesn't want me to stop watching Boggs altogether, just a little bit. I can do that if Spinner and Claryn will help. And she has a really good singing voice, she just hasn't used it much.*

His thoughts kept returning to her face. She was beautiful. He looked forward to tomorrow and seeing her again. He had no idea that by then, he'd have climbed the Singer's Tree to sing to the new spring sun.

EPILOGUE

ELI WAS HALF AWAKE. Roused by the storm the night before, he had been unable to return to his winter sleep. The thunder had awakened many, but it was the moisture and electricity in the air that had stirred Eli. Wind piled up ribbons of powdery snow in the long furrows that curved around his trunk. The electricity charged the melting snow so that a slight current ran around the trunk from the top of the tree to the ground.

Checks and cracks in Eli's bark had multiplied over the last several years as he lost his ability to grow fresh wood. Burned-out voids caused by lightning and fire allowed crystals of snow to reach through the damaged bark. The veins beneath it containing sap and water, now sluggish in their delivery, had been charged with a current of electricity which brought back memories.

Waves of wind and rain buffeting his thick canopy of leaves

were among his most common memories. His favorites were being part of the sea of giant honey locusts that reached to the horizon in all directions. The least-liked were of his siblings crashing to the ground. He had outlived all the others, and his mood usually matched the name given to him by the Tribe of banded squirrels—the Dark One.

He sang to himself, though it would sound like humming to anyone who could hear. And any listener other than a plant would have heard nothing. His singing was more a slow rumble, the living cells beneath his bark, filled with sap and water, vibrating ever so slowly. Beyond the meaning it held for him, the song gave Eli comfort—something he needed these days. It would pulse through his veins, easing his weary mind, until he slept again.

Acknowledgements

Thank you to the following, without whom *Leafensong: First Telling* would not exist.

My parents, John E. and Orpha, who showed me the value of hard work and education. With their steadfast support and spirituality, love of family, friends, music and nature, they have been my beacons of light. And to my sister, Carol, who epitomized unconditional love, goodness and sacrifice. These three have been my primary heroes in life.

The late Judi Geer Kellas, my mentor, teacher of art, and friend who first read *Leafensong* many years ago. She is deeply missed.

JoAn Pruyn. Without her insight, spirited encouragement and initial editing, I would not have continued my rewriting journey.

My wife, Claudia, who initiated and constantly encouraged my journey in art and stuck by me in spite of my ADHD-fueled wanderings. She taught me the love of language and the magic of rewriting. Most importantly, she gave me my best creations, our two beautiful children.

My beta readers, all of whom were generous with their time, critique and encouragement: Portia and Dave Blackman, Darwin Eads, Jenea Havener, Claudia, Becky Maletsky, Roxana Montgomery, Barbara Orsi, Kathryn Sheedy, Cindy Vinyard, Amy Lenharth, Alan Trites and Joy Underberg. Barbara and

Jenea's extensive critiques and suggestions went above and beyond beta reading and pushed me to make substantial changes. And Roxana Montgomery was tireless in her proofreading as well.

Michelle Leivan, who photographed and digitized my drawings, saw the worth in Leafensong and steadfastly encouraged me with great advice and expertise.

Robin Vuchnich, who expertly turned my drawing into a beautiful book cover and formatted the book as well.

Aimee Wuthrich, who proofread the final copy before going to print and caught all sorts of blunders.

Marc Havener, for his help with my headshot, the website, and all his encouragement.

My daughter, Jenea, whose expert editing; advice on writing, drawings and the book cover; creation of our website; formatting; and insight to ensure First Telling works both on its own and as a prelude to the rest of the series has made my vision come to life. It's been wonderful to have my daughter, whom I trust completely and is a far greater word stylist than I will ever be, as my partner in this creation.

Thank you all!

70637990R00183

Made in the USA
Columbia, SC
23 August 2019